Praise for *New York Times* Bestselling Author Diana Palmer

"Palmer proves that love and passion can be found even in the most dangerous situations."
—*Publishers Weekly* on *Untamed*

"You just can't do better than a Diana Palmer story to make your heart lighter and smile brighter."
—*Fresh Fiction* on *Wyoming Rugged*

"Diana Palmer is a mesmerizing storyteller who captures the essence of what a romance should be."
—*Affaire de Coeur*

"The popular Palmer has penned another winning novel, a perfect blend of romance and suspense."
—*Booklist* on *Lawman*

"Diana Palmer's characters leap off the page. She captures their emotions and scars beautifully and makes them come alive for readers."
—*RT Book Reviews* on *Lawless*

For a complete list of titles available by Diana Palmer,
please visit www.dianapalmer.com.

THE MORCAI BATTALION:
THE RESCUE

DIANA PALMER

HQN™

ISBN-13: 978-0-373-78991-7

The Morcai Battalion: The Rescue

This edition published by arrangement with Harlequin Books S.A.

For questions and comments about the quality of this book, please contact us at CustomerService@Harlequin.com.

® and TM are trademarks of Harlequin Enterprises Limited or its corporate affiliates. Trademarks indicated with ® are registered in the United States Patent and Trademark Office, the Canadian Intellectual Property Office and in other countries.

www.HQNBooks.com

Printed in U.S.A.

Dear Reader,

I honestly thought I would never see this day. To have a fourth novel in my Morcai Battalion series in print seems like a fantasy. Since the original was published in 1980, I tried for many years to get it back in print. I had no idea that it would be over twenty-five years before that happened.

I would like to thank my former Harlequin editor Tara Gavin for working so hard to help me get a spot for *The Morcai Battalion* at the former Harlequin imprint Luna Books. I would also like to thank Luna Books editor Mary-Theresa Hussey for giving me a chance to see the first book back in print. I owe these two editors a great debt for their kindness and their support. Thank you for believing in these books, against all odds. You both paved the way for me to get a three-book contract for new Morcai novels, of which *The Rescue* is the first.

In this book, I finally get to tell the bittersweet story of Rhemun, former Captain of the Cehn-Tahr Imperial Guard, now Commander of the Holconcom, and Dr. Edris Mallory, who replaces Dr. Madeline Ruszel as Cularian Medicine internist on the flagship *Morcai*. Edris is harboring a secret that could cost her her life, and Rhemun is her worst enemy. Only time will tell how the two of them resolve their conflict, and whether or not it will put Edris's life on the line. You'll have to read the book to find out. :)

On a final note, in my dedication in Wyoming Brave, the autumn 2016 release, I accidentally omitted the names of the grandchildren and great-grandchildren of my late brother-in-law, Doug Kyle. Here they are. Grandkids: Joshua and Angel McLendon, Chelsea Armour, Kaitlin Armour, Wayne Armour, Jr., Kylie Armour, Torrington Kyle and Justin Kyle. Great-grandchildren: Jordyn and Nolan McLendon, Breana and Gracie Taouis.

They're all terrific people, by the way, and all gorgeous. We miss Doug, but his legacy lives on in these young ones.

Diana Palmer

To the many kind and supportive people who kept my hopes up all the long years between the publication of the original book, The Morcai Battalion, in 1980 until the reappearance of the revised novel in 2007. You know who you are. Thanks for sticking with me for so long!

To Harlequin: thank you for taking a chance on my novels in a genre I'm not known for! And for that new three-book contract. If any of you ever need your car washed or your floor swept, here I am! Honest!

To new readers: thank you for taking this book home with you. I never forget that without my readers, I am just a former reporter with a word processing program. I hope you find something in the novel that you like. Check out the latest news on my websites: www.themorcaibattalion.com and www.dianapalmer.com. You can also find me on Twitter under @cehntahr, which is my gaming handle. I've played "Destiny" on Xbox One since it released, and "World of Warcraft" on Zangarmarsh and Hellscream servers for over eight years.

To my family: thank you for all the long years that you loved me in spite of my work. I know it was a sacrifice for you, as well as me, that I had to spend so much time at the computer. I hope you know that I love you more than anything in the world. I always will.

CHAPTER ONE

THE VOICES IN the medical bay aboard the Cehn-Tahr Holconcom ship *Morcai* were growing louder as the discussion progressed. Techs nearby were straining unashamedly to hear the outcome. Dr. Edris Mallory was small, blonde, blue-eyed and stubborn. Her opponent, Rhemun, was the new commander of the Holconcom. He was tall, with long, curly black hair down to his waist. Like all Cehn-Tahr, he had catlike features, predominantly his eyes, which changed color to mirror his mood. Right now, they were brown. Threatening.

"We must have a better allocation of space aboard the *Morcai*," Rhemun said in stiffly formal Standard. "Your sick bay has very few patients…"

"Begging your pardon, sir, it has quite a number of patients," she shot back, her cheeks faintly rosy with temper.

"Prove it," he said with a smug look.

"Delighted." She slammed a data padd against his broad chest.

"Mallory," he cautioned.

"Sorry, sir, my hand slipped." She didn't give him

a bland smile with the lie, as her predecessor, Dr. Madeline Ruszel, would have. But he got the point.

He looked at the padd with irritation. It did prove her point. Her sick bay had logged over one hundred visits from the Cehn-Tahr aboard ship in a week's time. In fact, Dr. Strick Hahnson, who took care of the humans aboard, had logged twenty fewer visits than Mallory.

He glared at her. His distaste for humans was painfully apparent to everyone aboard, but especially to Mallory, whom he rode mercilessly. She didn't understand his ongoing prejudices, but she caught the brunt of them. He seemed to go out of his way to make her life miserable. She couldn't think of a single serious infraction lately that would explain it. Of course, their mutual antagonism had a long history, all the way back to his first appearance aboard the *Morcai* when, as head of the *kehmatemer,* he accompanied Cehn-Tahr Emperor Tnurat Alamantimichar on a rescue mission to save Dr. Ruszel's life after a failed mission. She and Rhemun had been instantly antagonistic toward each other. Sadly, his appointment as Dtimun's replacement aboard the *Morcai* hadn't done a thing to reduce the friction.

"Very well," he said curtly. He handed her back the padd. "You can keep your present location, for the time being, until I can think of something more suitable."

"You could always have me set up shop in one of the cargo pods, sir," she returned, still standing at strict attention.

It was a calculated insult. He lifted his chin. His cat-eyes were still an angry brown. "You push too hard, Mallory," he said in a deceptively soft tone. "I have no love for humans, as you well know. Do not tempt me to have you replaced."

"I'm sure the commander would enjoy that," she said, averting her eyes. "However, I should point out that the only Cularian specialists at the Tri-Fleet Medical Authority at the moment are all assigned to permanent duty elsewhere."

"There are new classes graduating yearly, however," he returned, and his chiseled mouth approximated a very human smirk.

"Also true. Sir."

His eyes narrowed. He glared at her, as if the very sight of her offended him, angered him. He wanted to tell her why he hated humans so much; he wanted to tell her about his son, about the ragged tatters of his life that a human was responsible for. But Cehn-Tahr were forbidden to speak of personal matters with outworlders.

It was just as well. He wanted no personal conversations with this female, who reminded him so painfully of the past.

He turned on his heel while she was snapping to a salute and walked away.

EDRIS LET OUT a shaky sigh. She was afraid of Rhemun. It wasn't because he had authority over her. It wasn't even because he was her own personal devil.

It was because he made her feel things that she was forbidden by law to feel. She hid it as best she could, reciting multiplication tables in her head to keep her mind on the subject at hand, and not on how very attractive he was. She'd learned that trick from Madeline Ruszel, who used it to keep the former commander of the *Morcai*, Dtimun, out of her head.

Mallory knew that Rhemun couldn't read minds, of course. That was a trait only of the Royal Clan. But keeping her mind on work instead of her commander required all the mental tricks of which she was capable.

At least she'd saved her space here.

Tally, one of her medics, stuck his head around the corner. "Are we staying?" he asked in a whisper.

She laughed softly. "We're staying. At least, for the time being, until he can decide on a better place to put us."

"Like the cargo hold?" her assistant Tellas asked from beside her coworker, laughing out loud. "That was priceless, Dr. Mallory!"

She laughed softly. "I'll get in trouble again." She shook her head. "I can't imagine why he dislikes me so. I guess it's because we started off on the wrong foot, even before he turned a pot of soup over on my head."

"He what?" Tellas exclaimed, choking back laughter.

"See, there was this disagreement," Edris related, "when Dr. Madeline Ruszel was recuperating at the Imperial compound on Memcache. I thought she needed healthy vegetables and our new commander thought she needed meat for protein. There was a slight altercation." She made a face. "I threw a soup ladle at him."

They almost doubled over laughing. "Oh, my goodness, and he didn't demote you?"

"He couldn't," she pointed out. "At the time he was head of the *kehmatemer*, the emperor's personal bodyguard. Anyway, he took exception to having an object thrown at him, so he turned a whole pot of soup over on my head." She sighed. "It took forever to get the grease out of my hair."

"Did he get in trouble?"

She grinned and nodded enthusiastically. "Dtimun raked him over the coals and threatened him with the emperor. It was…"

"Nothing to do, Dr. Mallory?" a deep, irritated voice came over the intership frequency. It was almost purring.

She swallowed. She'd forgotten the damned AVBDs, the devices that were always listening, watching, aboard ship, to discourage potential spies.

"Sorry, sir." She stood at attention, as if he were actually physically present.

"Back to work." The circuit closed.

She rolled her eyes at the others, who gave her a thumbs-up and went back to their jobs. They were still grinning.

EDRIS SLEPT BADLY. There was a mission the following day, or what passed for a day in space. The unit was to rescue a pod of colonists on an outlying planet who had barely withstood an attack from Rigellian pirates bent on conquest. The colony was located on a princely node of emerillium, which the pirates wanted badly. They planned to drive away the largely unarmed colonists and claim the mines for their personal wealth.

However, the Cehn-Tahr Empire had sent the colonists there, and it took a dim view of pirates, in any case. So the Holconcom were requested, as the nearest vessel, to protect the settlers and solve the problem.

"Probably, it will only take a glance at us to send them running," Edris told her medics, "and I doubt we'll be needed."

"Considering how the Holconcom fight, I agree," Tellas said quietly.

Edris had rarely seen the Holconcom fight, and there were rumors that no human except Engineer Higgins had ever seen the way they went into combat before the Cehn-Tahr were combined with Terravegan humans from the lost SSC ship *Bellatrix*. She'd once asked Higgins about it. He'd excused himself on the matter of urgent business. He'd been very pale.

She did at least know the true form of her alien colleagues. Dr. Ruszel had persuaded Dtimun, after they bonded, to share it with the humans of the Holconcom. He'd done that, with great reservations. He'd been afraid that the humans would no longer want to serve with them, if they knew the truth.

But no one had been afraid. Their service with the Cehn-Tahr in the prison camp at Ahkmau had made them more family than comrades, removed all the intangible barriers of custom and behavior. So the true appearance of the Cehn-Tahr, who had some decidedly feline characteristics from the centuries of genetic tampering, had hardly created a ripple in them.

Personally, Edris thought Rhemun was the handsomest creature she'd ever seen, of any species. His nose was a little broader than a human male's, and he was immensely larger and more powerful, but in a crowd of humanoids, he would hardly have stood out except for his impressive presence. The differences were minor and not immediately noticeable, and the Cehn-Tahr had no tails or fur. Well, there was the strip of fur that lay alongside the spine, and which was never spoken of with outworlders, but that was the only real fur on their bodies. Edris only knew because of something Ruszel had once let slip, but she'd been sworn to secrecy.

She turned over in her narrow bunk, wishing her mind would go to sleep so that she could. She dreaded the confrontation. She was used to combat medicine, or as used to it as an overly sensitive woman could ever get. When she'd joined the military, after washing out as a breeder, she'd washed out of combat school with the lowest grade in the history of the Academy. She'd been given a berth in a

degree program in Cularian medicine instead, which
had kept her mostly on Trimerius. She'd worked for
years to get her certification after a minor accident
had caused some small loss of motor function. She'd
never expected to end up in a combat unit like the
Holconcom. She wasn't expected to actually fight,
but her profession did occasionally put her on the
front lines.

It wasn't what she wanted for her life. Her hunger for a child had led her to apply to a government
breeder colony, where she'd tried desperately to be
accepted. But she had recessive genes—obvious in
her blond hair and blue eyes—and recessive genes
were right out of fashion at the moment. The bureau-
crats in the Familial Requisitions Ministry decided
from generation to generation which traits should
be passed down and which suppressed. In this generation, only dark-haired, dark-eyed children were
wanted. Edris would mess up the works with her
sloppy recessive genes. So she'd been turned down,
and the only venue left to her was medical service
attached to the military.

She wasn't a military sort of person, really, but
she was a physician. So she became a frontline consultant in Cularian medicine, and agreed to the mental neutering, which was usually done at the age of
six. While Edris had been in medical school, and
not serving in active military, it had been deferred.
But once she went into a combat position, the neutering was requisite. It was dangerous in a woman

of twenty-two, and sometimes ineffective, but she'd faced it bravely. She had two strikes against her already: she'd failed to be chosen as a breeder and she'd washed out of combat school. One more mistake and she'd face Reboot, the most secret and terrifying fate possible to a Terravegan. She couldn't think about that. She didn't dare.

She could manage this assignment. Dr. Ruszel had trained her well. If only Edris didn't have the painful lingering legacy of an incident in medical school that had caused minor brain damage. Dr. Hahnson knew, and Dr. Ruszel. They'd shielded her from discovery, which would have meant washing out of medical school, and again facing the reality of Reboot. Fortunately, the doctors assessing her for breeding status hadn't bothered with her neurology, except a cursory look at its base cellular structure, because her coloring had already cost her any real consideration. They hadn't told her at the time, of course. She'd found out only later, when Dr. Ruszel had asked for her records and told her the truth.

The brain damage was very minimal, but she was slow. She would always be slow. Rhemun had already called her onto the carpet for it, during a rescue hop. She'd taken the punishment, days of detention and black marks on her record, without argument. But he was watching her, always watching, waiting for her to make a mistake so that he could punish her by having her decommissioned, thrown out of the Holconcom. It would be the end of everything. He didn't know what the consequences would be for her. Probably, she thought sadly, it wouldn't bother him in the least if he did.

She rolled over, closed her eyes and forced her mind to shut up. Soon, she was finally asleep.

SHE'D EXPECTED TO be put down in a combat zone; she thought she was prepared for it, but her wildest imaginings of horror hadn't prepared her for what she saw.

Most of the victims were children. The anguish almost paralyzed her when she saw the small victims tossed into a common grave, uncovered, because the fighting was still going on. She stared at them with anguish on her face.

"Mallory!" Rhemun's deep voice called. "Get to work!"

She turned, the pain so intense that he hesitated when he saw it. He knew about her history, her child-hunger. It disturbed him, so he didn't dwell on it. He motioned her toward the action with a curt gesture and averted his eyes. The sight of the children bothered him, as well. It brought back the pain of losing his son.

Edris ran toward him, dodging bursts of gunfire from plasma weapons, and rolled to the ground near a couple of refugees, one of whom had third-degree burns on his arm.

"Not to worry," she told him in Jibbet, the dialect of Altairian that these people, with their manner of dress denoting their Clan status, would speak. "I can heal him."

"You speak...Jibbet," the woman exclaimed. "No human speaks Jibbet!"

Edris smiled as she went to work. "I speak several very rare dialects," she said without conceit. "Yours is quite beautiful."

The woman touched her fingers to her mouth and then to the center of her chest, where the Altairian heart was located. She smiled. It was a gesture of perfect trust, perfect acceptance. Edris smiled again and began to heal the burned flesh of the woman's spouse.

He relaxed as her pain meds eased the anguish of the wound. "I am farmer," he said in halting Terravegan. "I will lose leg..."

"You will not," she replied. "You honor me, by speaking my tongue."

He managed a terse smile. "As you honor we, by speaking that of us," he replied brokenly.

"You will not lose your leg," she replied. "I will regrow the tissue."

"You can do such?!" he exclaimed.

She nodded, and continued to probe the damaged cells with a regenerative gel. Soon, the horrible gash that had almost amputated his leg began to close, cleaning itself of necrosis as it healed, until the skin was as blue and as perfect as it had been before he'd been wounded.

He cried out, delighted. He got to his feet and

stood up, without pain or loss of function. His purple eyes had great tears in them. "Thank you! Many gratitudes! You are great female," he choked. "My Clan is your Clan, forever."

She put her hand to her lips and then to her own heart. "You give me great honor."

The woman hugged her. "You are Web Clan. Never forget."

Edris smiled. "Thank you. I promise, I won't forget."

SHE WENT FROM patient to patient, doing whatever she could to mend the horrible effects of the radiation the pirates were using in their plasma weapons.

"Somebody should shoot them," she muttered as she finished the last suture on an elderly man.

"Are you finished?" Rhemun asked curtly. "We must move on."

"I am, sir." She smiled at her patient and fell in, behind the other Holconcom, as they advanced to the next pivotal point in the assault.

SHE FELL A little behind, stumbling over a piece of ship wreckage, and as she started to run to catch up with her comrades, a man stepped out of nowhere, one of the cold-eyed Rigellian pirates with a stolen chasat leveled at her chest.

Without thinking, she pulled her Gresham and fired. She gasped as she realized that she'd forgotten to lock the setting on stun. The pirate looked at her with wide, disbelieving eyes as he clutched his chest, groaned harshly and fell backward.

"Oh, no!" She ran to him, bent on saving him. But his eyes were open and dust was already settling on the pupils. They were dilated. Fixed. He was dead. One quick check with her wrist scanner confirmed that catastrophic damage had been done to his internal organs. Nothing could have been done for him, even on the ship.

Her face contorted. She shivered. She'd killed a humanoid. She'd killed someone!

"Mallory! Fall in!"

She heard Rhemun's deep voice, but as if in a dream. She was on her knees, staring helplessly at the man she'd just killed. She couldn't seem to move, to drag her eyes away.

"Come on!" Rhemun snapped.

She looked up at him with wide, innocent eyes that held a horror he'd never seen in them before. "I killed him," she said in a husky whisper. "I killed a man."

"Mallory…"

"I killed a man," she repeated. "I took an oath, 'Do no harm.' But I killed him. The setting was wrong. I've never killed anyone in my whole life," she added, her face contorted as she looked up at him.

He ground his teeth together. "You must do your duty, madam," he said curtly. "Other lives are at stake! Hurry!"

She swallowed. Her eyes went back to the dead man. "I'm sorry," she whispered.

"Now!" Rhemun snapped.

She gathered her wits and got to her feet. She straightened into a salute. "Yes, sir," she said formally.

He took off at a speed she couldn't imitate, but she ran as fast as she could to the next bunch of victims.

SHE WORKED MECHANICALLY, nodding as people confided their fears, their broken lives, their losses to her. She healed wounds and comforted the grieving. But her mind held the image of the dead man.

Rhemun was rarely concerned about the mental or physical health of a woman who reminded him so savagely of his son's death, but even he began to notice how Mallory was acting.

He paused beside her when she finished working on her last patient. The rest of the pirates had been routed, the colonists rescued. They were ready to lift. But Mallory was obviously not herself.

Hahnson had noticed it first and alerted Rhemun. It was up to the commander of the Holconcom to deal with her. He wished he could leave it to Hahnson, but the doctor was far too fond of Mallory to manage any harshness.

Pity and compassion would do no service here, he thought, as he contemplated her mental state. He'd seen this in battle, combatants who faced the horror of war for the first time and broke under the strain. They called it battle fatigue. But it was more severe in a woman of this sensitivity. It could not be allowed to continue. He needed her. There was no replacement available until the following year, until the next graduates in Cularian medicine.

"Mallory, we must lift," he told her curtly.

The woman she was treating, a little old Altairian woman, looked up at the Cehn-Tahr who had assumed his most human aspect—the woman was neither family nor Holconcom, so his true form was hidden from her.

"She is wounded, here." The old woman touched her own heart.

"That may be," he replied in Altairian, "but we must leave."

The woman stared at him. It was a little unnerving. "You have suffered a great loss," she said in a monotone. "But you will suffer a greater one. Your life contains another tragedy of your own making."

"Madam," he began, chilled by her perception.

She held up a hand. "The tragedy will lead to great joy," she continued, her eyes blank as she recited what she saw. "And to a place in history for your branch of the great Clan." She blinked. She frowned. She looked up at him as if she didn't recognize him. "What did I say?"

He gaped at her. "Excuse me?"

She smiled apologetically. "I see things. Sometimes I see things. I tell them. But I never remember what I have said. Perhaps it is a blessing. You look

very troubled. I am sorry. I should not have spoken.
It is a curse."

He went down on one knee. His eyes lightened.
"Never rue such a gift," he said gently. "On my
homeworld, there is a great seer, one whose proph-
ecies have all come true in the recent past. It is no
curse. And I thank you for your words."

She beamed.

Edris, who was trying not to listen, finished
cleaning the old woman's wounds. "There," she said
gently. "You'll be fine."

"I am grateful. Very grate..." Her eyes went
blank. "A terrible time is ahead for you," she said
hesitantly. Tears stung her eyes. "Such horror, for one
so kind...!" She swallowed. "You must not run. You
must not leave your ship because of harsh words...!"

Edris's eyes were like saucers. "What did you
say?"

The old woman's eyes cleared. "Have I done it
again?" She sighed and shook her head. "Twice in
as many minutes, perhaps I am going mad." She
laughed. "Thank you for your care. I hope that someone will be as kind to you."

"We must go," Rhemun said as he stood up. He
turned away and raised his voice, calling for the Holconcom to get ready to lift.

Edris touched the old woman's hair. "Thank you."
She turned away, chilled by the prediction, which she
didn't understand at all. Perhaps the woman heard
voices. There were some diseases which could cause

such symptoms. Then she thought of Lady Caneese, the bonded mate of the Cehn-Tahr emperor, whose visions about Ruszel had been absolutely accurate. And she wondered.

BACK ABOARD THE *MORCAI*, Edris went looking for Dr. Hahnson.

"May I speak with you?" she asked hesitantly.

One look at her pale, strained features caused him to turn over his latest patient to his assistant. He motioned Edris into the small cubicle that served as his office.

He closed the door and pulled some odd, white, ball-shaped device out of a desk drawer. He activated it with a sequence of touches, so that it began to glow white.

"Disrupts the AVBDs," he told her when she gave him a puzzled look. "It also blocks telepaths." He chuckled. "We never know when the emperor may be looking in. Now. What can I do for you?"

She sat down heavily in a chair. "I shot a man. A Rigellian. I think he must have been one of the pirates, hiding until he thought we were gone. I stumbled into him."

"And?" he prodded when she closed up.

She bit her lip. "He…died."

He drew in a long breath and perched himself against his desk. "I understand. I've only had to kill once or twice during my career. It was never easy, and I suffered long and hard for it. I'm sorry, Edris. I'm very sorry."

"I'll have to see his face every day for the rest of my life," she said, as if in a trance. "He looked so shocked. I tried to do something, to save him." She lowered her eyes. "But there was nothing I could do." She made a futile little gesture with her hands. "I've never killed anyone."

"Listen, kid, it goes with the job," he said gently. "I know that sounds harsh, but we are combat medics…"

"The oath we take says 'First, do no harm,'" she interrupted.

"Why did you shoot him?" he asked patiently.

"He was about to shoot me," she stammered.

"And you think your conscience would be fitter if you'd allowed yourself to die?"

She bit her lip. "I don't…know how to deal with it."

He made a face. "We don't have grief counselors aboard. Well, except doctors," he added.

"Yes. Not even an interfaith chapel. Nothing." She swallowed. "I don't suppose military Cehn-Tahr are religious, anyway."

"You'd suppose wrong," he said wryly. "They're deeply religious, in their own way. They have a deity, Cashto. You may see small statues of him from time to time…"

"The catlike busts, with glowing green eyes?" she asked, curious. "They're religious objects?"

"That's right. Even Dtimun had one in his quarters."

"I didn't realize…"

"They're very like humans," Hahnson said with a smile.

"Except for the new CO," she said heavily. "You'd insult him by even saying that." She frowned. "Why does he hate us so much?"

"I don't know," he replied. "Dtimun let something slip once to the effect that Rhemun had suffered a personal tragedy that was somehow associated with humans. But I don't know anything about the circumstances."

"How odd that he'd end up commanding an interracial group like ours."

"Their command structure is largely Clanrelated," he said. "I don't understand exactly how it works, but Rhemun was next in line for command of the Holconcom. He didn't have a choice."

"The men don't like him." She sighed. "He's put up more backs than a cat at a dog fight."

He laughed out loud. "Please, don't say that where he can hear you. I'd hate to have to repair the damage."

She smiled with faint mischief. "Shame on me."

"You get a good night's sleep," he said. "Let your assistant handle anything that comes up if there's an emergency." He sobered. "I can tell you that time really does make the difference. In a few days, the worst of the pain will ease. You'll get used to it."

"I suppose I don't really have a choice about that," she agreed heavily. "Thanks for listening."

"I'll always do that. Anytime you need an ear."

She smiled. "I owe my career to you. They'd have washed me out in a heartbeat if they knew how much damage that accident did to my brain."

"I only altered a couple of neurological profiles," he said with twinkling dark eyes. "No big deal."

"It was for me. You and Dr. Ruszel kept me safe." She grimaced. "If the CO ever finds out, he'll wash me out of the service, you know." She looked up with wide, worried blue eyes. "I'll be up for Reboot…"

"I will never let that happen," he said firmly. "I promise."

"Yes, but…"

"Mallory, you're the best friend of the wife of the heir to the Cehn-Tahr Empire," he pointed out. "Do you really think she'd ever allow you to end up in Reboot?"

She stood up. "It would depend on circumstances, I guess. But I can hope."

"Meanwhile, lots of rest. And take a sedative," he instructed. "I don't usually approve of them, but in this case, it's necessary."

She smiled. "Okay. Thanks." She hesitated and turned back. "This elderly woman, she was a seer. She said something to me about the future, about horror looming, that I shouldn't run from harsh words…"

"Seers are a dime a dozen on these fringe planets—you know that." He smiled. "Lady Caneese is the only person I ever knew who was accurate with her predictions. I shouldn't worry about warnings from strangers."

She laughed. "I suppose you're right. Well, thanks again."

"My pleasure."

He turned off the mute sphere and opened the door. "Lots of rest. I'll make it an official diagnosis. Okay?"

She nodded. "Okay."

She turned and walked slowly to her quarters. Hahnson waited until she was out of sight before he made his way to the bridge.

CHAPTER TWO

RHEMUN WAS DISCUSSING a new navigation program
with Holt Stern when Hahnson joined them on the
bridge.

Back when Holt was captain of the *Bellatrix*,
even with the usual military formality, Hahnson
would have thought nothing of greeting his commander with a smile. Here, on the *Morcai*, it was
like boot camp. Military formality was the order of
the day. Nobody used first names. Nobody acted in
a chummy fashion.

So Hahnson made a snappy salute. "Sir," he ad-
dressed Rhemun, "I need to speak to you for a moment."

Rhemun never smiled. His cat-eyes darkened to a
solemn blue. "Very well." He turned to Stern. "Keep
working with that program," he said curtly. "I will
expect it to be functioning perfectly before we lift.
Am I understood?"

"Yes, sir." Holt snapped him a salute, sat back
down and went to work. Hahnson, who knew his
friend very well, could see the hidden irritation that
accompanied the remark.

Rhemun led the way into the small cubicle off the bridge that was used for an office. He closed the door, but he didn't sit down or offer Hahnson a seat.

"Well?" he asked curtly.

Hahnson's dark eyes narrowed. "I've just spoken to Dr. Mallory," he began.

Rhemun held up a hand. "I know that Dr. Mallory has reacted badly to an incident earlier today," he said. "She will have to learn to cope. Even a combat medic must be expected to defend herself from attack."

"Commander Dtimun never allowed medics to be armed," Hahnson commented.

"I refuse to send any personnel into the field without weapons," Rhemun replied tersely. "But as to Mallory's condition, she must work through it herself."

He sighed. "Yes, sir, I realize that. But Dr. Mallory has never been in combat situations until quite recently."

Rhemun didn't speak. He folded his arms over his broad chest and stared at Hahnson.

"She really is doing the best she can, sir," he said finally.

"None of us has the time to shelter a physician from the harsh realities of military life," he replied curtly. "If Dr. Mallory finds her work too tedious, perhaps she should consider another branch of service."

"That is not an option," Hahnson said shortly.

Rhemun raised an eyebrow.

"Dr. Mallory washed out of combat school," Hahnson said stiffly. "Then she was rejected as a breeder…"

Rhemun's expression, in a normally expressionless face, was faintly surprising. "A breeder?" He said the word with blatant contempt.

"It isn't what you think," Hahnson replied. "She was kept in a lab while they decided if her genetics were sound enough for breeding purposes. They were not."

Rhemun's face hardened. "An inferior genome…"

"Recessive genes," Hahnson shot back, not caring if he had to take the loss of points on his military record. "They're not in fashion this year."

"Excuse me?"

"The government agency overseeing breeding decides from year to year which traits are acceptable, and as the board changes, so do the prejudices. The members of the board determined that recessive genes should be purged from the genome, so anyone who strongly depicted them was automatically rejected."

"Explain recessive genes."

"In a few words, blond or red hair and light-colored eyes."

"These traits are quite admirable," Rhemun replied. "Dr. Ruszel has beautiful coloring."

Hahnson wouldn't have touched that remark with a pole. He was aware that Rhemun had a soft spot for

Ruszel, which had caused some problems between him and the former commander of the *Morcai* before Dtimun and Ruszel bonded.

"Well, the board makes the final decision, sir," Hahnson replied tactfully.

"May I ask what those two rejections have to do with Mallory's current situation?" Rhemun asked after a minute, obviously impatient.

"It puts her in line for Reboot if she gets a third black mark on her service record. Sir."

"Reboot," Rhemun scoffed.

Hahnson frowned. "You know about it?"

"Yes. I know about it." He turned away. "Was there anything else?"

Hahnson was diverted. He hadn't realized that anyone outside the Terravegan medical corps knew the painful, horrible truth of that process. "May I ask how the commander knows of it?" he persisted.

"I was involved in a case where it was invoked. I will speak no more of it."

"Yes, sir."

Rhemun's eyes were dark with anger. "You humans protect your worst specimens in a manner that is repulsive to me."

"Sir?"

Rhemun waved a hand. "Dismissed."

"But, sir, about Dr. Mallory..."

Rhemun just looked at him. The look was enough. Hahnson saluted, turned and left the room.

How did Rhemun know about Reboot? Hahnson

asked himself. And not only that, why was he so dismissive of it, if he knew the truth? It disturbed him, but he wasn't going to try the alien's patience by referring to it again. Meanwhile, he'd do what he could for Mallory. Which was going to be precious little, he imagined.

EDRIS MANAGED TO get herself back together, after a fashion, but something inside her would never be the same after her brush with death.

She saw the alien face in her mind night and day, saw the horrified expression as life drained suddenly out of him. She slept badly, even with the sedatives. Her mental state made her more likely to make mistakes. When she did, the commander of the Holconcom was always ready to pounce.

"You have marked the wrong status on two of my crew," he growled at her when she'd presented him with the latest casualty list after a brief skirmish with renegade Rojoks on an asteroid colony world.

Edris looked at the padd and winced. "I'm sorry, sir," she said formally, still standing at attention. "It won't happen again."

He glared at her. Small. Blonde. Fair. Long, almost-platinum-colored hair tortured into a tight bun on top of her head. For one split second he wondered what it would look like loosened, and hated himself even for the thought. She was the image of a nightmare figure from his past, from a tragedy that he could never speak of to the humans aboard this ship. But it gave him reason to hate them, especially this one.

She swallowed. His hatred was almost palpable. She felt sick to her stomach. She didn't know what she'd done to create such antagonism. Well, she did snap back at him when he was at his worst. But that didn't really seem provocation enough for the anger he directed at her.

"Hahnson tells me that you aren't adjusting well after your…incident," he said after a minute. He lifted his chin and a cold little smile touched his chiseled mouth. "I suggested that a change of military assignments might be applicable."

She went pale. Her mind flashed with images of laboratories and body parts and agar in petri dishes.

Unknown to her, Rhemun saw those images. He didn't understand them. But, then, he understood very little about humans and their mental processes. However, her discomfort gave him pleasure. He felt a brief skirl of shame at his own behavior. An anniversary was upcoming. He couldn't share its import, but it was connected to his opinion of Mallory and her race and culture. He hated both. He hated the anniversary. His life was replete with torment, from adolescence onward. He had lost his father in a most terrible manner, in a way that shamed him and his mother even today, despite the emperor's kindness and support. Then he had lost another, to a human's stupidity. He closed his eyes. The pain was almost palpable.

"Sir?" she prompted, surprised at the anguish on his face.

He opened his eyes. They were dark brown, anger almost gone to rage. He hated her compassion. He didn't want it.

He handed her back the padd. "No more mistakes."

She saluted. "No, sir." Her tone was subdued.

His eyes narrowed. She was still pale. Why would the thought of reassignment be so disturbing to her? That was, after all, what Reboot was. The humans didn't punish their officers, not even for murder. They just reassigned them.

"Dismissed," he said in a cold tone.

"Yes, sir." She saluted and hurried away.

IT WAS ONLY going to get worse. She knew that. But she had no alternative, no place else to go. She was stuck here, Madeline Ruszel's replacement but never an acceptable replacement to the commander of the Holconcom, who revered Ruszel and hated Mallory.

"I should have known I couldn't make it here," she mumbled to herself as she ran blood samples through her small lab.

"Excuse me?"

She turned as Holt Stern entered. He was really a dish, she thought, smiling—dark wavy hair and dark eyes and a glorious physique. She wished she still had the crush on him that she'd had when she first served aboard the *Morcai*. But her heart was tugged elsewhere, to a person who didn't want her interest, who found her actually repulsive.

"Hey, Cap," she said with a grin. "How's things?"

He chuckled. She wasn't Maddie Ruszel, but he liked her. "Rough," he remarked with a sigh. "None of us are dancing with joy over the changes around here." He shook his head. "I never thought a court-martial would appeal to me more than staying in the Holconcom."

She lifted her eyebrows.

"Nobody back at Terravegan HQ knows I'm a clone," he pointed out. "If they found out, I'd be drummed out of the service. So would Hahnson. Only use we'd be then would be in some top secret government lab."

Sort of like me, she thought, but she only smiled. "It's not so bad. We just have to learn to get along together."

"Not going to happen, Doc," he replied, leaning back against a bulkhead. "I'm not the only one who has a problem. The new CO hates humans. Didn't you notice?"

She averted her eyes. "He's just not used to us yet," she said. "After all, he commanded the emperor's personal bodyguard for decades. All Cehn-Tahr. No humans."

"He makes his contempt for us known," Stern said quietly. "He doesn't even try to hide it."

"He wasn't with you at Ahkmau," she pointed

out. "Dr. Ruszel said that's what made the unit into a unit."

He nodded. "The enemy of my enemy is my friend," he agreed. "We pulled together and the CO got us out, with a little help from a real enemy, the Rojok Field Marshal Chacon." He chuckled. "When he took power, we thought the wars would be over forever, especially when he was given a seat on the Tri-Galaxy Council itself."

"We didn't consider that a lot of old, hard-line troops didn't want what they called 'handouts' from the Council. They thought of Chacon as a traitor and took to the field to oppose his rule." She smiled faintly. "How's that for a turnout?"

"Not what we all hoped for, for sure," he agreed. He studied her. "How's it going?"

Everybody knew what had happened to her. The humans had been sympathetic. Surprisingly, even some of the older Cehn-Tahr had been supportive.

"I guess I'm dealing with it," she said. "Not very well." She looked up at him. "How do you guys manage?"

He shrugged his broad shoulders. "After a few years in the field, it doesn't affect you so much. You still feel it, I mean. You just don't dwell on it. You can't afford to. It will get you killed. Worse, it will get your comrades killed."

She nodded. "The CO thought a change of military assignments might be the answer."

Stern's face went hard. "Does he know about Reboot?"

"Yes," she said, and he looked surprised. "He said he was familiar with it."

"And, knowing that, he still made the suggestion?" His face was like stone. "He's not getting rid of you," he said shortly. "Not unless he wants to lose the whole unit."

"Don't," she said. "Don't push him. You guys have as much to lose as I do. I already have one death on my conscience. No more. Period," she said firmly.

"We'd stand up for you," he told her.

She smiled. "I know that. Thanks."

He smiled. "What are friends for?"

THEIR NEXT ASSIGNMENT was to storm a suspected rebel Rojok base on Terramer, the former site of the Peace Planet that had failed.

Mallory was assigned to the forward unit, led by Holt Stern. But he kept her in the background, refused to let her advance with the troops.

She was treating a Rojok soldier for plasma burns when Rhemun rejoined the group, back from a scout with one of the Cehn-Tahr *kelekom* operators.

"What are you doing behind the lines?" Rhemun asked shortly.

She stood and saluted. "Captain Stern's orders, sir," she said formally.

"Pack your kit and get up with the line," he said coldly. "Your assistant can handle the job here!"

"Yes, sir." She didn't bother to argue. It would have done no good.

She found a place to work just behind a line of boulders and set up a temporary prefab medical hut with one of her techs.

"Go and do triage," she instructed. "I'll start with the men here."

"Yes, sir, Lieutenant."

She went to work, aware of Greshams firing and chasats returning fire all around her. The weapon fire didn't bother her as much as the thought of having to use a weapon. She tried to concentrate on her work, but the alien's face kept intruding.

"Dr. Mallory, there's a man over there," her assistant called.

She left the men with minor wounds and ran to her assistant. He was indicating a Rojok who was on a ledge, groaning loudly.

"Go take care of the abrasions in there." She indicated the hut. "I'll go over and look after this one."

"It's a long jump. Shouldn't I go?" he offered.

Rhemun would love that, she thought, having her delegate a dangerous chore to a subordinate. It would give him real grounds to demote or reassign her. "No," she said. "It's okay, I can do it."

She walked stealthily along the line of boulders, climbing up until she could see the ledge where the wounded Rojok was lying. His weapon was beside him, but when he saw Edris, he didn't reach for it.

"*D'egles* M'char Cha," she called across in the

old Rojok dialect, the one that Chacon had taught her while she was tending Dr. Ruszel's pregnancy on Memcache. "Don't worry. I come as a friend."

The Rojok, even through his pain, managed a smile.

She judged the distance fairly accurately, but when she went across, she dislodged the stone she'd used as a jumping point. It fell into the chasm below. She knew that she'd never be able to jump back across after she treated this poor fellow. But, she'd worry about that later.

She bent to her task. She questioned him and understood the answers as she treated his wound, which was a very bad one. A plasma blast from one of the Greshams had torn through his intestines. Untreated, the damage would have been quickly fatal.

She finished the sutures and smiled reassuringly. He would be taken to a prisoner of war camp, but nothing like Ahkmau. She reassured him that the Holconcom didn't torture captured prisoners. There was a treaty, under which such behavior was punishable. He only nodded, relieved.

He was able to jump the chasm. Edris, however, was stuck on the other side. The Cehn-Tahr who took the Rojok into custody stared across, motioning her to jump.

She sighed. "Can you send over a levibelt, please?" she called back. "I'm afraid I can't manage the distance—I knocked over the stone I used as a starting point."

One of them waved. She hoped they'd send Stern or even Hahnson. But it was Rhemun who came.

He glared across the chasm. "You can jump that," he scoffed. "It is hardly any distance at all!"

For a normal human, no. But Edris, with her gimpy motor functions, would end up dead and she knew it. For just an instant, she pictured the look on Rhemun's face as she fell to her death. It would almost have been worth it. She grimaced.

"I'm sorry, sir," she said, standing formally at attention and saluting. "I really will need the levibelt."

He jumped across as if he'd moved only a step. "Very well. I can carry you over," he said with long-suffering patience.

She backed away from him. "Sir...that would be unwise," she stammered.

He frowned. "Explain that."

She wasn't sure how to say it without giving offense and she didn't really want him to know how much she'd picked up about Cehn-Tahr customs— they were never shared with outworlders. But she was backed into a corner and she really had no choice.

"Sir, it would be unwise for the commander to touch me, sir," she said stiffly.

He looked down his nose at her with pure contempt. "I see. You've heard that certain behaviors in my race can be triggered by touching, is that correct?"

She didn't like the look in his eyes. "Yes, sir. Begging the commander's pardon, sir," she added.

"You think that I find you attractive, so that touching you would provoke me into unmilitary behavior?" he asked, almost purring.

"No…no, sir, of course not, sir." She hated herself for wimping out.

He smiled icily. "Mallory, I find nothing attractive about you. In fact, the only emotion you provoke in me is revulsion."

That was harsh, but she didn't dare reply. She'd gone right off insulting him ever since he mentioned reassigning her. She was afraid of him.

He realized that. And it was unfortunate, because nothing revolted a Cehn-Tahr more than fear. It had been Ruszel's incredible courage which had won his respect and his affection, despite her race. No Cehn-Tahr aboard the *Morcai* had more or better reasons to hate humans than Rhemun. Those whom he hated most were dead and out of reach of his vengeance. Mallory was close at hand, and vulnerable.

"Enlighten me, Lieutenant," he continued. "Why should I find you attractive?"

"Sir, I beg your pardon, but I never said I was…"

"You hardly had to say it," he shot back. "Apparently Stern finds you desirable, so perhaps I should send him to rescue you. Would that be more acceptable?"

She closed her eyes. "Sir, please…"

"Commander, we've got the last of them!" Stern called over, almost as if he knew what was going on there against the cliff. "Does Dr. Mallory need any help?"

Rhemun looked at Mallory as if he could have happily cut her throat. "Yes," he said. "She could use assistance." He turned and jumped lightly across the ledge. "Make haste," he added coldly. "These Rojoks may be only a splinter of a larger rebel group."

"Yes, sir."

Stern jumped across the distance almost as easily as Rhemun had. He was a clone, but with greatly advanced genetics, courtesy of the Rojok scientists who had cloned him from his original during the attack on Terramer. He was almost the equal of a Cehn-Tahr in strength, even without the help of the microcyborgs that the entire crew wore.

"Come on, Doc, I'll get you across," he teased. He bent and lifted her. "Old man giving you hell, was he?"

She nodded. "Thanks for the lift, Captain," she replied, and smiled up at him.

"Now, Stern!" Rhemun called angrily.

"Oooh, somebody's in a red-hot rage," Stern whispered in her ear, and she suppressed a nervous giggle.

"Coming, sir!" he called back to Rhemun with an angelic expression on his handsome face.

He landed in front of Rhemun with his soft burden, but he put her down almost at once when he registered the fury in the alien's expression.

"My hearing, like that of all Cehn-Tahr, is acute," he informed the captain, who was by now standing at stiff attention alongside Mallory. "Another infraction," he added softly, "and you will be up before a court-martial panel by the end of the day. Do I make myself clear, mister?" he added.

"Clear as mountain water, sir, yes, sir," Stern replied formally.

Rhemun looked down at Mallory with barely bridled anger. "Dismissed!"

The two of them almost ran for cover. Mallory didn't dare look at Stern. She was trying not to laugh at the brief glimpse she'd had of his rolling eyes before they left the commander standing there.

THE CAPTURED ROJOKS were turned over to a patrol ship for transport to the second of Memcache's moons, where prisoners of war were kept in a spacious, comfortable facility. One of the Rojoks was overheard telling his comrades about one of the humans who spoke the ancient tongue.

Hahnson wondered who they meant. He didn't know a single member of the human crew members who could even speak more than a few words of Standard Rojok.

He'd noticed that Edris had come back aboard even more depressed than usual, which prompted him to pay her a visit in her sector.

"How are you doing?" he asked.

She glanced up from lab results on a small padd. She smiled sadly. "Not so good. The CO's mad at me again."

"What did you do this time?"

She shook her head. "It's better not to discuss it," she said. She was wary of the AVBDs. It wouldn't do for Rhemun to catch her crying on Hahnson's shoulder.

He understood without a word what she was trying not to say. He closed the door and pulled out that little white ball and activated it.

"Nothing can hear through that, not even telepaths," he reminded her. "Spill it."

"I jumped across a crevice to treat a wounded Rojok and the rock displaced, so I couldn't jump back. The CO offered to ferry me across, but I wouldn't let him touch me." She winced. "He just went ballistic..."

"Humans aren't allowed to know such things about them," he pointed out. "They're very protective about their private behaviors, especially mating behaviors."

"Dr. Ruszel told me that," she replied. She drew in a long, heavy breath. "I know that if Cehn-Tahr males touch females, sometimes it triggers the mating cycle, even if I'm not allowed to know it. I wasn't sure if it was the same for females of other races..."

"It is," he interrupted.

She frowned. "I wasn't trying to insult him," she began.

"And how did he arrive at the idea that you had?"

"He hates me. He hates humans, but especially

me," she corrected. "He was insulted that I would think myself attractive to him at all."

"I see."

She lowered her eyes, almost in shame. "It's probably not noticeable to anyone except Cehn-Tahr," she began slowly, "but I...react...to him."

He frowned. "React?"

"Outbursts of pheromones," she said stiffly. "I know he can probably smell them, and that just makes it worse. Do you have something that inhibits hormone production?" she added plaintively.

"You get those at the same time you're mentally neutered for service," he began.

"Yes, but I tried to get into a breeding camp, remember? They did reject me but when they gave me the drugs later, I purged them, because I thought the board might reconsider my application. Bad move. Very bad move. Can you...?"

He sighed. "Yes. I can give you something. But there may be problems down the line. A lot of servicewomen who take them later in life have allergic reactions after a time."

"It doesn't matter about later, just right now," she replied. "I don't want to make things any worse than they already are."

"Okay, kid," he said gently. "I'll have my assistant bring them over when we get through talking. I noticed that it was Stern who ferried you over the chasm," he added with a grin.

She laughed. "Yes. Oh, I had such a flaming crush

on him when I first came aboard the *Morcai*." She shook her head. "In a way, I wish I still did. He's mourning for the woman he lost all those years ago, so it wouldn't be a problem." She looked up with a grimace. "Why am I getting a case on my hateful commanding officer? Sheer cussedness, you think?"

"You can sure pick them," he pointed out.

She grinned. "It's like people who hate cats, and cats always want to sit on them, you know?"

"He is a cat..."

"He has cat genes," she returned. "Besides, he doesn't want to sit on me. He wants to get rid of me. Maybe curtailing my pheromones will help."

"Maybe." He wasn't sure of that. No medicine known to science could completely override the human body's natural response to stimuli of that sort. Mallory had to know it.

He picked up the white ball. "Just try to stay out of his way. Maybe, eventually, he'll grow fond of us."

"Oh, sure."

He made a face and walked out.

CHAPTER THREE

NOT SURPRISINGLY, THINGS got decidedly worse on the *Morcai* after Mallory's involuntarily action on the cliffside. Rhemun gave her hostile glances every time he saw her.

He seemed to be the only Cehn-Tahr in the entire Holconcom who disliked her. Even old Btnu was kind, and he had enough reasons of his own not to like humans. Edris had heard that Btnu had been involved in a conflict with Alkaasar, the Cehn-Tahr who had rebelled against the empire and died as a result of it. An aggressive, and apparently mentally unstable, human advisor had provoked Alkaasar into a battle he couldn't win. But Btnu liked the little blonde doctor.

So, sadly, did Mekashe, Rhemun's friend. He came to see Edris often in her cubicle, just to talk. He was curious about humans and their social groups. He found endless questions about Terravega and the medical corps. He was always smiling, always in a bright mood. Edris warmed to him.

But he had a peculiar habit of trying to give her things. She didn't understand why he was so intense about it. He offered her everything from virtual pets to virtual flowers. She always refused, because the very intensity of his gift-giving made her uneasy. He was good-looking and kind. It didn't matter. Her emotions were centered on one very unpleasant member of his species, one who didn't want her interest.

Rhemun noticed Mekashe's visits to the sick bay.

"Why does he come here so often?" he asked Mallory coldly. "Mekashe is in perfect health."

"He's interested in Terravegan customs, sir," she replied, standing at attention.

"Yes?"

She swallowed. His tone was openly hostile. "He's curious about humans."

His dark eyes narrowed. "Let me give you some advice, Lieutenant," he said quietly. "Never accept anything from him."

She stared at him uncomprehendingly and flushed. "I...well, he's very kind," she began hesitantly, "and I don't want to hurt his feelings. But I can't, I mean I don't, accept gifts from him. Ever. Sir."

He lifted his chin. The way he looked at her was unnerving. She couldn't quite decide what that look really was. It was possessive. As if she belonged to him and Mekashe was trespassing. What an odd, and stupid, thought. She closed her mind on it at once. He hated her. She didn't need words to push that point home.

"I cannot speak to him about it," he said stiffly. "It is a breach of custom, a social taboo. But you must continue to refuse any gifts offered."

"I already do. Sir."

He nodded. "Very well. Dismissed, Lieutenant."

"Yes, sir." She saluted and almost ran from him.

He couldn't tell her that the giving of gifts was a prelude to courtship, or that Mekashe, unlike his own Clan, had accepted all the genetic modifications that Dtimun had. If Mekashe attempted to mate with the little blonde human, he would kill her.

As much as he disliked Mallory, he was also fond of Mekashe. They had been friends since boyhood. He didn't want the death of Mallory to lie heavily on Mekashe's conscience for the rest of his long life. Of course, that was why he was concerned. He turned and walked back toward the bridge. It was on Mekashe's account that he was concerned. Only that.

THE ENDLESS DRILLS continued aboard the *Morcai*. Rhemun timed the men on their response and rated them when they fell short of his idea of perfection.

"This is difficult for the men," Btnu cautioned gently. "Dtimun did this, but only at first, when the unit was formed after Ahkmau."

Akhmau was a sore spot. He had not shared that horror with the crew, so he didn't have the comradeship with the humans that Dtimun had forged. He was an outsider. They let him know it in many ways, most of which involved referring to their time in the Rojok concentration camp. It irritated him when the humans did it, but he hadn't expected his exec, Btnu, to join in.

His eyes narrowed over darkness. "We must have adequate response time. It might mean the difference between victory and defeat. When I captained the *kehmatemer*, these drills were conducted daily."

Btnu cocked his head in a very human way and even smiled. "I know, sir," he said gently. "But you were a bodyguard unit. Infantry. This is mechanized cavalry. They are different disciplines. As well, the *kehmatemer* was a very small group of men. We have hundreds aboard ship."

Rhemun didn't fly at him. He felt like it. "We might say that the difficulty is on both sides, but it remains that we must perform efficiently in combat."

"On that point, I agree," Btnu replied. "However, I will remind you, respectfully, that Dtimun led his troops more by affection and respect than by command alone."

Rhemun's jaw tautened. "I have no wish to befriend them."

"I know your past. The humans do not. You judge them by a tragedy. They are not evil. They have courage and good hearts."

"A human was responsible for my father's death," Rhemun said coldly. "A human killed my son."

"Yes." Btnu went closer and put a hand on Rhemun's shoulder, as a fond father might. "But these humans did not."

Rhemun felt cold. The memory of the past was covering him up, like ice. He never smiled. He never laughed. His heart was dead. And he was imprisoned here with the humans on a ship in space, because of his Clan status, because he was next in line to command the Holconcom. He wanted to go back to the emperor's bodyguard, but there was no escape.

"I do not belong here," he told Btnu, the words dragged out of him.

"You will belong here," the older Cehn-Tahr said quietly. "But first you must make the effort to earn the humans' trust."

Rhemun didn't reply with words. But he sighed, and nodded curtly.

Btnu smiled and went back to work.

THEY WERE ORDERED to Ondar, to pick up refugees from an ongoing conflict between a mixed culture community and a group of renegades who opposed Chacon's entry into the Tri-Galaxy Council with all the member worlds of Enmehkmehk's empire. The renegades struck unexpectedly, and efficiently, taking supplies, equipment, and sometimes even people when specializations were needed for some project.

Nobody could track them down, because they had no fixed base. The refugees were in a camp outside the largest city-state on the continent. This was where Madeline Ruszel had first encountered Tnurat. Edris had heard the story many times, so that she could almost picture it in her mind before Rhemun set the medical staff down in the camp and she saw the reddish landscape for herself.

"Prepare the refugees for transport," he told Edris

and her staff. "Hurry. The renegades strike quickly, and thanks to their depredations, they have equipment that equals our own."

"Yes, sir," she said, saluting him without quite meeting his eyes.

She led her medics into the camp, performing triage as she went along. There were only a couple of serious cases. One was a young Altairian boy who had suffered plasma burns when he ran unexpectedly between a Rojok and a colonist who were exchanging fire. The other was an elderly Altairian female with a concussion. Edris took care of the boy while Tellas, her assistant, treated the concussion.

Mekashe and several other soldiers who formed Rhemun's personal bodyguard unit had come down with them.

Ensign Lawrence Jones, the young blond weapons specialist, had accompanied them because of his prowess with a sensor cannon.

He paused beside Edris. "Ma'am there's a signal I can't read," he said.

She glanced at his monitor unit and grimaced. "That's a casualty," she pointed out. "See the life signs? It's Cularian, too." She looked past him. "Who's missing?"

"Not sure, sir. I don't see Mekashe, though," he added worriedly. Like Edris, he was fond of the commander's friend.

She finished healing the boy's wounds, smiled at

him and reassured him in Altair that he would heal and be whole again.

"You speak Altair?" Jones asked, grinning. "It's really hard to learn, Ma'am."

She smiled at him. "Really hard," she agreed. "I'm so slow that it takes me forever, but I've picked up quite a few languages in the past few years, even some that are an archaic form."

"I'm slow, too, Ma'am. Don't feel bad."

She nodded. "It's okay, Jones. You're doing great."

"Thanks." He glanced over to where the commander was just entering one of the scout ships. "He's going back to the ship to relay our progress to the military command," he told her. "We're having some comm issues on the ground. It's intermittent but it's causing him to be short-tempered. More short-tempered," he added under his breath. He shook his head. "I wish he didn't hate us so much."

She sighed. "You and me both, Jones." She got to her feet. "I'll have one of the air techs fly me over to the source of that signal. Darn, it's gone again. No matter, I saved the coordinates. If it's Mekashe, I'll send up a flare. You be watching, okay?"

"That's an affirmative, Ma'am. Please be careful."

She grinned. "You do the same."

A FEW MINUTES LATER, Edris wished she hadn't ordered the scout to leave her in the clearing. She'd been certain from the readings that a medical emergency loomed nearby—most likely one of their Cehn-

Tahr crew who'd gotten separated from the rest of the
landing party. It might be Mekashe who was missing.
The sensor reading indicated a wounded person, a
wounded Cularian person, in this vicinity. The sensors had suddenly fallen prey to an electromagnetic
interference of unknown origin, however, so it was
impossible to use a robot probe to find the victim.
She'd started to follow the sensor trail when her unit
began malfunctioning. It was almost, she puzzled,
as if the signal had been wiped out by some sort of
jamming device. It was quite possible that the renegade Rojok unit could still be camped near the refugees. They would certainly have jamming devices.

She checked her wrist sensor again. It was almost
useless. At least the drug banks would work if she
found an incapacitated soldier here. She only wished
she'd taken more time and refilled the med banks
first. As usual, she'd jumped in too quickly, without
enough preparation. It was a fault she'd tried to correct over the years. Her head injury from years ago
was still causing problems, even now.

Well, it would mean some walking, to use her eyes
and ears to search for a patient. But if it was Mekashe
lying there injured, it would be worth the effort.

A sudden, sharp sound made her turn her head.
She heard a voice speaking an ancient dialect of
Rojok, which only a few outworlders, including Edris,
could even understand.

"Holconcom!" it rasped. "Shoot!"

She felt a sudden burning pain in her lower rib

cage. "Stop! Medic, not soldier…!" she called back, in the same dialect, just before she hit the ground.

There was a scramble of feet and suddenly she was surrounded by Rojok soldiers of some elite group, all wearing black uniforms. The leader, who could be recognized by his long blond hair, stood over her with narrowed eyes. At that, he couldn't be the ranking officer, his hair only came to his shoulders, too short for even a company commander.

"Edris Mallory," she said, quickly using a light dose of her precious few meds to alleviate the pain. There was no time to diagnose the damage. "Dr. Mallory."

"Holconcom," the officer returned.

"Medic…not Holconcom soldier," she corrected. "I was searching for a wounded person. Our sensors…" She couldn't mention that they didn't work; this party of Rojoks was certainly one of the rebellious splinter groups that didn't honor Chacon's cease-fire with the Tri-Galaxy Fleet. "Our sensors weren't specific," she added.

"Our leader was wounded in a firefight with one of the refugees in a camp near here," the Rojok said. "You speak our dialect. This is unprecedented."

"I have an affinity for languages," she replied. "May I see your leader? I am a specialist in Cularian medicine."

He looked even more surprised. He glanced at the others, who were uneasy and coaxed him to let her try.

He sighed and signaled his men to holster their weapons. "Yes. We will take you to him."

It was hard to get up, even harder to walk. There was some internal damage, but not immediately life-threatening. Perhaps a slightly damaged lower lung. It was difficult to breathe normally, so it was probably the lung. The lower lobe was expendable, if necessary. Thank goodness the shot hadn't been better aimed. She'd already used a mild sedative, just enough to get her through the worst of the pain. She got to her feet.

She followed them to a speeder, got inside, and was whisked to their base camp. It was small. There were only about ten of them. They looked shocked when their comrades came into camp with a small blonde human female wearing the uniform of their enemy, the Holconcom, but they recovered quickly when the ranking officer explained why they'd brought her to camp.

He took her to a molded plexifab hut, inside which was a tall Rojok officer, middle-aged, lying unconscious on a pallet.

Edris went to him at once and prayed that her scanner would work long enough to diagnose, and that the electromagnetic field wouldn't interfere with the operation of her drug banks.

She grimaced, because the scanner wasn't working properly. "There's interference with my sensors here…" she began worriedly.

The ranking officer snapped something to a soldier, who saluted and left. Only a couple of minutes later, the sensors were working again. A jamming device. That made sense.

"Thanks," Edris said with a glance at him. "I'm afraid we've lost the ability to do examinations without our tech these days. Medicine, like weaponry, is dependent on it."

He nodded. He didn't speak. He stood, grim-faced, while she diagnosed the condition of their leader.

She sighed and smiled. "It's not as bad as it looks," she promised him. She went to work. It was a penetrating wound which had done damage to several internal organs and nicked his colon. She set about using her tools to do the necessary repairs.

Halfway through, he came around and groaned.

"Sorry," she said in the dialect, and used the last of her drugs to inject a powerful painkiller. "Better?" she asked.

He looked up at her, blinked and managed a rough laugh. "Better. A Holconcom? And you haven't killed me?"

"No, sir," she said, with a painful smile. Her own injury was uncomfortable. "We take an oath to treat any patient, regardless of political affiliation. Besides that, I know Chacon," she added softly.

He was impressed. "How?"

"My best friend is married to the son of the Cehn-Tahr emperor," she said easily. "His sister is the mate of Chacon. I attended the bonding ceremony on Memcache."

"We revere Chacon," he said heavily. "It grieves me that he joined the Empire with that of the Cehn-Tahr." He did not add that Chacon was a relative of his. It had saddened him to oppose the field marshal on this issue.

"It was to prevent the war from spreading," she said simply, "and claiming even more lives on both sides of the conflict. He sits in council now with the Tri-Galaxy and has a powerful voice in making policy. He will see to it that planets in the New Territory are shared equally between all worlds, including Enmehkmehk, your own homeworld."

He touched his stomach. "I feel the mending," he said, surprised.

She smiled. "We have powerful medicines, and even more powerful instruments." She closed her wrist scanner. Its drug banks were empty now.

The commander of the small unit got to his feet with a little effort, stood erect, towering over Edris, and managed a smile. "Thank you."

She smiled back. "Saving lives is an obligation, not a kindness," she said, quoting Dtimun, the emperor's son who had led the Holconcom for many years.

They moved outside, and suddenly the entire camp was on alert. A red blur materialized beside Edris with his big hand around the throat of the Rojok commander. Rhemun!

"No!" She jumped between them, pushing at Rhemun's broad chest. She grimaced at the pain.

Rhemun, shocked, let go of the Rojok. Edris moved between the two aliens, to shield the Rojok with her own small body. "No, he's a friend! I just saved his life. Don't you dare kill him!"

Rhemun gaped at her. She'd just spoken to him unthinkingly in the dialect the Rojoks used, the ancient tongue, which he spoke but no human ever had.

The Rojok commander laughed. "So everything written of the Cehn-Tahr Holconcom is true, I see," he mused. "Such speed is almost impossible to believe, unseen."

Rhemun nodded solemnly. "This is almost never seen outside a battlefield. Why is my medic here?"

The commander's lieutenant moved forward. "We brought her to treat our officer," he said. "She speaks the ancient tongue," he added with faint reverence.

"So I see." Rhemun lifted both eyebrows. "Impressive," he added, almost reluctantly.

"Odd that your commander would allow her to wander around hostile, contested territory alone," the older commander remarked, obviously not recognizing that Rhemun was the commander. Holconcon leaders never wore rank insignia.

"He had no knowledge of her deployment," Rhemun replied. "I came in search of her." He didn't add that Mallory's absence from the camp had first annoyed him, and then concerned him, as she'd gone in the direction of a suspected Rojok camp. Instead of deploying someone to check on her, he'd come himself. He didn't dare examine that thought too closely.

"I wasn't supposed to come alone," Edris told the Rojok with a grimace. "I suppose I'll be stood against a wall and shot for insubordination."

The Rojok commander laughed.

"I thank you for my life," the Rojok told her gently, and smiled. "We will tell tales of you around campfires."

"You honor me, when I am unworthy," she said, in the same ancient tongue.

He only smiled. He sighed as he looked at Rhemun. "Perhaps the old ones are right, and Chacon's government will be one to support." He shrugged. "My men and I will surrender ourselves and hope for clemency."

"I can tell you from my own experience that Chacon is the most fair-minded of military leaders," Rhemun told him. "He does not punish idealism."

The Rojok smiled secretly. He did not share his affiliation with the new head of the Rojok government. The Rojok bowed formally. So did Rhemun.

"May I know your name?" he asked the little blonde human.

She managed a faint smile for him. "Dr. Edris Mallory."

He made a stab at pronouncing it, which widened the smile.

"That's close enough," she said, encouraging him.

"My name is Soltok," he replied. "I will remember you."

"I will remember you." It was a formal leave-taking.

The men saluted her and Rhemun. The salutes were returned. The human and the Cehn-Tahr left the camp, walking.

When they were far enough down the dirt trail to be out of earshot, Rhemun glared at her. "I gave strict orders that no one was to do foot searches down here," he said curtly.

"Sorry, sir," she said, and managed a salute. "There was a wounded person. I recognized the physiology as Cularian. I didn't realize it was a Rojok. Nobody had seen Mekashe and I thought it might be him. The sensors weren't working properly…" She stopped walking, grimaced and caught her breath. There was a lot of pain. She felt unsteady on her feet.

Her remark about Mekashe had caught him on the raw. He didn't like her affection for his friend. He would have said something about it but her gasp caught his attention. "I smell blood," he exclaimed, turning to her. "And cauterized flesh."

She drew in a breath and went to sit on a large boulder beside the trail. "I was shot with a chasat."

"What?"

She held up a hand, because he was looking back in the direction of the Rojok camp with fiery intent. "They saw the uniform and fired first. Having seen you appear in their camp the way you did, I wouldn't have blamed them for shooting first. Holconcom have a fierce reputation among soldiers, and I don't wear a medical insignia that's visible at a distance. Something I'm going to recommend change for," she added.

"How bad is it?"

She swallowed. "I made running repairs. I think I may have some minor internal damage. I have nothing left in my medical banks. I used it all on the Rojok officer."

He drew in a rough breath. "I can carry you to the ship," he said.

She held up a hand. "No!"

He scowled, waiting for an explanation.

"I know that the commander doesn't find anything attractive about me, however, I am bleeding," she pointed out. "Even if I make a breach in protocol by mentioning it, if you come in contact with my blood, it could…" She bit her tongue. She was going to catch hell anyway, but she couldn't bring herself to say the words.

He lifted his chin. He was angry that she'd dared to say anything to him about intimate Cehn-Tahr behaviors. They were not discussed even between males, unless they shared Clan affiliation. Even then, it required at least family status.

Here she was, an outworlder, a human, presuming to lecture him on the dangers of touching her. And not for the first time. She'd made the same remark when he started to carry her across the chasm on an earlier mission. The trouble was, she was right. That made it worse.

He rubbed the crystal on his comm ring and Hahnson appeared.

"Mallory is wounded. I cannot touch her. This is our position. Make haste." He cut the communication and glared at Mallory.

"Sir, it's not my fault," she said, trying to stand at attention. "I was made aware of certain things during my time on Memcache when Dr. Ruszel delivered her son. I learned by things I overheard. I did not pry or ask questions."

He looked down his nose at her. She was in obvious pain and he felt guilty that he didn't just swing her up in his arms and run with her back to the refugee camp. However, she was correct. The scent of her pheromones was already disturbing. If he touched her, if he came in contact with her blood, it would almost certainly provoke a mating behavior. It was more dangerous than coming into contact with just her skin. It made him angry that she knew.

"We do not discuss such things, even among ourselves," he snapped.

"Yes, sir. I know that, sir. I'm very…sorry, sir." Her voice was getting weaker.

He rubbed the crystal again. "Hahnson, where the hell are you?" he demanded, sounding so much like Dtimun in a temper that Edris just stared at him.

"Five clicks away. Four. Three," Hahnson was counting.

Two seconds later, he landed in one of the small scout ships, piloted by Ensign Jones. "Hold it there," he told Jones. "We'll be right in."

He ran to Edris, examined her and grimaced. "You have a knack for accidents," he pointed out as he extricated his tools from his wrist unit. "You couldn't treat this yourself?"

"Used up all my meds treating a renegade Rojok."

"And they shot you?" Hahnson added coldly. "Some gratitude!"

"His men shot me when they saw the uniform, Doc," she replied, wincing. "We need bigger medical devices on our uniforms…"

"I'll put in a suggestion. Hold still."

He had to go close to work on her. Rhemun turned away. It was incomprehensible that he suddenly wanted to throttle Hahnson. A growl rose in his throat. He suppressed it by activating his comm ring and trying to get a message through to the crew at the refugee camp.

"All fixed." Hahnson chuckled. He hadn't noticed Rhemun's strange behavior or he might have remarked on it.

Edris got to her feet and drew in a long sweet breath. "Thanks," she said warmly.

"Back to the camp," Rhemun said icily, and gestured them toward the ship.

Mekashe was waiting at one of the preformed huts. He grinned when Mallory came into view. "You went looking for me," he exclaimed with a laugh. "You thought I was wounded and you were concerned?"

"She was wounded looking for you," Rhemun snapped. "A loss of time and efficiency." He glared at Mallory. "Your department would benefit from the same drills I require of command line soldiers. I'll initiate them when we're back aboard." He turned to Mekashe. "We have no time for pleasant conversation."

"Yes, sir," Mekashe said, saluting. But he had green eyes when he glanced at Edris.

She only nodded. She didn't want to see any more of the commander's temper. She was uneasy enough already. He didn't want Mekashe around her. She'd have to find a kinder way to deter his friendliness.

CHAPTER FOUR

EDRIS CONTINUED TO use the hormone suppressant that Hahnson had prescribed for her, but ironically, it seemed to increase the hunger she felt when she saw her commanding officer. It was much worse after her experience on Ondar, saving the Rojok commander. It had irritated Rhemun that she knew so much about his culture's intimate behaviors. Which didn't help his attitude toward her; it grew more acrimonious by the day.

His temper was unpredictable, and it escalated. He infuriated the human crew members by assigning them to off-duty education programs, reducing the already-small recreational time they were permitted by over half.

Stern, on behalf of the rest of the crew, protested.

"If you find the tasks aboard a Cehn-Tahr vessel too arduous, Captain," Rhemun said with faint contempt, "perhaps you would be more content to return to a Terravegan brigade."

Stern stared at his superior officer with cold eyes. "As I'm certain you already know, Commander," he said with quiet pride, "I would be used for spare parts, in such case."

"No military body would tolerate such abuse of its personnel," Rhemun discounted it. "You exaggerate."

"I assure you, it is no exaggeration of the facts," Stern replied. "Perhaps you might ask Commander Dtimun to acquaint you with Terravegan military protocols."

Rhemun lifted his chin. "I command the Holconcom. Not Dtimun."

"I know. Sir." The words conveyed enormous disdain.

"The adjunct educational requirements will be met. Or else. Dismissed!"

Stern saluted and went back to his friends, who were waiting for him in one of the storage areas.

Hahnson activated his white ball. "What did he say? Do we still have to do it?"

Stern nodded. "He's just looking for ways to provoke us. It's obvious we don't need retraining in our respective professions. There's not even that much new tech to learn, besides that nightmare of an updated astrogation program he dragged me through. Even that isn't much of an improvement over the software we're already using, as far as I can see." He huffed. "Listen, the guy's a ground pounder," he said shortly. "He led the emperor's bodyguard. Great job, he was good at it, but this is the space marines! If anybody needs retraining in his damned profession, it's him!"

"No argument there," Hahnson said. "He's grinding poor Mallory into the ground, for sure. He goes out of his way to stand on her."

"I noticed that," Stern replied. "He's baiting all of us, hoping to start a fight so he can kick us out of the Holconcom."

"It does seem that way," engineering exec Higgins said.

"Certainly does," Chief Communications Officer Jennings seconded. "He's ticked off most of the comm department with his new requirements and duty stations. Like he knows how to run a starship!"

"How the hell did he end up with Dtimun's command, anyway?" Stern wanted to know.

"Each military position has a Clan requirement," Hahnson said. "That's all I know, so don't start asking more questions. He was obviously next in line for this post so he got it. End of story."

"Suppose we pretend we don't know Dtimun is the emperor's son." Stern grinned. "Would they give him back to us?"

"Fat chance. He's got a son now." Hahnson chuckled. "He's not going off into space combat, not if Maddie Ruszel has anything to say about it."

"Well, back to the subject at hand. Just how long do you think we can hang on here?" Higgins asked Stern. "I mean, he's going out of his way to push us. He wants us off the ship!"

"Begging your pardon, sir, but he's right," Jennings seconded. "He couldn't make it much plainer."

"It's still early days," Strick Hahnson commented. "He's not used to a combined command, and he has deep prejudices against humans. He was thrown in headfirst when Dtimun's real identity as the emperor's son was divulged. He'd commanded the *kehmatemer*, the emperor's bodyguard, for decades. He can't be much happier than we are."

"The difference is that he's in command and we've got targets painted on our chests," Jennings pointed out. "The commander, even when he was furious, never treated us humans any different than the Cehn-Tahr crew members."

"We went through hell with the commander," Stern pointed out quietly. "Nobody who lived through Ahkmau could ever tolerate racial prejudice again."

"That's true," Hahnson had to concede.

"The commander saved us all," Higgins agreed. "What a hell of a rescue it was, too." He chuckled. "Do you remember how he came walking aboard the *Morcai* with Mangus Lo over his shoulder?"

"Yeah—" Jennings grinned "—and the way he walked all over Admiral Lawson to get us transferred to the Holconcom, and then led us out of the admiral's office while he was still in midtirade?"

"Nobody else in the three galaxies like the commander," Higgins said with pure nostalgia. "What a hell of a commanding officer!"

Stern sighed. "Good days."

"Never to be lived again," Jennings lamented.

There was a long silence.

"So, what do we do?" Higgins asked Stern.

Holt Stern's black eyes were sad. "We hold on for a little while longer, to see if things get any better."

"And then?" Higgins prompted.

Stern looked at him evenly. "You guys can go back to the Terravegan military without a single black mark on your records. The emperor would go to bat for you."

"Yeah, but you can't," Jennings said. "I'm not going without you, sir."

"Nor I," Higgins added.

Hahnson held up his hand and grinned. "Matched set. Can't break it up, Holt."

Holt swallowed, hard. "Well, we'll see how things go."

They all nodded.

So THE OFFICERS and crew, the human ones, went back to school, in a sense, during their off-duty hours. They grumbled, and nobody saw the sense in it. Rhemun ignored them. He'd never hated a posting so much. He even queried the emperor about returning him to the bodyguard unit, but without success.

He was angry, and he took it out on the humans. In all his life, he'd never been forced into a situation he hated as much—well, possibly once. That disgusting, ambitious female and her covert knowledge of herbs that provoked the mating cycle...

He turned his thoughts away from that pride-wrecking memory and the painful ones that followed it. He felt like a trapped animal, hating his surroundings and those he shared them with. But there was no recourse. He would have to cope, somehow.

MALLORY WAS SLOWLY regaining her self-respect, and the memory of the man she killed was fading into a still-painful but less haunting one. Meanwhile, she was developing a whole new set of problems.

Her interest in her commanding officer was growing. It had nothing to feed on. He hated her and made no secret of it. But her heart jumped whenever she looked at him. The hormone suppressants were working, after a fashion. But even if he couldn't smell the pheromones, he could certainly detect her racing pulse and shallow breathing when she was close to him.

It didn't make her life easier. He found new ways to annoy her, picking out flaws in her inventory system, dwelling on past mistakes. His newest requirement entailed noting every single injury ever suffered by Cehn-Tahr aboard the *Morcai* into a file.

IT HAD TAKEN two days, but she managed it. She was on her way to present it to him when Btnu stopped by, complaining of a headache that refused to go away.

She was very fond of the *Morcai*'s executive officer—Rhemun had replaced Stern with Btnu in that position—but she couldn't do invasive tests without permission from her commanding officer, Rhemun.

"It will take a little time to arrange," she said gently, and smiled. "I'll just speak to the commander about it."

"Thank you, Dr. Mallory." He hesitated. "I was also distraught when I killed for the first time. He was a Rojok, and we were at war, but my conscience was damaged," he said slowly. "I understand the difficulty. We are taught in our culture never to take life, but when we are in the military we are expected to do what is necessary." He smiled. "It is never easy."

"No. It never is. Thank you for sharing that," she said. "It's nice to know that some of you don't hate us because we're human," she couldn't help adding with some bitterness.

Btnu looked concerned. "You do not know, about him, about his past," he said softly. "There is a reason."

"We didn't do anything," she pointed out.

He sighed. "I know, Dr. Mallory. But you do not know. I wish that I could tell you. It is not my secret to tell."

"You're a nice man."

He made a sound like human laughter. "Not a man."

"You're a nice Cehn-Tahr," she corrected, and grinned.

He chuckled. "The commander is working out with the Kahn-Bo. He and Mekashe are in the gymnasium." He leaned down. "Mekashe is better, but only a little." He rose back up. "Do not tell him that I said so."

"Not to worry. I'm usually listening, not talking." Which was true. She rarely got a word in edgewise these days.

She closed the cubicle and went looking for the commander.

RHEMUN AND MEKASHE were locked in a heated struggle with the Kahn-Bo sticks. Rhemun was laughing as he applied all his strength to block the other alien's attack.

Mallory, her eyes on the padd, came into the cubicle and stopped dead when she noticed the intensity of the mock combat. She was shocked at the feelings the sight of her commander stripped to the waist engendered in her. She felt her heartbeat rocket as she watched the play of muscle in his massive chest and arms as he struggled with the other alien. His skin was pale gold, flawless. There was a thick wedge of curling black hair that ran down his broad chest to his abdomen. His spine displayed a thin band of fur that ran its length, barely visible above his waist where the flowing black curls of his hair draped in violent contrast to the golden skin.

He was laughing. He enjoyed a fight. The feline features of his face eclipsed into something almost human as his white teeth were displayed.

HE WAS, SHE THOUGHT, the most beautiful, magnificent creature she'd ever seen in her life.

As her mind worked, he suddenly stopped laughing and turned. His demeanor changed instantly. He lifted his chin. "Yes, Doctor Mallory?" he asked curtly.

She swallowed down the helpless awe and approached him with her eyes lowered. "Btnu requires an invasive scan," she explained in a subdued tone. "I can't do the procedure without your authorization."

"An invasive scan for what, exactly?" he snapped.

She held out the virtual comp. Her hands were shaking. He took it from her with something bordering on contempt and studied it.

"What did he do, swallow down a *cerat* whole?" Mekashe asked on a chuckle, referring to the small furry mammals that the Cehn-Tahr sometimes consumed for a protein jolt.

"He's complaining of violent headaches," she said, and managed a smile for him. "Nothing major, we just want to avoid problems down the line."

Mekashe cocked his head and studied her. The little human female was enticing, in many ways.

Rhemun became aware of his interest. It should not have disturbed him. He hated humans. He glanced at his friend. "We shall have to postpone the match."

"You are hoping that I will lose my edge over time," Mekache teased. "I will not."

"We will see," Rhemun replied.

"I will return to my duties. Sir. Dr. Mallory," he added in a soft, almost-purring tone, which earned him a cold glare from his commander.

He left the chamber, chuckling to himself.

Rhemun signed the virtual order and handed it back to Mallory. His nostrils processed the strong scent of pheromones that was issuing from her body. His jaw tautened.

"I find your interest offensive," he said coldly.

She had forgotten his olfactory superiority. She grimaced. "Sir..."

"You are human," he said, making almost an insult of the words. "Near the end of the Great Galaxy War, I had my young son moved to a military school in a system outlying the Megorian Sector." He waited for that impact on the small human. It seemed to stun her. "A female human pilot was playing some virtual vid with two companions on the nexus when she was ordered to use her strategic weapons on a Rojok emplacement. She mistook the target and dropped the entire cargo on the military academy. My son was incinerated in a flash."

Mallory's lips fell open. Her mind was on overdrive. He had lost a son. He was bonded to a female. She had been watching him, hoping for some sign of his interest, and all the time, he was in a relationship. He had a child who had died. She was ashamed of her behavior and her feelings for him. She had thought he was, like most of the Cehn-Tahr in the Holconcom, a solitary male.

HE SAW HER emotions clearly. He felt them. He lifted his chin. His eyes were dark with anger. "The human female was small, with blond hair and blue eyes. Like you."

She felt those words all the way to the soles of her feet. She looked at him with helpless comprehension. "I'm so sorry," she said huskily. "So very sorry, for you, and your mate."

He ignored the comment. "She was tried, court-martialed. But she was not punished. My government protested. It did no good. She killed my son and never paid for it!"

That was unusual. The Terravegan military was overly sensitive to such issues. But it had been long ago. Perhaps the law had been different then.

"Since I first saw you, when the emperor arrived aboard to help save Ruszel's life, I have felt nothing but revulsion," Rhemun emphasized, the injustice of the past making his tone harsh and cold. "Your continued presence aboard the *Morcai* is a constant reminder of the tragedy. I look at you and see the murderer of my son!"

Mallory had only basic psych training from the Tri-Fleet Medical Academy, but she understood what was happening. Rhemun had been unable to avenge the death of his child. The murderer was out of reach. But Mallory, who resembled her, wasn't. Much became clear in her mind. His continued antagonism, his constant criticism of her slowness, her ineptitude—now it made sense. It wasn't her skill or lack of it that prompted his distaste. It was a personal tragedy. Mallory was being made to pay for a crime she had never

committed. She had no defense. Her soft blue eyes
searched his angry ones and she saw secret dreams
fall to dust there.

"I don't want your interest," he gritted. "The scent
of pheromones that exudes from you is an insult! It
disgusts me!"

She swallowed hard and pulled herself to a rigid
stance. "I beg the commander's pardon," she said
unsteadily. "It isn't...intentional."

"See Hahnson," he said curtly. "There must be
some chemical means of disrupting the pheromones.
I want no repeat of this."

She didn't dare mention that she'd already been
taking the maximum dose possible. There was nothing stronger, and she was already showing symptoms of allergic reaction to the substance Hahnson
had prescribed. But she lied. "I'll speak to him at
once, sir."

He searched her blue eyes with contempt. "See
that you do."

"I am very sorry," she added, avoiding his gaze.
"So very sorry. But you're still young, sir. You and
your mate can have other children..."

"My personal life is not your concern!"

She stood straighter. "It is not," she agreed. "Sorry."

"And stop saying that you're sorry!"

She fished around for another word, couldn't find
it in her disturbed state and said nothing. She was
all but shaking.

He saw that. He knew, somewhere deep inside

himself, that he was being unreasonable, but the floodgates had been opened. He had never spoken of his loss to any other Cehn-Tahr. The emperor knew, of course, but it was a secret that the two of them had kept. He was sharing his grief with Mallory, an outworlder, a human who looked like the killer. It was incomprehensible to him. Such subjects were taboo except between family members or close friends, and Mallory was neither. His own behavior sickened him.

"Dismissed!" he snapped. "And you will never speak of this conversation!"

"Of course not, sir," she said, in a shaky voice. "Doctors make a vow never to discuss private revelations, you know."

He hadn't known. He didn't care. He saw again the ashes that had once been his child and felt again the rage and pain and...

He turned on his heel and stalked off.

MALLORY DIDN'T GO to see Hahnson. She went to her quarters blindly and began methodically packing her few possessions. The military didn't allow much. She had her uniforms and some personal bits of clothing that she wore off duty. She had a brush and a virtual Nagaashe that kept her company in her privacy.

When she was packed, she sent a flash to Tri-Galaxy Fleet HQ and resigned her commission. That done, she booked a seat aboard a passenger ship that would cross the path of the *Morcai* only scant minutes later. She would have to run to the airlock to make connections, and there was no time to explain what she was doing. Protocol demanded that she tell Rhemun of her decision and give him time to send for a replacement Cularian specialist. But she couldn't wait. She couldn't bear to see the contempt and hatred in his eyes. Stop the pheromone production? There was only one way known to contemporary science to accomplish that. Yes, she could use a drug, in fact she was already using one, but it clearly didn't work. She was aware that she wasn't thinking clearly. Rhemun's undisguised hatred confused her, panicked her. She had to get off the *Morcai*, get away from Rhemun, before she humiliated herself even more. The fact that he knew how she felt only made it worse.

No, drugs wouldn't suffice. The only way was to remove herself from his presence. And this was dangerous. By resigning her commission she was admitting to her third failure as a soldier. It would put her under the three strikes law and leave her vulnerable to Reboot. In fact, it was quite likely that Tri-Fleet HQ would send a team to arrest her and bring her back for a formal hearing. After which... She didn't dare think about afterward. There were rumors that one victim of Reboot had been kept in a lab for almost four decades, taken apart cell by cell for experimentation.

She ignored the possibility. Where she was going, they'd have a job trying to find her. She had a former colleague on Benaski Port who was the center of illegal activity there. She flashed him on scramble and asked permission to work in the Underway, as the underbelly of Benaski was known, as a medic. Permission was given at once, with an amused smile and a welcome. She had been kind to him at medical school, as many others had not, when he left because of his refusal to produce clones for medical experimentation. That practice had been ended by a Tri-Galaxy Council investigation. So now, the live human specimens collected legally under the guise of Reboot were even more precious.

She ran down the corridor, into the airlock and onward to the skimmer she'd reserved, pleading a medical emergency on the passenger ship.

The tech, a Cehn-Tahr with a kind face, smiled at her. "You will return shortly?"

"Of course," she lied, smiling back as she entered the skimmer. "But I'm sending the skimmer right back, temporarily. Don't know how long this may take, and the patient is a high-ranking Jebob diplomat."

"Very well, Doctor. Have a safe trip."

"Thanks."

She closed the skimmer, punched the ignition switch and hovered through the first lock to the second. It opened. She flew out into open space, toward a bright dot that was moving on her astrogation screen.

She'd thrown away her career, left her few friends, made a refugee of herself, all because her commanding officer found her very presence distasteful. It was shocking that she hadn't realized, until he spoke to her, how involved with him she truly was. Their arguments and disagreements had been only a symptom of her growing feelings for him, which she could not contain or remove. And he was bonded. He had had a child... The grief and shame she felt overwhelmed her. Her only option was to leave.

Strick Hahnson was going over scans when he heard the faint beep of the vid player. "Yes?" he asked.

The screen lit with Mallory's face. "Sir, I'm en route to...well, never mind where. I've resigned my commission. I'm sorry to leave so suddenly, but there's been a...well, an incident." She swallowed. "I can't discuss it. But I had to go."

He was thunderstruck. "Mallory, what have you done? You've put yourself under the Three Strikes provision!"

She drew in a long breath. "I know. I couldn't help it. They may send a team, but they'll have a long search. I can cover my tracks."

"Come back here, before it's too late!" he ordered.

She smiled sadly. "I can't. I've messed up too badly. I can't tell you what happened, but it's impossible for me to continue in the military. At least for now."

"Where are you going?"

"Can't tell you, Doc," she replied, and forced another smile. "But I have some skills. I'll get by. Sorry to leave you in the lurch about a Cularian specialist, but Tellas can take over until you get a replacement. We've got several residents at base who would love the assignment when they get their medical licenses. There might even be a female or two, to maintain the status quo."

"There was nothing about your resignation on the nexus here," Strick said worriedly.

"That's because I hadn't posted it until now." Her face was somber. "Please tell everyone I'm sorry. I loved serving aboard the *Morcai*. I know I made a lot of mistakes…"

"Head injuries leave minor disturbances in the brain," he replied gently. "I told you that you should discuss that with Rhemun, but you refused." He frowned. "He's always on about your lack of coordination and your slowness. You should have told him. It was another argument, wasn't it?"

She didn't answer. She smiled. "I'll miss you. Please tell the others I'll miss them, too, but anybody can be replaced. I was never an adequate replacement for Dr. Ruszel in the first place. You need someone more competent."

"You should have asked me for help, kid," he said gently. "I'd have done anything I could to get you out of whatever trouble you're in."

"There's no help for this trouble, I'm afraid." She reached for the kill switch. "See you around, Doc. And thanks for everything."

The screen went dead.

HAHNSON DID TRY to contact Rhemun about Mallory's abrupt departure, only to find that the Holconcom commander wasn't on the ship. Btnu said that he'd gone to Memcache on some top secret matter and he was maintaining radio silence, as the ancient language would denote it. Hahnson just smiled. *Karamesh*, he thought, remembering their former crewmate, Komak's, reference to that Cehn-Tahr concept of fate. He couldn't tell Rhemun, so that gave Mallory a little time to hide out, before her resignation became public knowledge and the black ops team at Terravegan Medical Command acted. He shuddered to think of her fate if she were found.

CHAPTER FIVE

EDRIS WAS LOST and alone in a colony of aliens who lived in abject poverty on Benaski Port. She was afraid to show herself anywhere she might be recognized. There were always spies who dealt in the sale of information. She didn't want the black ops group to find her.

She was grateful that she knew Percival Blount, whom everyone referred to locally as "Patch." He'd made her welcome, had one of his men forge documents for her so that she could practice medicine without being detected on the nexus, and forwarded her several hundred mems so that she had enough for food and what passed for lodging in the Underway of Benaski Port.

"You don't know how grateful I am," she told Patch.

He waved her thanks away. He only had one eye, but the other one was good enough to appreciate her delicate beauty. She really was a looker. Sadly, her neutered status made her an unlikely candidate for his affection, so he didn't try his luck.

"No, I'm happy to have you here. I'm the only doctor practicing here who has an actual medical degree. At least, until now," he chuckled. "Since you're available to my people, I can take a job out on the Rim that I want to do."

"You're leaving?" she asked worriedly.

"Just for a few standard weeks," he assured her. "There won't be any problems. Things run like a well-oiled machine around here."

"Thanks." She grinned at him. It was the first time she'd smiled like that in ages. She glanced at two little Parsifan girls who lived with the old woman who was giving her lodging in a sort of prefab dome. It was the best the Underway had to offer, which wasn't really saying much. It was pretty crowded with two women and two preadolescent children.

"Oh, a word to the wise," he cautioned, moving her out of earshot of the girls. "Cartha runs a brothel here. Several of them, in fact," he added coolly. "I tolerate him because he pays well, but he's developing a king-complex about who's in charge. Don't let him run over you." He nodded toward the girls, one who was eight and the other ten. "They're just the age he likes to get girls, to start them, if you know what I mean. Keep them out of sight. Their parents were lost in a terrorist attack. The old woman's taking care of them."

"Do they have relatives?" she asked.

"Yeah, somewhere in one of the outer colony worlds—not sure where. I'll have to track it down. It will be expensive to hire transport, and they don't have anything. They wouldn't be living down here if they did," he added solemnly.

"Maybe I can figure out some way to get them there," she said.

"Figure out how to keep yourself hidden, first," he said grimly. "You were good to me in medical school, a whole lot kinder than some of the other interns. You had a big heart. I'd hate like hell to see you wind up in Reboot."

"Me, too." She sighed and shook her head. "It really needs to be exposed. There's no need for such procedures anymore. We have such sophisticated testing apparatus in place..."

"You and I both know it isn't for any programs that help people. It's for bio research, ways to build better specific viruses keyed to DNA, even ways to send coded messages out of reach of regular intelligence corps operations." His face was grim. "You stay out of sight. If anyone asks, give them that fake ID I had worked up for you. Lie like a, well, like a soldier gone AWOL." He smiled.

She smiled back. "You're a nice pirate."

He made her a sweeping bow. "I do my best." He straightened. "Could I ask why you jumped ship?" he wondered.

Her blue eyes were sad. "Misdirected longing." She sighed.

He shook his head. "Hard to hide that on a shipload of humans."

She just nodded. No reason to let him believe that she had a case on her bonded alien CO.

"I really felt for Ruszel when she was carrying the alien commander's child," he said quietly. "Most human females can't survive pregnancy by a Cularian species male."

"Wh…what?" she stammered, not having been privy to the intimate details of Madeline Ruszel's pregnancy.

"You don't know?" He shook his head. "I thought you two were friends."

"Cehn-Tahr are very strict about sharing any information about their species with outworlders. I tended her, along with Dr. Hahnson, during her pregnancy. She had a hard time, but her physical strength was uncanny…"

"Genetic modification," he said shortly. He held up a hand. "I have my sources. It was classified above top secret and the sample was consumed in the process. They've been unable to replicate it."

She was devastated. She had no time to hide it from him. "I…didn't know."

"So it wasn't a human after all, hmmm?" he added. "That's a shame. Cenh-Tahr hide their true faces, and their physiology, but their altered DNA makes them several times more powerful than human males. Impossible for a human to mate with them, much less try to breed."

She just nodded.

He patted her shoulder awkwardly. "If it was a Cehn-Tahr, you're better off here, even in danger."

"Oh, it was only on my part," she said. Her eyes lowered. "He was bonded already."

"Just as well. They bond for life, you know. No such thing as separations or divorce."

She nodded again. Her heart was breaking in two.

He didn't know what to say. He felt bad that he'd even mentioned it. "They're coming up with new techniques every day," he said awkwardly. "Someday, maybe..."

"I have my own life to lead now," she said quietly. "I have to pick up the pieces and go on."

"Good thing he was bonded," he added.

"Why?" she asked. "I mean, I didn't want to accidentally provoke any mating behaviors with my uncontrollable pheromones, but why was it a good thing?"

"Because you don't just provoke mating behaviors in them, you provoke the mating cycle. Once it begins, they'll kill any other male who even looks at the female they're pursuing—family, friends, anybody, doesn't matter who. And the only way to end it is by mating. They'll follow the female of their choosing straight to hell, never stop, never go back, until they achieve the objective."

"I didn't know," she said.

"Most humans don't. I've had some good relationships with Rojoks, and they know more about their old enemies than humans ever will. Two millennia ago, the Cehn-Tahr combined genes from the galot species of giant cat and *canolithe* plants, which change color with emotion. They added those genes to the base genome of the Cehn-Tahr race."

"So that's why...!" she exclaimed.

"Why they're so strong and have such feline features, and why their eyes change color with emotion. Yes. But a few centuries back, old Tnurat Alamantimichar decided to improve that genome even more and he put his scientists to work on ways to enhance strength and stamina. He insisted that his military be endowed with it. This was during the time he made contact, and a treaty, with the *kelekom* race. I don't have to tell you how clones from those aliens have boosted the Cehn-Tahr clones' strength and ability."

"No, I'm very aware of that," she replied.

"Well, Tnurat wanted to go even further with his tech, do more DNA adjustment using other alien species as material. But one of his people, a soldier named Alkaasar rose in rebellion, and went to the Rim in exile to build an army. He went to war against old Tnurat to resist the drastic change in the genome. He lost, long story short, and he was killed by the Holconcom."

"Gosh, you know a lot!" she exclaimed.

"More than I should. Like I said, I have sources. Anyway, the death of Alkaasar did have one major impact on old Tnurat's ideas—he shelved them permanently. So the earlier genetic adjustments were the only ones that prevailed, and no more Cehn-Tahr, to my knowledge, were subjected to genetic modification."

"Who was Alkaasar?" she wondered.

"No idea. The Cehn-Tahr keep their Clan information so secret that even my best sources can't sift through the disinformation and dig anything up. He must have been at the very least an aristocrat, however, and in the military. They don't use those modifications on private sector individuals. Just the elite. And, of course, the clones of the Holconcom."

"It's not a good idea to mess around with genetic modification," she said. "There are myths about the home planet of all the Terravegans, that scientists there, with the best intentions, began modifying agricultural assets. It was all right at first, insect resistant, high yield. But after a generation, horrible mutations in humans started showing up, deadly viruses, immune system dysfunction—things like that. The governments at the time kept all that secret, but eventually an enterprising reporter managed to go public with it. There was such an outcry that they had to open up a centuries-old seed bank and go back to heirloom plants." She sighed. "Sadly, they had no reserve banks for the animals. All those were lost or destroyed. People became vegan through necessity. When they spread out into space, the colony worlds they were allowed had no native animals, so the vegan lifestyle continued, and all the humans there were known as Terravegans."

"Fascinating," he said, impressed. "I don't read history, or I would have known that."

She smiled a little self-consciously. "History is my hobby. I do a lot of reading in my off-duty time." She sobered, thinking that she would never be able to refer to duty again. She'd resigned her commission.

"Don't look so sad, Doc," he said gently. "You'll get over this. It just needs time. You can get used to anything if you have to. A few days and you'll improve. A few weeks and you'll laugh again. A few years, and it will only be a pinprick at the back of your mind."

"You really are a nice pirate," she reiterated.

He grinned. "I do my best." He checked his communicator ring. It was flashing. He rubbed the crystal and a man appeared in a pale blue haze.

"Time to go, Captain." He chuckled. "At your pleasure, of course, but the engines are on line and ready. Already did the walkaround."

"Good job. I'm on my way."

He turned off the crystal. "I'm away. Keep safe, Doc. I'll be back in a couple of weeks. Well, it may take longer. A couple of months at most. Honest."

She smiled. "I'll be okay. Thanks for all you've done."

He shrugged. "Wasn't much."

As DAYS TURNED to weeks, she began to learn the names of her patients and their histories. The old Altairian who lived in the prefab hut near them was

Megwa. He came from one of the Rim planets, but hard times had cost him his import business, so he lost it all and ended up here. She was treating him for an alien form of tuberculosis, long eradicated in the core planets of the Tri-Galaxy Council, but prevalent elsewhere. He was, of all things, Web Clan, and the Altairian farmer whose leg she'd saved on a far-away planet had given her Clan status. The old Altairian was shocked, because to give an outworlder membership in that Clan was almost unheard of. He treated her with amazed respect, which both amused and delighted her.

Another of her favorites was the old woman, the Parsifan, Ahrani, who was looking after the children, Marcella, who was 10, and Minat, who had just turned eight. In her spare time, which became less and less as time passed, she amused the girls by telling them tales of Terravegan history. She brought the past alive for them, and in return, they told her stories of their own distant homeworld.

"Our aunt lives on Tol Shalad," Marcella told Edris sadly. "We would like to go and live with her, but nobody here has the mems to get us there. So we will be happy here with Madam Ahrani," she said formally, smiling. "This is a good place. Nobody tries to hurt us."

"You will stay, will you not, Dr. Edris?" Minat asked, smiling up at her.

The children both had long, curly black hair down to their waists. It reminded her painfully of Rhemun. She must not think of him. He was bonded. He was Cehn-Tahr. He hated her. She must remember, and not mourn herself to death over another female's mate. But it was hard.

"What? Will I stay?" She pulled herself back to the present when Minat tugged at her sleeve. She smiled. "Yes. Of course I will!"

Minat hugged her and laid her soft face on Edris's throat. Marcella suddenly did the same. All Edris's thwarted maternal instincts took over. She hugged the girls close, her eyes tearing as she thought how wonderful it would have been to have children of her own.

But that would never be possible. Meanwhile, here were these two precious orphans who offered her their trust and love. She would care for them. It would be almost enough, along with her new job. It was the most amazing thing, to treat people who were desperate for even the most basic medical care, and see them respond as if she'd worked magic. Percy had left her two boxes of modules for her wrist scanner, obtained from God-knew-where, so she had plenty of drugs to use in her treatment programs. She also had an update for her diagnostic minicamp, done with a scrambler that wouldn't allow her signal to be traced by anyone listening.

As another precaution, she took the white ball, the disrupter, with her everywhere and had it turned on constantly. It wasn't likely that Rhemun would do anything to get her back, but Hahnson might mention to Madeline Ruszel that she was gone. Dtimun, Madeline's mate, was a telepath. She couldn't risk having him seek out her mind for Madeline. It was best if nobody had any way to find her.

She thought back through her life, to her childhood in the government nursery, always alone, because she didn't fit in anywhere. The other children, most of them destined for the military, as she had been, ignored her because she didn't like combat practice. She kept to herself, reading everything she could find about medicine, and herbs, and treatments for various diseases. It was almost a foregone conclusion that she would end up in medical school, even before she washed out of combat training. It was a good thing that the military allowed her to pursue a career in specialized medicine within its ranks. But when she tried to get into the breeder sector, it had not gone well with her superiors. She retained her rank, because only if she were chosen would she withdraw from the service, but there were prejudices against her. The main one was that she had deferred the neutering until she graduated from medical school. She never seemed to do the right thing. She never fit in.

That had changed when Dr. Madeline Ruszel took over as medical chief of staff for the Holconcom flagship *Morcai* and recruited Edris as her assistant. It had been, despite her fear of the alien Cehn-Tahr, and her difficulties with adjusting to the routine of assistant Cularian ship's surgeon, the happiest time of her entire life.

Her only real difficulty had been when she went with the ship to rescue Madeline Ruszel, after her return to the Amazon Division and an attempt by a Terravegan politician to see her killed in action. Old Tnurat, the emperor himself, had come along for the secret mission to save Madeline's life, and with him came his exceptional bodyguard, the *kehmatemer*. The captain of the guard was Rhemun, and he hated Edris on sight. Their relationship had gone from bad to worse, even when Madeline was struggling through her first pregnancy and the crew was on shore leave on Memcache. Edris and Rhemun had set new records for disagreement.

Then he'd removed his helmet at the official bonding between Dtimun, who turned out to be the emperor's only surviving son, and Madeline Ruszel. And Edris had watched his gorgeous hair, black as space, deeply curling, fall down around his broad shoulders and flow all the way past his waist. She'd stared at him, mesmerized, until he noticed her intent stare and glared at her with angry dark eyes.

That was when it started. Afterward, when he took command of the *Morcai*, their arguments increased as he found ways to provoke her temper and she found ways to provoke his. Not one kind word passed between them in those few months.

Like her, the crew found their new commander a cold taskmaster, who made new duty assignments and walked roughshod over their pride by mandating new training sessions and implementing an even more rigorous formality than any of them were used to.

While Dtimun had grown fond of the human comrades who suffered with him in Ahkmau, and stayed with him for three years through thick and thin, Rhemun had deep prejudices against humans. He hated them and made no secret of his contempt. This did not sit well, even with the Cehn-Tahr aboard the *Morcai*. They protested the treatment of their fellows as much as possible, but Rhemun was ice-cold and unapproachable, even by members of his own race.

Edris hadn't known why until he'd blown up at her in the gymnasium, while he was practicing the Kahn-Bo with Mekashe and she'd almost swooned at just the sight of him stripped to the waist.

Now she understood very well his hatred of humans, of her. She understood that it was impossible for her to mate with him, even if he hadn't already bonded with the female who bore his son. His son. A child who looked like him. A child he loved. A dead child, because of a human female's horrible mistake. So Edris's sad unrequited love made her an object of utter contempt to an alien who didn't want her interest. Moreover, an alien who, if he had ever been attracted to her, would likely have killed her in any mating attempt.

It broke her heart, to think of what might have been. She was a physician. She knew, better than most people did, the damage the Cehn-Tahr did to their enemies on the battlefield. Rojoks also had altered genomes, making them far stronger than humans. A Rojok patient had fractured her wrist, unintentionally, by grabbing it when she attempted to perform a cursory examination on him with her wrist sensors. She'd quickly repaired the damage and she hadn't told anyone.

That should have set off alarms in her brain. She knew the Cehn-Tahr used microcyborgs. She just hadn't known that their base DNA was modified. Her scans should have picked it up. There should have been notations about it in the Cularian database. But she vaguely recalled that Madeline Ruszel had said something about the Cehn-Tahr being able to modify any information on their species that was disseminated through other computers.

She thought of Rhemun, his black hair curling down his back, his muscles straining, his laughter as he engaged in mock combat with Mekashe. She shut her eyes against the torment. She had to stop thinking about him. He was part of a past that she could never regain. This was her life now, here, with these poor people who needed, more than anything, a physician. They were her only concern.

One night, she brought out the little virtual Nagaashe that kept her company in her lonely, off-duty hours. She'd had it since she was an intern at the Tri-Galaxy Medical Academy. The virtual alien was like the real, miniature Nagaashe sold on the black market as pets on Dacerius. The military didn't allow pets of any sort on starships, but they had no qualms about virtual pets. On the *Morcai*, the incredible 3-D projectors allowed her to interact with her pet in a way that would have been impossible anywhere else.

She missed that interaction when she activated the tiny disc in which the creature resided.

It came to life, although it was opaque at best here on Benaski Port. It purred, opened its blue eyes and mimicked rubbing against her cheek.

The Parsifan girls were fascinated with it.

"He has blue eyes!" Marcella exclaimed.

"It is a serpent, but it purrs!" Minat gasped.

Edris laughed softly. "His name is Liscashe," she told them. "It's a Dacerian word for 'small creature.'"

"What is Dacerian?" Marcella wanted to know.

"Dacerius is a planet many, many light-years from here," she explained. "It's a desert planet. There are real, tiny Nagaashe there. They also have mounts called Yomuth, huge rodents with thick fur that they ride."

"I should love to go there and ride one!" Minat enthused.

Edris chuckled. "I'm afraid that's a pipe dream."

"A what?" Marcella asked.

"Sorry. It's an impossible thing," she explained. "Dacerius is a very long way from here."

"So is Tol Shalad," Marcella said sadly. "We should love to go there. Our aunt and uncle are farmers, you see. They grow many things."

"Isn't Tol Shalad a desert planet?" Edris asked.

"Oh, yes, but there are pressure domes which contain the farms. I had a vidcatch of it, but my player was stolen," she said quietly. "One cannot keep many things here. There is no safety for possessions."

"You should be asleep," Ahrani fussed, peering into the large hut.

"Sorry," Edris said, smiling as she cut off the projector. "I was showing them my virtual Nagaashe."

"Serpents." Ahrani shuddered delicately. "I do not like them."

"Oh, the Nagaashe aren't like any serpents you've ever seen, I imagine." Edris defended them. "These are the height of two-story buildings," she explained. "They have blue eyes and they're telepathic. And they purr, like cats."

Ahrani was curious. "They do not attack?"

"They belong to the Tri-Galaxy Council," she said. "They're sentient. Very intelligent."

"I have never heard of this race."

"Until quite recently, most people thought they were a myth," Edris pointed out. She almost spoke of Madeline Ruszel crashing on Akaashe, the Nagaashe planet, but she caught herself just in time. She didn't dare speak of her past. Ahrani would not mean to betray her, but she might let something slip accidentally.

"They are sentient," Ahrani said, shaking her head. "I have never seen such a serpent."

"If they are so big, they must be very frightening to people," Minat said.

Edris smiled. "They really are. We had a recruit…" She bit her tongue.

Ahrani saw her sudden fear. She put a gentle hand on her shoulder. "We will never speak of anything you tell us. Is this not so, girls," she asked, and they nodded. She turned her attention back to Edris. "We know that you are not here by choice. All of us are hiding from something, Dr. Edris," she said gently. "You must not be afraid."

"Fear has become my constant companion," Edris said heavily. "But I really must not speak of where I came from."

"I understand." She looked at the girls and wagged her finger at them. "Bedtime. Right now."

They laughed, but they ran to their pallets and pulled up the torn, ragged covers which were all they had.

Ahrani went outside with Edris. "They have so little. I bought dolls for them with some mems I exchanged for an old container with a lock. But they were stolen." She shook her head. "Nothing is safe here."

"It's just as well that I have nothing worth stealing," Edris commented sadly.

Ahrani lowered her voice. "Those medical supplies have attracted attention from a man here," she said under her breath. "He sees much profit in their sale."

Edris pursed her lips and smiled. "I rigged a fail-safe on them."

"Excuse me?"

"If anyone attempts to steal them, they're in for a very unpleasant surprise. I've laced them with a particularly nasty virus. The culprit would start throwing up before he got five paces, and he wouldn't stop until I administered an antidote." She leaned toward the older woman. "You might pass that around. It's immune to antibacterial mist, also."

Ahrani laughed with real pleasure. "You are a mean doctor."

Edris chuckled. "In the interests of my patients, yes, I am." She shook her head. "I'm having to adapt. I wouldn't want to hurt anyone, but those medical supplies mean life and death down here, especially with Percy off-world. Or off-asteroid, at least," she corrected.

"I am concerned that he will be away for so long," Ahrani said quietly. "Cartha is looking for new girls. He has never dared to take the youngest on Bena-ski Port before, because Patch watches him, and he is afraid of Patch. But now..." She spread her hands expressively.

"If we have any problems about the girls, I'll handle it," Edris told her. "I may not look like it, but I can handle myself in close combat."

Ahrani just nodded. She didn't remark that many hefty, burly men had been killed quite rapidly by Cartha, who used weapons outlawed in most civilized societies. "Just the same," she said, "be wary of Cartha, and his son. They are the worst of the criminals here."

Edris smiled. "Duly noted. Now I'd better get to sleep before you start pointing that finger at me!" She laughed.

Ahrani laughed, too. "It is good to see you smile, Dr. Edris. You were very sad when you first arrived."

"I still am. But it takes fewer muscles to smile than it does to frown, in a human face," she confided. She grinned. "Good night, Ahrani. And thank you. For giving me a place to stay, for keeping me informed of dangers, for taking such wonderful care of the girls."

"You are growing fond of them, and they of you," Ahrani commented. "That is good. Have you never had a child?"

Edris was somber. "In my society, people have to meet certain strict specifications in order to be chosen as breeders. I don't fit them."

"That is such a pity. It is obvious that you love children."

"I do." She smiled. *"Karamesh."*

"Kara...what?"

"It's a Cehn-Tahr word, one in midformal usage," she explained. "It means something like, 'that's fate.'"

"Midformal..." The old woman was still trying to comprehend the word.

"There are many levels of conversational rules of

usage in Cehn-Tahr," Edris told her. "It depends on the relationship, the length of the relationship, the class affiliation, the Clan affiliation, and many other factors, how you address a person." She shook her head. "I'm still learning...was still learning them..."

"You worked with Cehn-Tahr," the old woman said under her breath, shocked. "They are savage, brutal people. They kill in the most horrible way...!"

Edris put a hand on her shoulder. "You know only the worst of them. I know the best." She smiled. "They're not as bad as they're pictured. Certainly not to women and children."

Ahrani was less tense. "If you say so." She put her hand on Edris's shoulder. "I will never speak of this, have no fear."

"I know that. Good night, Ahrani."

The old woman smiled. "Dream of happy places."

Edris sighed. "Wouldn't it be nice?"

She went into the hut, snuggled into her pallet and pulled up the covers. At least she had a place to stay, friends and food. That was certainly all she needed, for now.

CHAPTER SIX

IT DIDN'T TAKE LONG, even aboard a ship as big as the *Morcai*, for word to get around that Mallory had resigned her commission and left. It hit the humans hard.

"What the hell happened?" Holt asked Hahnson.

Strick made a face. "She wouldn't tell me. Apparently it was an altercation of some sort with Rhemun."

"Figures," Holt said tautly. "He's given her hell ever since he assumed command."

Strick ran a hand through his thick blond hair. "Well, she has friends all over from medical school. I imagine she's gone to one of them for shelter, in some backwater dive where people can keep secrets." He shook his head. "Damn it! She wouldn't let me tell Rhemun about the head injury, either. If he'd known, it might have made a difference. She's slow for a reason."

Holt nodded solemnly. "I suppose she thought he'd use it as an excuse to push her off the ship. She's a good medic, one of the best I've ever seen. This was pure bad judgment on her part. She should have sent a comm to Maddie on Memcache and complained. The emperor would have had words with Rhemun. He's fond of Mallory."

"She hasn't been the same since she shot the pirate," Strick replied. "It did terrible things to her, mentally. I tried to counsel her, but she needed someone with really good psych training. I don't have it."

Holt's black eyes flashed menacingly. "I told you it would only take one more little thing to push the crew over the edge. This is it. Jennings already sent in his request for transfer," he added heavily. "So did Higgins."

Strick cocked his head. "What about you?"

"What about you?" Holt replied with a sad smile.

The older man sighed. "Yeah. We're both clones. But they don't know that at SSC HQ. The commander— the real commander, Dtimun—hid the fact even from Lawson. I'm sure I can do a little creative alteration on the med files to keep us from being found out. If you want to leave, that is."

Holt nodded. "I want to leave. I've had it with trying to adjust to the new CO's idea of what his crew should look like."

"He wants it to look nonhuman," the burly physician said quietly. "Dtimun would hate this. He worked so damned hard to build up an interracial crew, to get us to work together, grow together. And it takes his replacement—what?—a few months to destroy that comradeship and split us into mutineers." He shook his head. "It will kill Maddie if we go home."

Holt grimaced. "I know." He laughed softly, but without humor. "She'll be the only human on Memcache."

"She's a royal now, though," Strick said. "She'll manage." He turned back to his computer bank. "I guess I'll add my name to the pot." He glanced at the other man with a wicked smile. "You know, it will almost be worth the risk just to see Rhemun's expression when he notices all these requests for transfer."

"From the entire Terravegan complement, if I'm not badly mistaken, once they know Mallory's gone, and they know why." He frowned. "I'd give a month's mems to know exactly what happened." His dark eyes narrowed. "You know, don't you?"

Strick hesitated. After a minute, he nodded. He and the captain had been through ten years of military hell together. They really didn't keep secrets. "She's got a case on the CO. And he hates humans. I imagine his senses, as acute as they are, would tell him how she felt. She did use hormone inhibiters, but a Cehn-Tahr, even a non–genetically enhanced one, can smell a fly speck in a swamp."

"Poor kid," Stern said sadly.

"I just hope the black ops guys won't be able to find her," Strick said. "I would have tried to stop her, if I'd had the chance."

"Me, too." He shrugged. "Well, I'm going to file my request for transfer. Let's hope Mallory lands someplace safe. That damned Three Strikes provision should be lifted. It's archaic. And I won't even bother to give my opinion of Reboot. Damned sadists! Like they need live humans for experimentation, with all the advances in medicine!"

"I know," Strick agreed. "It shames everyone who practices medicine."

"Hey, it's not the doctors doing it," Holt reminded him. "It's the damned government." He sighed. "You know, they say old Earth had a whole continent that was advanced almost to the point we are today, with a republic form of government. People voted to elect leaders. There was freedom of individual pursuits, freedom of religion and speech. Nobody was persecuted."

"Myth," Strick said. "Legend. Such a society couldn't exist."

"Maybe. Maybe not."

Strick clapped him on the shoulder. "We make do with what we've got, son." He chuckled. "I'm going back to work. Might as well do the best job I can, while I'm here."

"Yes. You're going to be out of patients pretty soon, when those transfers go through."

Hanhson just nodded.

RHEMUN HAD PREVARICATED with Btnu about his reasons for leaving the ship quite suddenly. He didn't usually employ falsehoods, but after his confrontation with Mallory, he needed time to cope with the violent emotions her interest in him had kindled. He invented an urgent message from Memcache about a military op. He had to go, he told his second in command. He left the ship without a word to Holt Stern or any of the humans. He felt such distaste for them that he was unnerved by it. His contretemps with Mallory had awakened all the old pain, the old prejudice. He was deeply troubled, not only by his memories but by his treatment of Mallory, who had done nothing to deserve it.

He needed to speak to his mother. When his reason was dimmed by emotion, she was his anchor. They had become close after the death of his father. That, too, was a sore spot. His father had defied the emperor himself to avoid menacing his own family with the required genetic modifications. His son, he told Tnurat, would never be used for a test subject in some insane quest for physical perfection in the species. He gathered other dissidents and declared war on the Cehn-Tahr Empire.

Sadly, it was a short-lived war. His father permitted himself to be killed to spare his Clan the utter disgrace of a public trial and execution. Rhemun had the emperor to thank for his position as head of the *kehmatemer*, against the advice of some senior members of the Dectat. Over the decades, Rhemun had proven himself trustworthy and loyal. But with Dtimun's true heritage disclosed, someone had to take over command of the Holconcom, and Rhemun was next in the chain of command. This was millennia old, this Clan status and responsibility. He could not refuse the position. His hatred of humans, however, had not been taken into account when he assumed command of an interracial battalion. He could not help his prejudices. But they complicated things.

Sfilla was at home, on R & R from her last assignment as the emperor's spy chief. She smiled at her son's approach, went forward, touched his cheek with her soft fingers and rested her forehead against his.

"My heart is happy to see you."

"And mine, to see you."

She studied him quietly. "You are troubled."

"Deeply." He followed her out to the balcony that overlooked the lush valleys of the temple province of Memcache, near the compound that the emperor called home when he wasn't in the planet's capital.

"Mallory," she guessed, and smiled with affection when his head turned sharply toward her.

"Stop reading my mind," he said firmly, and then laughed to soften the words.

She shook her head. "Your feud with the little blonde human is quite notorious. Even the emperor speaks of it."

His powerful shoulders rose and fell. "This has gone further than any feud." He lowered his eyes. "She is...attracted to me."

Her eyebrows rose. "And this is a bad thing?"

He glared down at her. "You must surely recall the human pilot who killed my son," he said stiffly. "She was like Mallory, small and blonde and fair," he added with contempt.

Sfilla's eyes faded from an amused green to a

somber blue. "It is your memory which seems to be at fault, my son. Come with me, please."

He followed her back into the spacious living room, curious as she went directly to a hidden console and pulled up two vid frames, side by side, projected on a bare wall in holographic form, but with the physical reality that covert Cehn-Tahr tech could provide. He could, if it pleased him, touch the humans in the vid frame and actually feel their warm skin. It did not please him to try.

He didn't recognize the women. He frowned and turned to his mother. "Who are they?" he asked, curious.

His mother's eyes widened. "Surely you recognize the murderer of your son?" she asked.

Shocked, he looked back at the wall. One of the projections was tall, dark and very slender, with a somber face and sad eyes. The other was a small blonde human female, laughing and animated, beautiful in her happiness.

"No," he said abruptly, disturbed.

Sfilla joined him. "The female on the left, very dark and very young, dropped her bombs on the military school where your son was enrolled," she said quietly. "She was convicted of the crime and sent to what the humans term 'Reboot.'"

He was still trying to cope with his uncommon lapse of memory. He was shocked that he didn't recognize the human who had destroyed his life. "Reboot. Yes," he said sarcastically, "for the crime of murder, they reassigned her to another military command."

Sfilla's face was very still. "She was taken to a Terravegan government medical lab," she corrected, "where she was used for experimentation projects over a period of decades. After the first two years, she mercifully lost command of her mind so that she no longer realized what the medics were doing to her."

He was shocked speechless.

"I have only recently come into this knowledge, through a contact. This is a shameful, murderous process employed by the humans to gain legal rights to other humans for their biological weapons division, since they are no longer permitted to create clones or use incarcerated subjects for the purpose. They go to great lengths to acquire any human soldier convicted of capital crimes. Once, I have heard, a medical commando unit went all the way to the Rim and provoked a riot in order to subdue an escaped prisoner. Dozens of innocent people died in the process." Her face hardened. "The humans never speak of this. Some of those in the military are even unaware of the unit's existence. Perhaps the medical corps is more aware than others, but I doubt that even they know the true extent of the butchery involved."

"It should be exposed."

She shook her head. "We have no right to involve ourselves in the internal affairs of ally civilizations." She sighed. "But the emperor has said that he would welcome the chance to make the Tri-Galaxy Council aware of the classified project. They create biological weapons, which are never used, which could never be used without provoking planetary war," she added, frowning. "Can you see any point to such experimentation?"

"No." He was deep in thought. He had lived for decades with the certainty that his son's killer had never been punished. But this punishment exceeded anything a Cehn-Tahr court would ever prescribe. It was something worthy of the Holconcom in their most savage battles, but even then, a quick death was most often the punishment for provoking them. Decades in a lab, being used for experiments, cell by cell.

"Barbarians," he muttered.

Sfilla smiled at the irony of the product of a savage race such as her own referring to another race in that manner.

He glanced at her. "I had no idea," he confessed. "It is extreme punishment, even for the crime."

"I agree."

He was studying the blonde woman with unusual interest. She was like sunshine itself, radiant and fascinating. "Who is the other human?" he asked.

Sfilla gaped at him.

"Have I said something confusing?" he teased.

"The other human is Dr. Edris Mallory," she said hesitantly.

His lips fell open. He stared at the animated image again, shocked.

"That vid was captured during the time she served with Ruszel under Dtimun, when he commanded the Holconcom," Sfilla said.

Rhemun was very quiet for a moment. He drew in a breath. "I have never seen her laugh."

It was a telling admission.

He turned to his mother. "I said some terrible things to her," he confessed. "I also spoke to her of my son's murder." His eyes fell. "Two lapses of behavioral protocols. I lost my temper."

"Something which is not without precedent," she mused.

He smiled. "Yes." The smile faded. "My son's death wasn't her fault," he continued. "But her interest provoked me. I…have not wanted to become involved with a female since the death of my mate."

Sfilla's eyes darkened. "Your mate was dishonorable."

"Yes. And her brothers corrupted my son. I should have fought her through the courts for custody. But I was away with the emperor while I captained his bodyguard. I thought the boy would be safer with her."

"She left your home when she was barely pregnant and used the child to procure wealth for her and her family," Sfilla said coldly. "I grieve for what my grandson could have been, without her influence."

"I grieve, as well," he confessed. "I placed him in

the military academy, to try and undo the damage his uncles had done to his character. The blame is mine."

"No," she said, turning her face up to his. *"Karamesh,"* she said softly. "Our fate is written the day we first see light. There is no way to change it."

He bent and rested his forehead against hers. "Your words give much comfort."

"You must find a way to make peace with Mallory," she said unexpectedly. "She is a sweet child."

He made a face. "Even though I find her distasteful, the effect of the pheromones over time may produce unwanted complications."

"Your father and I refused any of the genetic enhancements that troubled Dtimun's relationship with Madeline Ruszel," she said quietly. "She required classified tech, genetic enhancement, in order to bond with him. Your strength comes from tech that can be disabled." She held up a hand. "Yes, we are not to discuss such matters, of this I am aware. And you hold Mallory in contempt—I am also aware of this. I am simply stating a fact."

He frowned. It was unlike her to speak of personal issues, not to mention that it was a serious social taboo. He wondered why she would bring up such a thing, and he turned to ask.

But she was staring at a holographic projection that had just emanated from her ring, in a scrambled transmission that only she could read. This was one of the tools of her profession, of which she rarely spoke. Her responsibilities to the emperor often included covert assassination.

She ended the transmission and her face was troubled.

"Can you speak about it?" he asked, indicating the holographic ring she wore. "Or is it classified?"

She smiled faintly. "You have classified clearance. It would not matter. However, this is nothing to do with my job." She cocked her head. "When did you last see Lieutenant Commander Mallory?" she asked.

His eyebrows arched. "Just before I left the ship," he said, and grimaced as he recalled the conversation and the expression on her face. He contrasted it unwillingly with the happy, smiling face in the projection nearby.

"Why do you ask?" he wondered suddenly.

"I am informed that Mallory is no longer aboard the *Morcai*."

"What?" he exclaimed.

He turned to the communicator and punched in his access codes. Btnu's heavily lined face was enhanced in a small glowing field above the communicator.

"Sir," Btnu said respectfully.

"Where is Mallory?" Rhemun asked without preamble.

Btnu looked uncomfortable. "I do not know, sir. I only know that she has left the ship. It was in the duty log. I meant to contact you…"

"Never mind. Patch me through to Hahnson," he said with sudden inspiration.

Btnu, relieved to pass his angry commander along to someone else, agreed and pressed the controls immediately.

"Hahnson," the human doctor answered, his broad face outlined now in the vapor.

"Where is Mallory?" Rhemun asked curtly.

Hahnson's eyebrows rose. "I tried to contact you..."

"Where is she?"

Hahnson grimaced. "Well, the thing is, she wouldn't tell me. She just said that she wanted to go to someplace where they couldn't find her."

"They?" Rhemun asked with cold, dark eyes and a sense of utter foreboding.

"Yes. The black ops medical unit. She's just become subject to the Third Strike Provision in our military statutes. If they can find her," he added sadly, "she'll be sent at once to Reboot, without even a trial."

Rhemun exchanged a disturbed look with his mother. He turned back to the comms. "I will return shortly."

He cut the connection. "I must go at once," he told Sfilla. "Despite my prejudices, I have no desire to see the little blonde human subjected to vivisection."

"Nor do I." She touched her hand to his cheek and laid her forehead against his. "Save her, if you can."

He looked troubled. It wasn't what she said so

much as the way she said it. "What more do you know?" he asked.

"I cannot say. It is not my secret."

He didn't reply. He touched her cheek and left for his command.

HIS FIRST ACT when he boarded the *Morcai* was to summon Hahnson to the bridge. He took the other man into his small office and closed the door. He noted that not one of the humans on the bridge would even look at him. Apparently, Mallory's abrupt departure was no secret.

"Why did you let Mallory leave?" Rhemun demanded.

"I didn't," Hahnson replied curtly. "She was gone before I had any chance to stop her. She contacted me after she'd already left the ship."

"My mother told me about Reboot," Rhemun replied. "How is it used?"

"We have what's called a 'three strikes' provision in our constitution, which applies to military service. God knows where the term came from, but it's applied in cases like Mallory's. Resigning her commission will be considered the third strike and they'll move heaven and earth to send her to Reboot."

Rhemun was very still. "She resigned her commission?" he asked, stunned. He thought she had simply gone AWOL.

"Yes."

Rhemun had moved to his desk and punched in

a code. He saw every name of every single human on the *Morcai* listed with requests for reassignment to the Terravegan Strategic Space Command—even Hahnson and Stern, who were clones and would suffer horribly if their state was discovered. It made him sad to realize how far his prejudices had driven those decisions. But Mallory's name wasn't among them.

He turned back to Hahnson. "Why is there no request from her for reassignment?"

"That's because she isn't just leaving the Holconcom, she's leaving the Terravegan military, as well. That's what I'm trying to tell you. She booked a seat aboard a passenger ship and didn't tell me where she was bound. It won't matter. Tri-Fleet military will be on her trail in a heartbeat, and when they catch up with her, she'll go straight to Reboot."

"Reboot. I thought for years that this meant only a reassignment to other duty," Rhemun said, trying to understand. The same had been done with the murderer of his son. He looked up. "But my mother recently learned that it is not. She gave me a brief overview of the process. It is barbaric."

"Indeed it is. Reboot is a living death, one of the best-kept dirty secrets of our service," Hahnson said angrily. "She'll be placed in stasis and used for donor tissue for medical experiments. She'll be conscious and aware of every damnable thing that's done to her. She could survive for a century or more like that. It's the most barbaric practice left over from ancient Earth. It used to be used as a punishment for crimes, terrible crimes. Now it's standard OP for the third infraction."

Rhemun moved away to stare at the virtual wall. He was shocked speechless. He had assumed, furious, that the female pilot had not been punished. Now he knew that his son had been avenged, even more horribly than he had imagined in his fantasies of revenge. It was a fitting punishment for murder. But Mallory, who had committed no real crime, would be treated the same. It was his fault. He had overreacted to her interest in him.

Images of her flashed through his mind. Mallory, compassionate with refugees, shocked and fascinated the first time she saw his helmet come off and his long, curling hair fall to his waist and around his shoulders. Mallory, tender with children when she had to treat them. Mallory, white and shaking as he berated her and shared his anger and disgust over her helpless infatuation for him…

"She's just a kid," Hahnson said heavily.

Rhemun turned. "Mallory is a mature female…"

"She's twenty-three years old," the doctor said quietly. "In my culture, that's barely an adult."

Rhemun had never considered her age before. It was suprising. She seemed mature.

"She's tried so hard to perform her duties efficiently. Considering her handicap, she did extremely well."

"What handicap?" the alien asked.

"She had a brain injury, in medical training, on

a field trip. I knew about it and kept it to myself—it would have washed her out of medical school."

"Her episodes of clumsiness," Rhemun recalled.

"Yes. And the slowness. She's very good. She just takes longer than some physicians to do procedures. But she's greatly loved by the humans aboard." He shook his head. "She'll be missed."

Rhemun was still trying to wrap his mind around her abrupt departure. So many complications in so short a time. "We will be without a Cularian specialist."

"Indeed. I can do some of the exams, but we'll have to rely on Mallory's assistant, Tellas, for the more difficult ones," Hahnson said, with no real enthusiasm. "Of course," he added with dry sarcasm, "I won't be needed much longer. I'm sure the commander noted that the entire human contingent is up for transfer, pending your approval."

Rhemun glanced at him, but he didn't react to the sarcasm. The alien seemed unusually disturbed. He stared at the vid screen and did not see it. Hahnson was speaking of a future that did not include Mallory. He should be relieved. She was a painful reminder of all that he had lost. Her absence would make his life easier. He should be grateful that she had solved the problem for him...

He moved to the intership comm, and talked to one of the Cehn-Tahr comm techs in his own tongue, the ancient dialect that none of the humans in his crew could speak. He directed the officer to track all departures from passenger ships that had been nearby around the time of Mallory's departure and report when he found Mallory.

Rhemun turned back to Hahnson. "If you have any contact from Mallory, any at all, you are to tell me at once."

Hahnson was undecided about that. Rhemun might decide to help her into Reboot as quickly as he located her.

"I am not the enemy, Hahnson," Rhemun told him quietly. "I have no wish to see the small blonde human used as material for experimentation. Despite our disagreements."

Hahnson wasn't convinced, but he didn't say so.

"Think," Rhemun said with some force. "You know Mallory. If she ran, where would she go?"

Hahnson drew in a breath. "Well, I'm not sure, but if I were to run, I think I'd head for Benaski Port. It has everything a fugitive would need to stay alive. Mallory could barter her medical skills for food and lodging." He shrugged. "Anywhere else, it would be hard for her to hide."

Rhemun nodded slowly. It was a good assumption.

"Is that all, sir?" Hahnson asked formally.

Rhemun studied him for a long time. His face was taut and drawn. He wanted to apologize for Mallory's danger, for the mess he'd made of the *Morcai* and her crew. But he was too proud. His whole life had been one of toughing it out, pretending that his father hadn't been a traitor, that he was worthy of his Clan. So pride stilled his tongue.

"Yes, Hahnson," he said quietly. "Dismissed."

He saluted and left the alien alone.

Rhemun stared at the request for transfers with blank eyes. This was the result of his maltreatment, not only of Mallory but of the human crew. Dtimun had called them the finest fighters in the three galaxies, second only to the Cehn-Tahr themselves. He had trained them, rated them, pushed them to the limit—but they had loved Dtimun. They would, as the emperor said once, laughingly, follow their commander straight into hell if he asked it of them. All that work had been lost, that loyalty discounted and discarded, by one alien. By himself.

He turned and looked out the viewscreen that covered one bulkhead, looked into the blackness of space, dotted here and there with color, stars in their various classifications, steady lights in the nonatmosphere of the infinite dark. Somewhere out there was a small blonde human who must be terrified at the fate that awaited her if she was discovered. And Rhemun didn't know where to find her.

CHAPTER SEVEN

LATER, WHEN HE considered what Hahnson had told him, Rhemun went to the communications console in his quarters and sent a comm to his mother, speaking in the old tongue.

"She has gone to Benaski Port, the human surgeon believes," he told her. "But it is a lawless place, and the black ops unit might well take her without opposition, if she can be found."

"Give me a moment." His mother was briefly absent. When she came back over the comms, there was a lilt in her tone. "I have located her. She is practicing medicine in the Underway, living with an elderly Parsifan woman and two little girls."

"You really are a magician," he said fondly.

She laughed. "I have spies everywhere." She sobered. "However, even under the circumstances, if you go near Benaski Port, the emperor himself may not be able to save you," Sfilla said heavily. "The Dectat, as you know, placed a severe penalty for any attempt to port there during the war. The restriction is still in place. And the emperor will have to deal with the Dectat if you persist. I do not tell you this to discourage you," she added surprisingly, and with a smile in her voice. "It will simply require some diversion to cover your actions."

Rhemun chuckled. "I will think of something."

He cut the connection and opened a communication channel to Dr. Strick Hahnson. "I found her," he said.

"Where?" Hahnson asked, forgetting to salute in his excitement.

"Where you thought she might go—Benaski Port."

Hahnson grimaced. "The one place we can't go look for her," he groaned.

"Perhaps there is a way," Rhemun replied. "I have an idea."

HE FELT THE chill when he walked onto the bridge of the *Morcai*. The humans were unusually quiet. Their responses were in strictly formal monosyllables and they didn't quite meet his eyes when he gave commands.

Mallory was loved by the Terravegans. It was expected that, when they knew why she'd left the ship, they would blame Rhemun. But apparently some of the Cehn-Tahr also had affection for her. Mekashe was cold to his friend, as well as some of the other crew. It irritated Rhemun, even as it amused him, because until the *Morcai* Battalion was formed, most Cehn-Tahr hated humans.

HE CALLED A BRIEFING. The room was packed with department heads, both Cehn-Tahr and human. Ignoring the hostile looks he was getting, he began.

"I've called this briefing to inform you of a practice drill," he said curtly. "Our reaction times are down. We need to reduce them. Our maneuvers usually take place near planetary systems. However, I have been thinking that we need to consider other venues for this purpose." He looked around the room. "We are experiencing some minor problems with our emerillium boosters, and we need to make port to address them. Benaski Port is the closest source of the part we need. So, since our engine problems require immediate attention, it is my intention to use this situation to our advantage. Since we must port to make repairs, and acquire a rather rare piece of equipment for the endeavor, we will utilize the time we must spend at the stopover in Benaski Port for our next military drill. We will proceed there, as quickly as our strained engines allow…"

Rhemun touched a button on the console. "How strange—I seem to have effected a momentary recording disturbance. Accidentally, of course." His eyes dared the officers to contradict him.

His deep voice dropped in pitch. "Dr. Mallory has resigned her commission in the human military," he told the officers assembled in the briefing room. "This places her, according to Dr. Hahnson—" he indicated the cold-faced physician at the table "—under a classified medical code, in great jeopardy." He pulled up a star map. "According to my best resources—" he wasn't mentioning his mother "—she's practicing medicine in the Underway, a part of Benaski Port that lies beneath the tourist district. It is the dominion of thieves, murderers, refugees and escaped criminals."

Hahnson looked shocked. He'd only guessed at her whereabouts, but Rhemun seemed to have private intelligence about the location. He wondered if it was Sfilla. She was a master assassin. And she was Rhemun's mother. She would have resources that even Admiral Lawson would envy. Lucky for Mallory.

"A pirate is the unofficial leader of this confederation," Rhemun continued. "However, he is off-planet on a job and another resident has claimed control in his absence, an Altairian named Cartha, who owns several houses of prostitution and a casino there." His eyes narrowed angrily. "His enterprises include extortion from refugees, and his methods are, shall we say, dire."

"Can't we go get Dr. Mallory, sir?" Ensign Jones, who was one of two crewmen assigned as Rhemun's personal guards, asked softly. "Begging your pardon, sir." He saluted and flushed, having spoken out of turn.

"Sir, there's an edict from the emperor forbidding contact with Benaski Port under penalty of court-martial, held over from the war with the Rojoks," Stern said curtly. He didn't look pleased to be reminding them about it. "It has never been rescinded."

Rhemun lifted an eyebrow. "Yes. I am aware of this. Which is why I interrupted the recorder." He indicated it. He stood up and paced the room, with his hands locked behind him, his long mane of curly black hair moving with each graceful step. "I have put on record my decision to practice maneuvers near Benaski Port, and also the existence of problems with our emerillium boosters."

There wasn't a sound in the room.

He turned to expectant, hopeful faces.

"Of course," he said, appearing to think out loud, "our potentially damaging engine problems give us a logical excuse to make port there. Just long enough for repairs, of course." He turned to the ship's engineer. "Lieutenant Commander Higgins," he continued, "I mentioned engine problems. I believe that you recently encountered a disturbance in the emerillium flux, in the booster matrix, that has been producing intermittent problems with the reactors, have you not?"

"Sir?" Higgins asked hesitantly.

He stared at Higgins. "A deft hand could produce a mechanical problem that would not be disputed by the ship's computers. And Jennings could make sure of that, yes?" he added, glancing at the communications officer.

Jennings was quicker than his friend Higgins. "Oh, yes, sir," he agreed, nodding.

Higgins caught on and grinned. "Damned Chi-Bahn Stabilizer, I'll bet it's what's causing that problem, sir," he said at once. "Only place in this part of the galaxy where you can get one is at Benaski Port."

"This would produce an excuse to port there while we make repairs. A few of us can leave the ship covertly and search for Mallory. The AVBDs must be modified into a loop of the bridge to conceal my absence. This," he added curtly, "is off the record. I will not expect to hear any gossip about it. Is that understood?"

It was. They knew that if they discussed it, even among themselves, the AVBDs would record it and they would all be up for court-martial. Which would leave Dr. Mallory at the mercy of the medical unit's black ops division. There were somber faces as they nodded agreement.

"Very well." Rhemun touched the recorder again. "Accidental remission of log due to mistouch by commanding officer," he read into the log. "Now, gentlemen, where were we? Preparing for maneuvers, I believe?"

This time, the cold faces wore hope.

RHEMUN WAS SO impatient that his temper, never well kept, overflowed onto the bridge crew. A communiqué from the Tri-Fleet had requested the unit to respond to an emergency only a brief distance from their current position. It would be a quick response, but any loss of time was dangerous to their chances of saving Edris Mallory.

"This is unbelievable," he raged at Chief Communications Officer Jennings. "I told you to refuse transmission of any requests from Admiral Lawson!"

Jennings was standing at strict attention, his face flushed, his body rigid. "I am deeply sorry, sir. You must know that it was unintentional! I'm just as concerned about Lieutenant Mallory as…"

"Stow it!" Rhemun snapped. He ran a hand over his face and turned away, bristling. "We have no choice—as the closest vessel available, we must respond to the emergency." He turned back to Jennings, who looked mortally wounded by his own mistake. He moved closer and actually laid a hand on the young human's shoulder. "Forgive me," he said quietly, breaking the habit of a lifetime. He never touched people. "That was uncalled-for. Of course we can't ignore any urgent request for aid from the Fleet."

Jennings beamed. "Thank you, sir." He hesitated. "Sir, I did tell them about our engine malfunction, and they said it would be a quick hop and we could proceed to Benaski Port after."

Rhemun forced a smile. "Very good. Go back to your station." He had touched a switch on the comm board, giving him a very brief window of privacy during the discussion. "Monitor Benaski Port for any information that comes out of the Underway," he added. He touched the comm switch again and turned away from Jennings, who was grinning now.

"Plot a course to Ven Wahran," he told Holt Stern. "And use that new system we installed."

"Leaving over now, sir," Holt said quietly. He was surprised at how well the upgraded program worked, and the ease of programming. He glanced at Rhemun.

The commander laughed softly. He read that thought in Stern's mind, although he made certain it didn't show. He was responding to the surprised look, as any human might.

"Sir, these modifications, well, they're quite an improvement," he said, and then gritted his teeth for speaking out of turn. "Begging your pardon, sir."

"Unnecessary. They are an improvement. We have some good things coming out of Kolmahn-kash," he added, naming the top secret research facility on Memcache that produced the most amazing 3-D tech of any in the three galaxies. Most of the humans, and many Cehn-Tahr, used it for virtual gaming. But it had other, more secret uses, than these.

"Yes, we do," Stern replied, and bit his tongue again. "Sir, sorry, sir."

Rhemun shook his head. He'd been unnecessarily harsh with his human crew. He was hoping to make amends, by first relaxing the atmosphere on the bridge a little. Just a little, however. One couldn't turn it into a rec hall, after all. So he waved away Stern's apology and turned back to his command chair.

PRIVATELY, HE WAS very concerned about Mallory. He couldn't read her thoughts because there was some sort of major interference. He knew about Hahnson's white ball that interfered with thought transmission, but Mallory had no knowledge of his ability to read minds. She would not have known to use it against him.

On the other hand, she did know that Dtimun was a telepath. Surely she also knew that Madeline Ruszel, if Hahnson told her about Mallory's absence, might ask her mate to search for her mind. That would explain it.

He hoped that she was in a safe place. Benaski Port was a den of thieves. She would be at risk for many reasons, not the least of which was her medical skill. He thought of all the potential dangers, and his mind simply shut down on the subject. He didn't want to admit how guilty he felt for the danger he'd placed her in.

He had let her think that he was still bonded. It was a defense mechanism. Mallory was very attractive. He shook himself mentally. It was best to keep such thoughts out of his mind altogether.

He pulled up the global maps for Ven Wahran.

MALLORY WAS TREATING a line of patients that seemed to go on forever. People found out about her presence in the Underway and came to her in droves. Many had skin conditions for which they couldn't afford treatment. Others had more serious complaints that required surgery.

Still others were suffering from drug withdrawal, alcoholism or mental problems. Pregnant women had no midwives to assist at births. By the end of her first

month on Benaski Port, Edris looked back at her
time spent in the Holconcom as a veritable rest stop.

"This is very hard for you," Ahrani said gently,
when she was taking a brief break. "I am very sorry.
Perhaps it was I who told too many people of your
medical skill."

Edris smiled. "I don't mind, really I don't. This
is what I took a vow to devote my life to," she explained. "There are so many sick people here," she
added quietly. "How horrible, to have no medical
care at all."

"The only physicians on Benaski Port are above,
in the elite sectors, where the hotels are located," the
old woman said sadly. "None of us have many mems.
None of us can afford to get care above." She sighed
and smiled. "You are like a gift from the gods," she
added. "You have helped so many!"

"It is a privilege," she replied, and meant it.

"You still think of the male you left behind," she
said softly.

Edris shook her head. "I try very hard not to
think of him. It's better this way, you know. He was
bonded."

"So many females, especially here, would think
of him as a challenge, in such case," the woman said
disapprovingly. "They think bonding is stupid."

"Not in my culture, it isn't," Edris replied. "Not
everyone feels the way I do, but I did belong, very
briefly, to a religious group. It gave me courage at

a time when I needed it badly. I miss the people I knew then."

"We have little religion here," was the reply. "But I, too, in my youth was a person of beliefs. When we are in peril, those foundations support us."

Edris smiled. "They do indeed."

"And here are still more patients!" she exclaimed, nodding toward a group of newcomers.

"I have plenty of supplies. We're good."

"You will get to bed very late tonight, I fear," Ahrani said.

Edris grinned. "But happy."

IT WAS, INDEED, very late before she settled onto her pallet. The girls, who were supposed to be asleep, moved their pallets on either side of hers.

"Dr. Edris, can you tell stories?" Minat asked.

Edris laughed softly, despite her fatigue. "Not very many, and most of the ones I know are not fit for young ears," she added.

"There must be one," Marcella coaxed.

Edris frowned, staring at the stained ceiling of the prefab hut. "Well, I do know one, about pigs."

"Please, Doctor, what is a pig?" the youngest girl asked, all eyes.

"I'm not really sure," Edris confessed. "I read it on a textdisk—there were no vids and no explanation. I think it might be some sort of small Yomuth," she concluded.

"I see. And what of this pig thing?" Marcella asked.

"It was something about three of these creatures building houses..."

She recalled what she could remember of the story. It was funny to think of a small Yomuth with its hooves trying to build a house. She had no reference point for animals from the ancient Sol system, and there was nothing left in the history, most of which had been destroyed by planetary cataclysms long before the first Terravegan colonies in the Tri-Galaxies had even been established. But she went ahead gamely, describing the construction of the houses and the predatory creature who was stalking the "pigs," which sounded much like a galot, so that was how she described it.

"Oh, we have heard of the galot," Minat said, all eyes. "They are fearsome creatures, Dr. Edris. They eat people!"

"Not all of them," Edris replied with a smile.

"Are you certain? Because this is what we have been told," Marcella interjected.

Edris was recalling Kanthor, the galot who had known Dtimun from childhood and was his friend. The big galot had been often in the house where Madeline Ruszel was waiting to give birth, and he and his friendly enemy, Rognan the Meg-Raven had refused to leave when Komak was being born. That had been almost comical, the big cat and the big bird sitting side by side, defiantly in place despite Dtimun's admonitions to them to go out of the room.

"Yes," she said finally. "I am certain. Not all galots kill without reason."

"I still would hope not to meet one," Minat said, and shivered delicately.

"Nor I," Marcella added.

Edris gathered them close. "I would never let anything harm you. I promise."

THE NEXT MORNING, she had cause to remember those words.

Just as she finished with her last patient in the group that had been waiting since what passed for dawn on the asteroid colony, two blue-skinned Altairians dressed as aristocrats showed up at the door of the prefab hut.

She stared at them with faint surprise. She'd never seen patients of their obvious wealth and position.

"Can I help you?" she asked.

The old woman, the Parsifan, was making frantic motions to Edris to run. She frowned, not comprehending the warning.

The eldest of the two men, bald and purple-eyed, with a bland expression, looked her over. "You might do for the business. What do you think, my son?" he asked the younger alien.

"She is too small," he scoffed.

"But comely, in a broad sense." The older Altairian laughed with barely concealed contempt. "Not my taste."

"Nor mine. But we have customers who might enjoy her."

Edris was beginning to understand the comments, and she didn't like what she heard. Her eyes narrowed. "You're Cartha," she said. "You run a brothel here."

"A brothel? I run many brothels," he said haughtily. He looked down his blue nose at her. "Where are those girls?"

Edris's heart did leaps. "They're not here," she said firmly. She said it very loudly, so that Ahnari, in the prefab, could hear her. The girls were huddled at the old woman's side.

"Lies," the younger alien said calmly. He turned and quickly went into the prefab. "They're here," he called to his father. "I'll get them…"

"No, you don't!" Edris said shortly. "You're not taking them!"

She rushed into the hut and got between the alien and the girls. "Get out," she said, and dropped into a martial arts stance she remembered from her sad attempt at combat training. Perhaps it would make them hesitate, at least.

"Get out of my way," the alien said with contempt. He jerked her by the arm and threw her against the opposite wall. "You will come with me," he told the two frightened girls. "Now,or we will kill your friend, there," he added, indicating Edris, who was getting to her feet despite being disoriented by the sudden hard contact with the wall.

"Dr. Edris!" Minat cried, and tried to run to her.

The younger Altairian caught her around the waist, laughing. "She has a temper. This is good. Many of our customers like spirit in their women."

"Let her go!"

Edris tried to kick him. He caught her heel, turned it and flipped her onto the ground.

She lunged at his leg and unbalanced him, so that he fell. Furious now, he caught her by the hair and threw her, literally, out of the hut and onto the hard wooden surface of the walkway outside, at Cartha's feet.

"You think to stop us? You human?" Cartha said with utter contempt. He drew back his hand and slapped her across the mouth as hard as he could. "Hold her!" he told his son.

"With pleasure," the younger alien snapped.

He held Edris's arms while Cartha worked her over. The first blows were the most painful. The alien was very strong, and she could feel the impact on her lungs and her stomach as the blows rained on her. She felt a rib crack, and then another. She could barely breathe. The girls, she must protect them, she must…!

"Get them…away!" she called to Ahrani.

Ahrani, to her credit, tried to run with them, but Cartha dropped Edris, who was now limp, bleeding and barely conscious, to the wooden flooring.

He caught Ahrani and knocked her down. Then he picked up Marcella while his son threw Minat over his shoulder.

"If she lives," Cartha told Ahrani contemptuously, indicating Edris, "tell her this is what she may expect when she defies her betters!"

"Please let them go," Ahrani pleaded.

He shot back a curse in Parsifan.

"There are many medical supplies in there," Cartha's son said, indicating the prefab hut. "We should send someone for them. They will sell well on the market."

"I will have them fetched."

"How will we live, without medicine?" Ahrani pleaded.

"That is hardly any concern of mine," Cartha said harshly. He and his son walked out of the sector, with many frightened citizens hiding behind their makeshift barriers, praying that he wouldn't notice them.

Two of the old men helped a weeping Ahrani get Edris back into the prefab hut. But there was nothing any of them could do for her.

She was bleeding all over from the blows, and from her mouth, which indicated internal injuries. Her breathing was shallow and she winced, as if it hurt to breathe. She was barely conscious. Ahrani turned her on her side, in case she threw up, so that she wouldn't choke. She patted her shoulder gently.

"It will be all right," she whispered. "It will be all right." But she knew that it wouldn't be all right.

There was no doctor on Benaski Port to save Edris, who had saved so many poor souls here.

The old woman remembered the talk she and the little blonde human had, about faith. She closed her eyes and began to pray.

MANY PARSECS AWAY, Rhemun and his crew were finally almost finished with the impromptu rescue operation. It had been a very brief operation, and it went smoothly. The refugees were loaded aboard the ship with the single assistant physician left who was willing but hardly had the supplies to treat them.

"There is a band of Rojoks here," one of the settlers told Rhemun. "They are not with an army—they are renegades. They raid us for food and medicine, while they hope that they can attract more numbers to fight the government of Chacon."

"Fools," Rhemun muttered. "Chacon has won territory for his people that all Mangus Lo's and Chan Ho's wars could not manage." He also recalled another group of Rojok renegades whom Edris had impressed enough to foster their surrender. It was a painful memory now.

"Yes," an old man said, "we tried to tell them of this. They have no radio communications with their homeworld. They have broken off all contact, so they have no access to news on the nexus. But they would not believe us."

"It is of no consequence," Rhemun said. "There are few colonies left here. One by one, they will be relocated, as this one is being, and the Rojoks will be forced to practice their mutiny elsewhere."

"We are most grateful to you for sparing us from more of their predations," the old one added.

"You are most welcome."

RHEMUN MADE HIS way to the bridge and filed a report with the military authority and the Tri-Galaxy Fleet indicating that the mission was concluded and the refugees were to be dropped off at the first Terravegan colony relocation center. It was, luckily, on the way to Benaski Port.

"Now," Hahnson said under his breath, "can we get back to maneuvers, sir?"

Rhemun glanced at him. "Yes, and fortunately our emerillium relays were temporarily functional. However, I believe I noted a surge in the power indicators. Higgins?"

Higgins played along. He snapped a salute. "Yes, sir, you did, sir. If I don't get those engines in full repair soon, we'll blow apart, sir."

"Benaski Port is the closest resource for emerillium repair modules," Rhemun replied. "Stern, get us underway for the relocation center on Magdos Three, and then we'll go at best speed to Benaski Port. However, do not think that I have forgotten the drills we will need to perform to optimize our alert skills," he added firmly. "You will not be allowed access to Benaski Port's recreational facilities. That is in defiance of standing orders not to port there except in cases of extreme emergency—which, of course, this is," he said in a very convincing tone. "We will conduct our drills on the ship."

He looked around, irritated that nobody was complaining. He lifted his hands up and down with a frustrated expression, indicating that he wanted a response.

The bridge crew belatedly got the idea.

"Darn," Jennings muttered under his breath. "No shore leave, sir?"

"Double darn," Astrogation specialist Ole Crandall echoed.

"Can it," Rhemun said, using an old human expression. "We do what the law says we must. R & R must wait until we reach our own port."

"Yes, sir," they echoed, and managed to sound very disappointed.

Rhemun, with his back to the nearest AVBD, grinned at them.

THE REFUGEES WERE sent down in a scout ship. While they waited for it to return to the ship, Rhemun answered a sudden, urgent call from his mother. He took it in his quarters, on scramble.

"I'm here," he said when he engaged the comms.

Her face was troubled. "I have only a snippet of news from Benaski Port, but it is not good. Word is spreading that Cartha and his son have caused some sort of trouble in the Underway, and medical supplies have suddenly come on the black market. I think they may have taken them from Edris."

"It indicates that she is in the Underway, at least," Rhemun said.

"You must find a way to hurry there," she said. She bit her lower lip in a very human manner. "I have not your mental gifts, but I sense that something is very wrong."

"I sense it, too," he replied. His expression was one of concern. "The little human is in great danger because of me."

"Yes, she is." She studied him quietly. "It is more than anger that drives you."

He closed up. "There is no future in such conjecture."

"Your father died to spare you the difficulties Dtimun has faced because of his choice of mates," she reminded him. "Your genetic structure was never modified."

He averted his eyes. These were things that they were not permitted to discuss.

"Yes, again I am speaking of things which are taboo," she mused. "However, you might consider speaking to Hahnson. If you had any interest in such subjects. Which, of course, you do not."

"I need my Cularian medicine specialist back," he said noncommittally. "That is my only concern, at the moment."

"Bah. She had a capable assistant."

He glared at her. "I need my..."

She held up a hand. "Hide, then. I will say no more." She sobered. "But you must hurry."

He nodded. "I know."

"She has a big heart for such a small human," Sfilla said softly. "I am quite fond of her."

Rhemun unbent, but only a little. "She thinks I have a mate."

Sfilla's eyes twinkled. "You need the protection of such a falsehood, then…?"

He gave his mother a glowering look and cut the connection deliberately. He was not going to start thinking in those terms.

THE COLONISTS WERE TRANSPORTED, and the scout ship was back in the hangar. The *Morcai* left orbit and headed for Benaski Port. Rhemun had them throw the lightsteds to make better speed, but it was still a day away at best.

He worked out with Mekashe with the Kahn-Bo to relieve some of the stress he felt at the length of time it was taking to get to the asteroid.

"You are concerned for the little blonde human," Mekashe mused when they were resting from two continuous bouts—both of which Mekashe had won.

He looked at his friend. Mekashe had stood by him in the old days when many others had turned away because of his father's rebellion. He owed the other man a lot.

"Yes," he said. "She washed out of combat training. If she is attacked, and she might be, she might not survive."

"She is a physician," Mekashe reminded him. "And no human would be more welcome in the Underway than someone with medical training. Who would want to harm her?"

"I don't know," Rhemun replied heavily. "But I feel that someone is thinking of it."

Mekashe knew everything about his friend, including his Clan affiliation—something that none of the humans was privy to. He put a large hand on Rhemun's shoulder. *"Karamesh,"* he said quietly. It was a comfort.

"We are leaves on the water, being carried downstream by fate," Rhemun mused, translating the old axiom.

"Yes, to a fate that only Cashto knows," the other alien added, smiling, as he referred to the Cehn-Tahr deity.

Rhemun drew in a breath. "The not-knowing is the worst," he pointed out.

"It always is."

"It was my fault that she left," he confessed heavily. "I should not have been so harsh with her, over something she could not help."

"What a pity that she went soft for you," Mekashe said with pursed lips and amused green eyes. "When I find her delectable. I should very much like to have her for my own."

Rhemun glared at him.

Mekashe cocked his head. "Why should that anger you? You do not want her. You hate humans."

Rhemun didn't even answer him. He got to his feet. "You have won twice. Now it is my turn."

"Good luck with that." Mekashe chuckled. "If Master Cotashe was still here, instead of exiling himself to the Rim, he would tell you that you will never unseat me. I am Fleet Champion."

"Not for long." And Rhemun extended his Bo stick.

DOWN IN THE engine room, Higgins had succeeded in making a problem where none had existed before. He was ably assisted by Holt Stern and Communications Specialist Jennings, both of whom had stalled the comms while he performed his sabotage.

Jennings glanced at them and, when they nodded, he rooted out the interference he'd made to keep the operation secret. "There," he said loudly, "I got the recorder working again. Damn, we're having a lot of these failures lately."

"It's the blip in these engines," Higgins lied. "But I'll get them in shape. How long until we reach Benaski Port, Cap?" he added to Stern. "My little bit of jury-rigging isn't going to last long. We need that Chi-Bahn Stabilizer part, and no supplier even has one except at Benaski Port. Expect to pay an arm and a leg for it, too. I hope our credit's good."

"Once they know it's a Holconcom ship, I don't expect them to haggle over prices." Stern laughed.

"Well, there's that, of course. I wish we could go

downside, and see some of those hotels and casinos," Higgins said dreamily.

"No problem," Holt teased. "Resign your commission, get into civvies and go play with the natives."

"Leave the Holconcom? In your dreams!"

Stern grinned at him. "That's what I thought. Sorry, it's a standing order that we can't port here."

"We're not at war anymore," Higgins ventured.

"Yes, but there was an incident here that caused the Dectat to keep the restriction on the books, and that law hasn't been changed yet. Until it is, Benaski Port's entertainments, as fine as they are, are off-limits to us. Sorry."

Higgins grimaced. "Well, at least I can go down to get my part. Can't I?"

Holt shook his head. "Sorry, old pal. They'll have to bring it up on a shuttle. No contact. Period."

Higgins made a terrible face.

"Not my fault," Holt replied. "Go talk to the emperor."

Higgins sighed. "Not a chance in hell of doing that out here with a bad Chi-Bahn Stabilizer," he repeated.

"In that case, my advice to you is to borrow a handful of sand, spread it on the deck in your quarters, light a candle, order up a synthale and pretend you're on some exotic beach."

"Thank you, Captain, sir, for the great advice." Higgins glared at him.

Holt just chuckled.

RHEMUN'S STERN LOOK stopped the banter as he entered the engine room unexpectedly. "Status of the engines?" he asked Higgins.

"The Chi-Bahn Stabilizer is failing. If we don't make Benaski Port soon, sir, we may blow apart, despite my jury-rigging," Higgins replied, standing at attention.

"Damn," Rhemun said, sounding just like a human. "Very well. Path us to Benaski Port at best speed," he told Holt Stern. "Lay over when ready."

Holt saluted. "Yes, sir!"

"Higgins, do the best you can. We'll keep the engines sublight in the meantime."

Higgins saluted. "Yes, sir."

Rhemun flashed them a green-eyed smile and went back up to the bridge.

CHAPTER EIGHT

THEY DOCKED IN the harbor at Benaski Port. Rhemun called the officers into the engineering sector and gestured at Jennings to screw up the comms, which he did quickly and efficiently.

"Jennings, you will need to run a loop of the normal operation of the bridge on screen for the recorders," he informed the officers. "Btnu, you and Hahnson and I and three of my bodyguards will go down to Benaski Port in a scout, camouflaged..."

A blond head peered into the compartment. A slender body followed it and stood at rigid attention. "I know, sir, I'm crashing a meeting of officers. I'm very sorry, sir, but this is important. Can I speak? Please?"

Rhemun nodded.

"Sir, I know you're all planning to go rescue the doctor. Can't I go, too?" Ensign Jones asked hesitantly. "Sorry, sir, begging your pardon but...you see, Dr. Mallory was always kind to me. A lot of people weren't when I came on board. I'm sort of slow..." He cleared his throat. "I'd just like to go. If you don't mind. Sir."

Rhemun was honestly touched by the young man's dedication. Fortunately he was touched enough that he didn't growl or take the man by the throat, both of which reactions had suddenly risen in him, to his own amazement. "You may come, Jones," he said gently, and he even smiled.

Jones grinned. "Thank you, sir!"

"But you do as you're told and keep in the background."

"I will, sir, yes, sir!" He saluted again.

Rhemun turned to the others. "This will be a court-martial offense. I can only take the risk for myself. Each of you must decide if…"

"We should get going, sir," Hahnson interrupted. "Begging your pardon."

"As soon as possible, I should think," Btnu added. Of the command crew, he had the most to lose, because of his seniority. It touched Rhemun that he didn't even hesitate.

Rhemun's eyes burned a soft brown as he looked around at his officers, and Jones. "She would be gratified at such support." He turned to Stern. "You have operational command. And this I must add—placing you back at the post of astrogator was not intended as a slight. You are the best we have. Dtimun was privileged to appoint as he pleased in command staff. I am not. I must follow protocol and that requires Btnu, due to his Clan rank, as my exec."

Stern's eyes warmed. "Thank you for explaining it, sir."

Rhemun smiled. "Your ability to command was never an issue with me. A captaincy at your age is a mark of achievement. You earned your command. I would be honored to have you as my exec."

Btnu made an amused sound deep in his throat. "My Clan is second only to his, but I have seniority. Dtimun told me once that, had Komak not had the position of executive officer, he would have been proud to have you in it."

"Thanks," Stern said, with heartfelt appreciation. He grinned. "But it's still the Holconcom, sir, even if I only sit at a desk."

"True," Rhemun replied. He looked around at his men. "We will need long cloaks to disguise our uniforms. We must wear them to avoid a charge of espionage if there are...complications."

"Complications, sir?" Ensign Jones asked, saluting again.

"He means, if we have to kill somebody." Higgins chuckled. He saluted. "Begging your pardon, sir."

"In which situation you will not be involved. You put in the requisition for your missing part, Lieutenant," Rhemun told him, "and wait here to receive it."

"Darn it. I mean, yes, sir!" Higgins said.

"Meanwhile, sir, I'll have you rating the bridge crew for inefficiency in your absence, sir, in the finest bit of tech espionage possible," Jennings said with a grin.

Rhemun just laughed.

But as he donned the long brown cloak, he worried about how they were going to locate Mallory. The Underway was a big place. It covered much of the asteroid. Finding a small human in such a place, when she didn't want to be found, would be a challenge. He only hoped she was safe, or safe enough, and that they could find her before the human black ops team did. He had spoken to his mother just before the meeting with his officers. There were whispers on the nexus that a small party of humans had landed on Benaski Port and were asking specific questions about any other humans in residence. And they weren't looking for them in the hotel district.

RHEMUN AND HIS small party pulled up the hoods of their long robes to hide their faces as well as their Holconcom uniforms. Benaski Port was dangerous enough for civilians. There would be those who saw the uniforms and deliberately started trouble, thinking the Holconcom reputation was overstated. Rhemun couldn't risk it, not with Mallory's life in the balance.

He glanced at Jones, the only human besides Hahnson in the search party, who was fumbling to get the hood over his head. He was still surprised that the young Terravegan weapons specialist had pleaded to go with the shore team. Rhemun had almost hesitated—if they had to fight, he had every intention of letting his Cehn-Tahr officers live up to the old reputation they enjoyed in the galaxy, and he wouldn't want the humans to see it. But Jones was so sincere that he relented and let him come down. He hoped he wouldn't regret it.

"We must spread out to search for her," Rhemun said quietly. "Hahnson and I will go to the bazaar in the Underway and see what we can find. The rest of you, search in the bars and restaurants below, question the port workers, see if anyone knows of a human doctor working here."

"Yes, sir," they agreed and only just managed not to salute him before they separated.

"Where will she be, do you think?" Rhemun asked Hahnson.

"I honestly don't know," the human replied. "But I'd bet we have a better chance of finding her if we just look for a group of sick people, where the rogues hang out. There would be the best chance of avoiding any black ops human team."

Rhemun nodded. "Let's start there." He keyed the transmitter in his ring and pulled up Holt Stern's image. "Any luck with deciphering her last messages?" he asked.

Stern nodded, "Yes, in fact, we found something. She sent a communiqué to a human who has underworld connections on Benaski Port—some people say he runs the place. A Terravegan reject named Percival Blount."

"Patch!" Hahnson exclaimed.

Rhemun frowned.

"I've heard Mallory speak of him. He was in her class in medical school. He was expelled because he refused to grow clones for organ replacements. He thought it was unethical."

"I like him already," Rhemun said baldly.

"Yeah, me, too." Stern chuckled. "I mean, yes, sir."

"Thanks. That bit of information may lead us to her." Rhemun cut the connection. "Let's find this man Patch."

THEY WENT BELOW, but nobody knew where Patch was. Hahnson was told that Patch had taken a merc job off-station and that in his absence the owner of a local brothel had pretty much taken over the place.

"I've heard of that man," Hahnson said coldly as they left the bar where they'd been asking questions. "Cartha. He press-gangs young females into service. He has a son who's even worse. They have a bad reputation here, even in a place where bad reputations are nothing special."

"Let's try down here," Rhemun said. He'd had a whiff of some aroma that reminded him of Mallory. His sensory development was uncanny. Although his father had refused the elite biological enhancements of Alamantimichar, even went to war to avoid it for his son, he did have some inherited sensory superiority, like the clones of the Holconcom except that his was natural, not engineered. He knew Mallory's scent. It haunted him.

He followed it to a makeshift tent. An old woman was sitting in front of it, rocking herself, crying.

Rhemun knelt beside her. She was Parsifan. He knew the people. They had similarities to the Cularian genome, although their race had followed a separate evolution.

"Mother, what is it?" he asked in her own tongue.

She looked up at him, startled. "You speak my language!"

"Yes."

She bit her lip. "There are two children, girl children. They were placed in my care when their parents were killed. I had no money to take them home...he took them!"

"He?"

"Cartha." She spat the name. "One is eight years old, the other is ten. I could not stop him. She tried." She nodded toward the tent. "I think she will die. She fought so hard for the girls. She loves them... I have prayed so hard!" She sobbed again.

Rhemun's nostrils caught the scent of blood and bile, mingled with another scent, one he knew well.

He got up and thrust the curtains aside. What he saw dragged an exclamation from his very soul. *"Maliche Mazur!"* he exploded in rage.

At the sound of the curse, one of the most virulent known to the Cehn-Tahr tongue, Hahnson looked past him and paled. Edris Mallory was lying in a pool of blood. Her face was swollen. Her arm was lying at an extreme, odd angle. There was a seeping wound in her stomach. She was barely breathing.

"Let me in there!" Hahnson exclaimed, pushing

past him. He opened the wrist scanner and started his examination, trying to be objective and failing miserably. "The filthy bastard who did this should hang for it!" he exploded.

Rhemun was kneeling on the other side of her. He touched her purple, swelling cheek. "Edris," he whispered roughly.

But she didn't hear him.

Hahnson was cursing with every movement of the wrist scanner.

"Well?" Rhemun asked.

Hahnson's jaw set. "I can heal her. I just don't know if I'll have time... Her injuries are lethal... There are so many...!"

Rhemun closed his eyes and tossed his mind across time and space to Memcache, to the Imperial palace itself. "Sir," he asked respectfully, "Mallory is damaged almost beyond the reach of medicine. Can you, will you, intervene?"

"Of course," came the immediate reply.

Rhemun touched Mallory's hand. It was cold, life-less. But as he watched, he began to see evidence that the powerful old mind was touching the human's, and was beginning to do its work. Tnurat Alaman-timichar, emperor of the Cehn-Tahr, convinced Edris Mallory's mind that it could help heal her body. He put it to work.

Minutes later, Mallory began to breathe normally, and her blue eyes opened, in horrible pain.

Rhemun let out the breath he'd been holding.

"Thank you. I am forever in your debt," he said in his mind.

There was a smile in the old voice that replied. "It was no difficulty. Mallory is important to the timeline."

"She is?"

"Yes. I cannot tell you why." There was a hesitation. "You are on Benaski Port, Rhemun."

Rhemun sighed. "Yes, sir. I could not permit the human black ops team to take Mallory. I have been guilty of some little subterfuge..."

There was a chuckle. "I will make an exception this time, and so state with the Dectat and the military authority. There will be no repercussions."

"I am most grateful. I should hate to see my men penalized for a choice of mine."

"You have made great progress with them," the old one thought. "Because of Mallory?"

"Because of my failure with her. Her pain is my fault." There was a pause. "I intend to invoke *Sharah-Malach*," Rhemun said silently, and with venom in his tone.

The emperor seemed to not be shocked. "That is your right, if you choose it."

"There may be political repercussions, even here."

"If so, I will deal with them," the emperor said. There was sudden steel in the other's tone. "Avenge her."

"Yes, sir!"

He opened his eyes and found Hahnson watching him with frowning curiosity.

"The emperor," Rhemun replied. "I asked him to intervene." He let Hahnson think the emperor read his mind. None of the humans needed to know that he was a telepath. It might lead to questions he was reluctant to answer.

He used his comm ring to call to the other members of the search party. In seconds they gathered around him. There were exclamations from the humans, especially Jones, when they saw Dr. Mallory lying in her own blood. The Cehn-Tahr stood solemnly, with grim faces.

"Will she live?" Jones asked for all of them.

"Yes," Hahnson said. "It will mean a long recovery, but she will live."

Rhemun stood up, cold-eyed. *"Sharah-Malach,"* he said in the old, high Cehn-Tahr that was only understood by members of his Clan or by the *kehmatemer.*

Btnu stepped forward. "Agreed. We will find him. And the others," he replied.

"His scent is on her body," Rhemun said in Standard. "Track him."

The Cehn-Tahr took a long smell.

Rhemun noticed the young man's curiosity. He smiled, though he felt no humor in the situation itself. "We can find the perpetrator in this manner, Jones," he explained.

"You can track him by smelling him?" Jones asked hesitantly.

Rhemun nodded. "You humans could smell a stew and tell perhaps what sort of meat was used. We could smell the same stew and tell you each ingredient and its exact point of origin."

"That's amazing. Can I go with them?" Jones asked. "Please, sir?"

Rhemun's lips made a thin line. But the boy was upset and he wanted to be useful. "Very well." He looked at Btnu and spoke in the old tongue. "Do not let the boy watch. Send him after the Parsifan girls while you deal with the perpetrator and his son. Two little girls were taken to the brothel owned by Cartha, one aged eight and one aged ten. Dr. Mallory attempted to prevent them from being abducted. You can see the result."

Btnu nodded. *"Sharah-Malach."* He cocked his head. "It will be dangerous for her. More dangerous than this."

"I know," Rhemun said solemnly. "I will deal with it when I must. For now, she must be avenged. And the punishment must be made known among those who might repeat the offense."

"I understand. We will not fail you." He saluted. So did the others.

"Make sure he knows who came for him," Rhemun added coldly.

Btnu smiled with ice in his eyes. "Of course."

He motioned to Jones, who took a last, wincing

look at the prone human female and followed the tall Cehn-Tahr out of the small nest.

HAHNSON WAS WATCHING RHEMUN. *"Sharah-Malach?"* he questioned softly. "I thought you hated her."

Rhemun's dark eyebrows arched. "You speak the Holy Tongue."

Hahnson nodded. "At least, my original did." He was working on Mallory with a healing device. "I was bonded to an outcast Cehn-Tahr female, during the Great Galaxy War. Her brother invoked the retribution over his mate when she was assaulted."

Rhemun's eyes narrowed. "Cehn-Tahr cannot mate with human. I know because the emperor told me that Ruszel had to be genetically altered in order to bond with Dtimun, who had the full complement of genetic manipulation in his youth."

"Yes. I know it's impossible. At least, I know now. Dtimun tried to warn me, but I wouldn't listen." He swallowed. "My mate's family also had the genetic enhancements. When we tried to mate, she broke my back. If Dtimun hadn't acted quickly, I would have died." His eyes lowered. "She committed suicide, when she knew we could never be truly together."

"I'm sorry. Very sorry." Rhemun sighed. "That explains how you know so much about us."

"I know a lot more than that. Things I would never share with other humans." He glanced at Rhemun. "I've seen you fight without restraint. I know your true face."

Rhemun nodded. "I understand." His eyes softened. "You have great courage, to stay with us and know that."

"Not courage. I admire your race. I have no fear of you." His face hardened. "And I approve of your actions. Nobody should do something like this and live to brag about it," he added coldly.

"I agree." He looked down at Mallory and winced. "I can never mate with her, of course, but I can protect her."

Hahnson gave him an odd look. "I know that you aren't permitted to discuss intimate subjects with members of your own species," he began, without looking at the alien. "And of course, I'm just talking to myself now, not to you. But your great strength is almost totally dependent on classified tech. You don't have the genetic modifications that I noted in Dtimun when I ran a scan on him in Ruszel's absence."

"That is true," Rhemun said, shocked. "My father went to war with the Cehn-Tahr government to make certain that I was never subjected to genetic manipulation."

"Which means that you could, theoretically, mate with a human. If you disabled your tech and had a couple of shots of dravelzium after the bonding."

Rhemun's heart shot almost into his mouth. He looked at Edris with new eyes. "I did not hear you say these things, of course," he added solemnly.

"Of course. I would never presume to initiate such a discussion with you, although I am a physician and anything we speak about comes under the confidentiality rule." He looked absolutely innocent when he glanced at the alien. He turned his attention back to Mallory as he continued treatment. It was going to be a long recovery. He was grateful for the emperor's intervention. She had three major injuries, any one of which could have ended in terminal organ failure. Now he had time to treat them.

"Sharah-Malach." He drew in a long breath. "If she ever finds out, she won't approve. She's quite softhearted, even over people like Cartha and his son."

Rhemun nodded. "She wouldn't approve." His face hardened. "But there must be retribution. She is Holconcom."

"You won't tell her?"

"About Cartha? No. You won't tell her, either, nor will my men," he added firmly. "It would lie on her conscience forever." He glanced at Hahnson. "It will not disturb mine in the least, nor that of the men I sent to enforce the sentence. I told them not to let Jones see it, however. He has a sensitive nature. Somewhat like Mallory," he added gently, and smiled.

Hahnson smiled back.

Btnu and the other Holconcom surrounded the man, Cartha, and his grown son, Debkar. The criminals were Altairian, blue-skinned and haughty. They stared at the newcomers without any particular interest. They only saw hooded males, nothing to alert them to the true identity of their visitors.

"If you want girls, go see Makmak," Cartha said dismissively. "I do not deal directly with the women."

"We have not come for women," Btnu said quietly in Altairian.

While Cartha puzzled about that, Btnu turned to the young human beside him. "Jones, will you go and search for the little girls, please?" Btnu asked politely in Standard.

Jones studied the older alien curiously. "Me, sir? But why?"

Uncharacteristically, Btnu, who never touched humans, put a kindly hand on his shoulder. "Because you are our friend. And you should not witness this."

Jones was touched beyond words. He wanted to help, but he knew he wasn't needed. "Very well, sir." He smiled, turned and went to the next level of the building to search the cubicles for the little girls.

Btnu stared at Cartha coldly.

"What girls?" Cartha asked belligerently, rising. "You have no right to take my servants!"

"You had no right to take them from their protector," Btnu said quietly. "Or to injure the little human female who attempted to stop you."

"She was human," he said with contempt. "Why should that concern you? As for the girls, they are now mine. You cannot frighten me into giving them back." Cartha laughed contemptuously. He looked at the tallest alien more closely. "What race are you, anyway, Cehn-Tahr? The tales we hear of you are those of reclusive farmers." He made it sound contemptuous.

Btnu glanced at his companions and nodded. The Cehn-Tahr threw off their robes.

Cartha knew a Holconcom uniform when he saw it, and he knew what would happen next. Somehow he had offended these soldiers. The results would be...unpleasant. He gasped and started to run, but of course, there was no possibility that he could escape. The Holconcom herded him and his son to the center of the room.

"You have no authority...!" Debkar cried.

"You beat one of our own almost to death," Btnu said quietly.

"The female?" Cartha exclaimed. "She was only a female!"

"She was Holconcom."

Cartha's face went white. Even he, with all his wealth and power, feared the retribution of the Holconcom. No criminal had ever dared to provoke the elite unit. Nor would he have, had he known.

"I did not know," he said, trying to persuade. He managed a smile. "We can come to terms. I have great wealth, great power."

Btnu took a step forward. "I am Holconcom. That is my wealth. That is my power." He nodded to the others. The soft, slow growls began and slowly intensified. Almost casually, Btnu let the biomechanical claws extend from his fingertips and abruptly he shifted into his true Cehn-Tahr form.

Cartha had just enough time to scream, once. His son did not have even that.

MINUTES LATER, EDRIS was stabilized. Hahnson just shook his head. "I've seen combat wounds that weren't this bad," he said heavily.

"So have I." Rhemun was kneeling beside Edris. His big hand smoothed her matted hair. "She is so fragile."

"Yes, but she has great courage."

Rhemun nodded. "She will live?"

"Yes," Hahnson said. "But the recovery will take time."

"That doesn't matter. Her assistant can fill in for her until she is healed completely."

They heard footsteps approaching. Rhemun stood and turned. Jones had two little girls, one in his arms, and one by the hand. The children had bruises and their clothing was torn. Rhemun's face hardened.

"They're all right, sir." Jones spoke for the others. "I was just in time to spare them any lasting damage. But they were treated pretty badly by that madman."

"They were avenged." Rhemun looked at Btnu, who nodded grimly.

"What kind of monster would do this to children, or that to a human woman?" Jones added with a painful glance at Edris, lying so still and white. "She'll be okay, won't she, sir?" he asked Hahnson.

Hahnson smiled. "She'll be fine, Jones. Honest." He looked at the two little girls with painful compassion. They were traumatized, that much was visible. "Now if you little ones will let me examine you, I can treat those cuts and bruises." He smiled. "I won't hurt you. I promise."

"You will come with us, Jones, sir?" the eldest girl asked worriedly.

Jones looked down at her and smiled. "Of course. This is Marcella." He indicated the young girl clinging to his hand. "She's the oldest. And this is Minat," he added, nodding toward the smaller girl curled up against his chest. "Marcella is ten. Minat is only eight."

"It's nice to meet you, girls. My name is Dr. Hahnson."

"Oh. The Doctor Hahnson." Marcella let go of Jones's hand and walked right up to Hahnson. "Dr. Edris speaks of you. She says you are very kind."

He smiled. "I try."

For the first time, she saw the blonde human woman, lying bruised and bloody on a pallet inside the prefab dome. "Dr. Edris!" she exclaimed, and ran to the injured physician on the pallet. "She will not die?" she asked in Standard.

"No. She's going to be fine."

"She was so kind to us!"

"We love her," Minat said shyly, but in Parsifan, still clinging to Jones.

"Let the doctor examine you," Rhemun said gently, kneeling in front of the children. He spoke in Parsifan, like Minat. "I promise he won't hurt you."

They looked at him warily. "You are Cehn-Tahr," Marcella said. "We are afraid of your kind."

"I know. We have a sad history of conflict. But I have no quarrel with you." He smiled. "No one will hurt you again. I promise."

Minat asked Jones to put her down. She went to Rhemun and cocked her head at him curiously. "Your hair is like ours." She fingered her own long, wavy hair that fell to her waist. "It is quite perfect."

"Thank you," he said, and smiled again.

"You speak in our tongue," Marcella observed.

"Yes. I speak many tongues."

"We speak only Standard and Parsifan," Marcella replied. "I would like to learn your tongue."

"That would take a very long time. And you must let the doctor see you. We have to get Dr. Mallory to our ship, so that she can be properly treated."

"I see. Very well, sir." Marcella went back to Edris. Minat joined her. They were silent and sad.

Jones stayed with them, very protective and supportive while Hahnson treated their injuries. He was happy to see that there were no injuries to them other than superficial ones.

"Shameful, to treat children that way," Jones muttered.

Hahnson nodded. "This place is a thieves' den, all right. Hell of a shame that Patch wasn't here..."

"Did I hear my name mentioned?" a deep voice asked from just behind him.

CHAPTER NINE

HAHNSON TURNED. OUTSIDE WAS a tall man with a patch over one eye. He wasn't smiling. Behind him were three humans, raging about illegal detention, held by three burly Rojoks in what passed for Benaski Port Security uniforms.

"Patch?" Hahnson asked, moving outside the prefab dome.

The one-eyed man raised both eyebrows.

"Sorry." Hahnson chuckled, extending a hand to shake the other man's. "Glad to meet you, Mr. Blount. I've heard a lot about you from Madeline Ruszel and Edris Mallory."

"I was at the bonding ceremony." Patch smiled. "In disguise, I might add. I was glad to hear that her delivery went smoothly. Delicate thing, pregnancy between species."

"Quite delicate," Hahnson replied.

Patch looked beyond him at Mallory, and he winced. "God, I hate that!" he exclaimed. "If I hadn't been off-world, it would never have happened. She's one of the kindest human beings I've ever known."

He moved into the hut and knelt beside Mallory.

But as he extended his hand, there was a blur of red and he found himself confronted by a tall Cehn-Tahr in a red uniform with long, curly black hair and murderous black eyes. Rhemun growled, once.

Patch, who knew mating behavior when he saw it, stood up and moved away from Mallory. "Sorry," he said quickly. "It's a very human trait, trying to give comfort."

"Fatal, I'm sad to say, if you had touched her," Rhemun said tautly. "Although I am grateful for the aid you gave her."

Patch nodded. He smiled. "Percy Blount," he said, introducing himself.

"Rhemun. I command the Holconcom."

"Who are they?" Btnu interjected, indicating the three humans in custody.

Percy's one eye narrowed and his face hardened. "They say they're human military on a layover. But I can tell you from personal experience that they're Terravegan Medical Corps black ops. They came to take Dr. Mallory into custody."

Rhemun faced them with the same black-eyed ferocity he'd shown to Patch at Mallory's side.

"Holconcom!" one of the humans gasped.

"Mallory has Cehn-Tahr citizenship," Rhemun informed them. "She also has reserve status with the Holconcom. Either of those appointments gives me the right to order a summary execution on the spot, under Cehn-Tahr military regulations."

"You can't...!"

"We have to have a trial…!"

"We have rights…!"

Percy Blount smiled at them. "This is Benaski Port. We have no law here." He leaned toward them. "We're pirates."

"There's the Malcopian Articles of War!" one blustered.

"Nonapplicable in a neutral port," Percy said blithely. "Would you like me to furnish you a copy of them, so that you can read the fine print? The one listed exception to the Articles is Benaski Port."

"We're entitled to legal counsel," one of the humans stated.

Rhemun's eyes were still dangerous. "You will be transported to Memcache, where you will face formal charges at the hands of the Dectat for harassment of Cehn-Tahr Holconcom personnel."

"Oh, yeah?" one of the humans said. "Well, I say Dr. Mallory asked us to come and take her back to Trimerius!"

Before he could even get the last word out, Rhemun had him by the throat. "Do you pray?" he asked the human in a voice that sounded like a cat hissing. "Now is the time." He permitted just the tip of his genetically engineered claws to extend so the human could feel them. "Tell the truth, or die."

The human was clawing at the hand. "We were sent to…apprehend her," the man choked. "She broke the law. Third…strike…provision…means Reboot."

"You may explain Reboot to the Dectat," Rhemun said, dropping the man to the wooden flooring with magnificent distaste. "And you might recall that our emperor's son is bonded to a former Terravegan physician."

The humans looked much less belligerent now. "Please," one of them said. "There's no need for this…"

Patch looked at Rhemun quietly. "There is a very nice compromise I could suggest."

"Suggest it."

Patch pushed in a code and brought up a Tri-D journalist from the nexus. "Hi, John. Have I got a story for you!"

The humans paled.

Patch muted the feed. "You can talk to him." He indicated the journalist in the nexus feed. "Or you can go home with him." He pointed to a still-fuming Rhemun.

The human who'd irritated Rhemun touched his throat. "Uh, how do you feel about refugees here?" he asked Patch.

"Oh, we take anybody. This is a haven for people running from the law." Patch chuckled. "We're family, you might say."

"In that case," the black ops man said, noting that his friends were nodding furiously, and that the tall Holconcom officer was almost purring at the thought of taking them away, "I think we'd like to join the family and move in with you."

"Excellent!" He touched a button. "John, these gentlemen have some very interesting information to impart. I hope your publisher is still as fearless as he once was…?"

"Even more so since he has the backing of several extremely wealthy politicians," the other man laughed. "Let's hear it!"

MALLORY WAS STILL unconscious when they took her back aboard the *Morcai*. The old woman who had been helping them look after her was sad to see her go.

"She helped many to live who would not have." The woman sighed. "But what of the girls?" she added, wincing when she saw their terrified little faces, still white and strained. They had bruises from the rough hands of the men who had taken them back to the brothel, although Hahnson had treated their injuries.

"Can you take care of them?" Rhemun asked gently.

She had been more nervous of the tall aliens when she saw the red uniforms, which were quickly recovered with cloaks once the girls were returned to the place from where they'd been abducted.

"Comcaashe," he said softly, in the familiar usage which was reserved for family or the children and elderly of any race, noting her fear. "The Holconcom do not make war on women or children."

She relaxed, but only a little. "I have heard terrible things of you."

"After today, you will hear more," he promised,

and his eyes glittered. "The creatures who did that to Mallory—" he indicated the still form in the floating ambutube "—paid a very high price for their brutality."

The old woman looked at him with new eyes. "They will not come back for the children?"

"Cartha and his son are no longer alive," Rhemun said flatly, and without guilt.

She sighed. "I am grateful." She glanced at the girls. "But they must not stay here," she emphasized. "Cartha and his son had friends. They will seek vengeance where it is easiest." She indicated the children with her head.

Rhemun searched her eyes. "Do they have family?"

"Yes, on Tol Shalad," she replied. "Her uncle and his mate have a green farm there, in a pressure dome, along with a few other settlers."

"Do you know how to contact him?"

She nodded, and handed him a chip for his communicator ring. He inserted it and watched the information scroll on the virtual display.

Two STANDARD HOURS LATER, he had diplomatic status and was appointed legal guardian of the two Parsifan girls for the trip to Tol Shalad, where their uncle and aunt had eagerly agreed to accept custody of them.

"The emperor is truly a worker of miracles." Rhemun chuckled. He didn't add that Tnurat had already seen the news feed on the nexus, exposing Reboot and the black ops team. Tnurat had also filed a formal complaint with the Tri-Galaxy Council against the Terravegan Medical Authority for its attempted abduction of Mallory and demanded a formal apology from the medical corps.

"I never thought he could manage it in that tight time frame," Hahnson said, shaking his head. "But I'm glad he did. I would have hated leaving the girls behind, especially if Cartha's friends looked for someone to blame." He looked up from Mallory's chart. "What about the old woman?"

Rhemun chuckled. "I gave her mems and temporary Cehn-Tahr citizenship. She's on her way to the Rim colonies. She was quite excited about the trip. A great adventure, she called it."

"Nice of you," Hahnson commented.

The alien shrugged. He looked through the plexiglass at Mallory, lying very still in a bed in sick bay. "She hasn't regained consciousness. Is this normal?"

"Yes. I've placed her in stasis while her injuries continue to heal. No distractions." He looked up. "The emperor has a rare gift."

He nodded. "Quite rare. His ability to heal is legendary. Like his temper," he added with a chuckle.

"Jones is looking after the girls," Hahnson commented. He pursed his lips. "That was an odd choice, if I may say."

"He rescued them," Rhemun said simply. "They look to him as a relative." He made a face, an odd

YOUR PARTICIPATION IS REQUESTED!

Dear Reader,

Since you are a lover of our books — we would like to get to know you!

Inside you will find a short Reader's Survey. Sharing your answers with us will help our editorial staff understand who you are and what activities you enjoy.

To thank you for your participation, we would like to send you 2 books and 2 gifts — **ABSOLUTELY FREE!**

Enjoy your gifts with our appreciation,

Pam Powers

SEE INSIDE FOR READER'S SURVEY

For Your Reading Pleasure...

#1 NEW YORK TIMES BESTSELLING AUTHOR

NORA ROBERTS

DANGER, SECRETS AND LOVE IN THE SCOTTISH HIGHLANDS

THE MacGREGORS

REBELL FREE!

#1 NEW YORK TIMES BESTSELLING AUTHOR

DEBBIE MACOMBER

the sooner the better

A Deliverance Company Novel

We'll send you 2 books and 2 gifts
ABSOLUTELY FREE
just for completing our Reader's Survey!

thing for an impassive Cehn-Tahr. "They're afraid of me. Of all my race. They've heard tales of us."

"I've never known any Cehn-Tahr to harm a child of any race."

He smiled. "We don't make war on children. Perhaps in the time it takes to convey them home, they might change their minds."

Hahnson just nodded.

RHEMUN KNEW THAT children loved stories. His own son had been fond of books. Rhemun had sent him several, and at least was allowed by his vicious mate to read to the little boy over the holon, the exotic, top secret virtual comms unknown to all but Cehn-Tahr. They allowed the actual physical presence of a person through an avatar who could touch and be touched. It was never spoken of to any outworlders, even Holconcom humans.

He had learned some stories by heart and the child had enjoyed them, for a time. Then came the day when his mate broke off all contact between the two. A price had to be negotiated, allowing him to contact the boy no more than a few times a year. Eventually, those visits ceased, when the boy, brainwashed by his uncles, refused to speak to his father at all. It had been painful. Even more painful when his mate had died unexpectedly and Rhemun managed to obtain legal custody of his son. The boy didn't know him, and didn't want to know him. He hated the military, wanted nothing to do with the military school to which Rhemun had sent him, and found ways and means to cheat on exams and bribe staff to sneak him exotic goods for resale, at high prices, to the other students. The boy's behavior shamed both Rhemun and Sfilla, his grandmother. But years of conditioning were going to be hard to undo. Rhemun had resigned himself to a long, drawn-out process, but he was hopeful that he could turn the child. Soon afterward, the bomb fell on the military academy and his son was lost forever.

He had blamed Mallory, and all humans, for the accident. That shamed him even more in memory. She was kind and openhearted. He had treated her shabbily, made her pay for what the female pilot had done. Now that he knew the true punishment to which the pilot had been subjected, he was horrified, even more than vindicated for his son's death. The humans were barbarians.

He wondered if the little Parsifan girls might respond to some of the stories he remembered from decades past.

One night, he walked into sick bay where the girls were staying, with a small, square reader in his hand. He shape-shifted into his true form, the form that was only ever shown to family—or enemies as they were about to be dispatched.

At his approach, the girls stood up, clutching one another.

"I mean you no harm," he said in Parsifan, placing his hand over his heart. "I share my true form with you because we are now family. I have come to tell stories."

The little one, Minat, stared at him from a face that had fading bruises from her rough treatment on Benaski Port.

"Stories, sir?" she replied, watching him unblinkingly.

"Stories. They are Cehn-Tahr, but perhaps they might apply to all cultures. Would you like to hear one?"

"What are they about?" the older girl, Marcella, asked gently.

"One is about a lone galot—one of the giant cats who prowl my homeworld of Memcache and have a colony on Eridanus Three. The galot cub is lost and wanders through the land in great danger until he finds a home with a family of *copcas*—small rodents like mice." He smiled. "It is an adventure."

"I should love to hear it!" Minat exclaimed.

"Oh, yes, please!" Marcella enthused.

He sprawled on the carpeted floor with them and opened the reader.

THE GIRLS WERE so enthusiastic that Rhemun had to find time each night to tell a new story. It amused and touched him that he had won their trust.

Mallory's trust was harder to reacquire. She was out of intensive care, but still mostly bedridden, wary and nervous and very frail.

"I deeply regret your treatment on Benaski Port,"

Rhemun said quietly when they were together, in sick bay.

"Yes. It was...very bad. But we rescued the girls." She shivered. "It would have been unspeakable for them to remain in such a place." She cocked her head. "What happened to Cartha, and his son?" she asked.

He lifted his chin. "Things we should never discuss," he said flatly.

"But they might do it again, to other little girls..." Her expression was plaintive.

"They will never touch another child," he promised her. His face was ice-cold. "Their reign of terror is over."

She swallowed. "Do I want to know how?"

He looked at her quietly, his eyes almost gold. He smiled and shook his head.

"All right." She searched his eyes. They were such an odd shade of gold. She'd never seen it before. Well, maybe once, when Dtimun was looking at Madeline Ruszel. She'd never been able to get Madeline to explain the color to her.

"The ops team, they wouldn't try to take me again while I'm aboard the *Morcai*?" She was worried about that.

"It would be instantly fatal. Besides," he said, with some secret humor, "your Terravegan Medical Authority has enough problems right now with the Terravegan judiciary. And the Tri-D press."

"Excuse me?"

"It seems the emperor expressed public disdain for the process called 'Reboot.' Your friend Percy Blount had the black ops team tell the story to a Tri-D journalist, who broadcast it all over the nexus. In the aftermath, the emperor even gave an audio interview to the Tri-D press, condemning it. He brought the matter to the attention of the Tri-Galaxy Council, as well. The men in the black ops team sent to apprehend you are now living on Benaski Port, after revealing everything they knew about what amounts to an illegal practice." He smiled. "I understand that many people are now struggling not only to retain their employment in the Terravegan medical service, but also to avoid being spaced. Interesting, is it not?"

"The black ops team told on them?" she exclaimed.

He chuckled, or what, in a Cehn-Tahr, equated to that. "With elaborate detail."

"Good for them!" she said firmly. "It's a shameful, barbaric practice. I never approved of it."

He studied her quietly. "Your friend Blount was responsible for convincing the black ops team to speak publicly. With some inspiration from me," he added without telling her what had actually happened.

"Percy hates our medical service," she replied. "When he was a resident, there was a program responsible to create clones for, well, spare parts for the wealthy people in our society. Percy refused to do it. They threw him out of the medical profession. That's why he's on Benaski Port now."

"A pirate with ethics," he remarked. "Astounding."

"Yes."

His eyes narrowed on her body. She was very thin. Almost frail. "Hahnson prescribed increased rations for you, I believe?"

She shrugged. "I'm not hungry, sir."

"Then perhaps we might import something exotic to tempt your palate. I'll see to it."

"But, sir..."

He held up a hand. "It does no good to argue with me. You should know that by now."

She opened her mouth, and then closed it.

"Hahnson is not comfortable having you alone during your sleep periods," he added solemnly. "He says that the AVBDs indicate that you have nightmares."

"I'm sorry, sir..."

He held up a hand. "I may have a solution," he said. "We will discuss it later."

She swallowed. "Yes, sir." He was trying to make things up to her. It made her uncomfortable. She didn't want pity.

He moved closer to the bed. "You think I act out of guilt, yes?"

She was surprised at his perception. "Well...yes."

He drew in a breath. "In a sense, I do. In another..." He hesitated. He locked his hands behind his back and stared down at her solemnly. "Mallory, my mate died before my son did," he said quietly.

She didn't reply. She frowned through the pain-killers, her blue eyes wide and questioning. In spite of everything that had happened, her heart skipped when he stared so deeply into her eyes.

He smiled faintly, with something akin to relief. There were dangerous times ahead, but at least he hadn't managed to kill what she felt for him.

"I'm sorry, sir, for…"

"You have nothing to apologize for. I, on the other hand, have a great deal to atone for. Your treatment at Cartha's hands shames me, shames my Clan. It was my own senseless prejudice that put you in danger." He drew in a breath and stood straighter. "I hope you can forgive it."

She swallowed. She wasn't sure what he meant. "I…thank you for telling me the truth, sir. I'll try to keep my…my hormones…under control while I'm here…" she faltered.

"I'm afraid that it's far too late for that to be of any help," he mused, recalling his near-fatal reaction to Patch's attempt to touch her. "We must speak of it, but at a more appropriate time. Now, you must rest." He dimmed the light above the medi-bed. "Try to sleep. We will talk again later."

She closed her eyes. "Yes, sir."

Her hair was around her shoulders, blond, almost platinum blond, and curling. He loved the way it looked. It made her even more feminine than she already was. But it was dangerous to look too closely.

He needed another injection of dravelzium. There could be no slipups. Not yet. She was much too frail.

THERE WAS A briefing as the crew prepared for another short rescue hop to lift colonists from a populated asteroid in the Algomerian Sector. Pirates coveted the minerals there. Rhemun was going over the mission with his executive officers and one of the *kelekom* operators, Jefferson Colby, when the door opened and two little girls came running in.

"He said we couldn't, but we did!" Minat laughed and flung herself into Rhemun's lap. Marcella followed her sister, laughing, but she perched on the edge of Rhemun's chair.

Ensign Jones rushed into the room, also. "Sorry, sir, they escaped!" Jones said, saluting smartly. "Girls, you have to come with me."

"No. Oh, please, can't we stay?" Minat asked Rhemun. She was perched on his lap with one arm around his neck, her hand tangled in his long, thick, curly hair. "Please, sir?"

"Please?" Marcella seconded. She was sitting on the wide chair arm on Rhemun's other side.

He looked at the girls and at Jones's worried expression and laughed. "Let them stay." He looked from one child to the other. "But you must sit very still and not speak. All right?"

"All right, sir!" Minat spoke for both of them. She curled up in his lap. Marcella sat beside him in another chair that was quickly provided.

He drew Minat close with a smile that was full of affection and amusement.

Rhemun and some of the crew had been having a hard time adjusting to each other, even after Mallory's rescue. But the tenderness he displayed with the children that day melted even the hardest of human hearts. After the briefing, when gossip got around the ship about the intruders at the briefing, the last two crewmen who had filed requests for transfer quietly withdrew their requests.

THAT NIGHT—OR WHAT passed for night on the rotation shifts of the *Morcai*—Rhemun found a new story to tell the girls. It was a Terravegan tale about a reclusive bear and a stubborn fox who insisted that he was also a bear and should share the larger animal's den while they hibernated.

While he was telling it to the girls, he heard odd sounds nearby, but he discounted them as some distortion of regular ship noises. He continued with the story, to the delight of the two little girls, who were becoming quite close to him.

"But then what happened?" Minat asked when he finished the narrative.

"Well, then the fox and the bear hibernated together," he explained.

"Yes, but then what happened when it became warm weather again?" Marcella seconded.

He thought for a minute. "I expect they went hunting for fish. Bears love fish. I'm sure the fox would have been happy to eat them, too."

"Ah," Minat sighed.

"Thank you very much, sir. I shall miss the stories," Marcella agreed.

"I shall miss both of you," he said quietly, and meant it.

They hugged him warmly. He hugged them back, and then made a quick exit, because he was feeling quite emotional at the thought of giving them to their uncle and aunt, which was to happen the next solar week.

He walked out of the room and straight into Stern, Hahnson, Higgins, Jennings and even Btnu.

His eyes widened.

Stern whipped out a handkerchief. "Sorry, sir, place needed dusting. Delicate computer equipment in here, you know."

"Computer...yes, I was checking the mainframe!" Higgins said quickly and went looking for it.

"Communications...uh...flubbed. I mean, sporadic." Jennings cleared his throat and reddened. "Just making sure everything was all right."

"Uh, Jennings had a sore throat. Right?" Hahnson asked Jennings, who nodded enthusiastically. He pulled out an instrument. "I'm just giving him a once-over."

Btnu didn't even speak. He looked absolutely disoriented.

Rhemun was staring at them as if they'd gone

mad. At that moment, Jones came into the room without looking. His arms were full of snack bowls, prefilled. "I got the snacks. What's the next…story…" He stopped in midsentence and gaped at Rhemun. His whole face turned red. "Oh. Sir. Yes. I, uh, I…!" He tried to salute with his hands full.

Rhemun burst out laughing.

"Aw, now, sir, don't do that," Jones said, hurt. "Listen, we all grew up in government nurseries. None of us ever got told a story in our lives. We stumbled on story time accidentally, and then we, well, we just sort of eavesdropped every night. We didn't mean any harm."

Rhemun was still smiling. "I haven't told stories in many decades." He shrugged. "I enjoy them, too." He glanced around the room at the embarrassed officers and Jones with his arms full of treat packs. "Why don't all of you go to the rec room and watch a vid?"

"Could we?" Jones spoke for everyone. "Really?"

"If anything comes up, we'll call you," he promised. "Get out of here."

They laughed, saluted and ran for it. Btnu, more somberly, saluted and retreated behind the humans.

RHEMUN JUST SHOOK his head.

Mallory came slowly out from the closet she'd been inhabiting. She was redder than the men.

Rhemun was fascinated. "I suppose you grew

up in a government nursery also and never heard a story?"

She nodded. "It's rather…nice, listening to stories."

He moved closer with a long sigh. "I will miss the girls."

She studied his face. "I will miss them, too." She hesitated, started to speak and closed her mouth.

"They must go to their kin," Rhemun said kindly. "You know this. They are the only survivors of the tragedy that befell their parents. Their aunt was their mother's sister. She wants them very much."

"Yes, I know, but the uncle is involved in illegal activities," she blurted out.

"So you have been making inquiries," he mused.

"Not really. I just hacked the judicial mainframe and pulled out his priors." She flushed.

"Hacked the mainframe. I see."

"It's not illegal if you're doing it for a good cause," she said stubbornly.

He reached out and touched her blond hair lightly. "All right. Do you want to come with me when I take them down to the planet?"

She was shocked that he touched her, and it was deliberate. Was it guilt? Or something more? She swallowed, tried to force her mind back to the question he'd asked. "Yes, I'd like very much to go with you. With them." She flushed. "May I?"

"Of course. We'll leave at planet dawn. I'll flash you when to meet us on the flight deck." He hesitated. "You must not weep in front of the girls. It will only upset them and make a difficult time more difficult."

"I understand, sir."

He withdrew his hand. "Good."

THE GIRLS WERE reluctant to leave. They picked up their small backpacks and boarded the scout ship. Rhemun flew them, and Mallory, down to the surface of Tol Shalad. It was a barren, cold place with green oases in constructed domes all over the southern continent. The others were covered with ice. Only this one was even remotely inhabitable, and even then only with pressure domes.

Rhemun piloted the scout ship through the force field of the largest dome, a huge agricultural complex, and put it down gently on the runway. There were only two other ships there, both dilapidated and run-down and rusted. Rhemun grimaced at their condition and wondered if any pilot here would dare trust himself in space in one of those hulks.

"You're the Holconcom commander?" the fixed base operator asked when he approached them. "I'm Tal Chavoz. I keep what's left of the space vehicles and maintain the runway for landings." He shook his head. "We don't get much traffic. And those—" he indicated the two ships "—will most likely never lift off again." He shook his head. "Just can't get spare parts out here, even with Tri-D replicator tech. You here to see the Pivons?" He smiled at the girls. "That must be Marcella! I haven't seen you since you were born and your parents visited here. Sorry about your folks," he added gently.

"Thank you," Marcella said softly.

He looked up at Rhemun and Mallory. "You two serve together? I heard there was a female Holconcom. Never believed it. Not until now. You must be a heck of a woman," he added. "Sorry, if that sounds forward."

Mallory laughed. "No apology necessary. Thanks."

Rhemun was fascinated by the change laughter made in her appearance. It was the first time he'd seen her do that. It made her whole face radiant. On the other hand, he didn't like the way the operator was looking at her. His eyes narrowed and a low, soft growl escaped his tight throat.

The operator looked at him and stiffened. "Uh, the Pivons live right over that hill. Here, you're welcome to borrow my skipper. Ignition key's enabled."

"Thank you," Mallory said. She was looking at Rhemun curiously. She'd never heard him growl at anyone. She wondered if he sensed something about the fixed base operator that she didn't.

But Rhemun didn't say anything. He lifted the girls gently into the back of the skipper, motioned Mallory into the passenger seat and lifted off, soaring just a few feet off the ground.

THE PIVONS LIVED at the outer edge of the force field dome, on a small plot of property where they grew indigenous vegetables and fruits. It wasn't a huge property, but it was well kept and fertile. Many crops were maturing, under the soft misting irrigators and the gentle buzz of the small surface tillers that worked automatically to remove weeds and insects. No chemicals of any sort were allowed in these green colonies. Thanks to the little machines, they weren't needed.

Two people came out of the small, prefab house when they landed. The man was tall and thin and seemed very nervous. The woman was smaller, rounder, and she had a huge smile on her face when she saw the girls.

Minat ran right into her arms. Marcella followed suit. They rambled on in Parsifan, crying and talking, crying and talking.

"I'm Rado," the man said, nodding formally. "My spouse is Jessa. The girls are ours now." He looked at Rhemun with mingled interest and fear. "What are you?"

Rhemun transformed. The man gasped and moved back, both hands out.

"We have done nothing. We are not your enemies!" Rado exclaimed.

Rhemun didn't stir. "I mean you no harm," he said in the softly accented tones that accompanied the shape-shifting to his natural form.

As if to prove that statement, Minat and Marcella went to him and curled against his side.

"He is our friend," Minat said. "He tells us stories!"

Jessa was hesitant.

"Cehn-Tahr never reveal themselves to outsiders, except in battle," Mallory explained. "Or to close family."

"Family." Jessa relaxed. She smiled. "You honor us."

He bowed. "The honor is mine, to meet the family of our young friends."

Belatedly, Rado moved forward and extended his hand. "Sorry. Very sorry. We've heard stories about the Cehn-Tahr, especially in the Holconcom. That's what you are, yeah?"

Rhemun nodded, shaking the hand. "I am Rhemun. I command the Holconcom."

"You are most welcome here," Jessa said, moving forward a little reluctantly. She peered up at the tall alien curiously. "The girls said that you saved them from a very bad man on Benaski Port who hurt them."

"Yes," Rhemun said coldly. "A man named Cartha, who used to run several illegal operations there."

"Used to, sir?" Jessa asked.

Rhemun's chin lifted. "He will never harm another child."

Jessa relaxed a little. "I thank you for that."

"He was brutal to the girls." His eyes were ice-cold. "And Mallory." He indicated his companion. His eyes lingered on her face, and her thin body, which was still fragile. "Much skill was required to save her life. She attempted to stop Cartha from taking the girls."

"Oh!" Jessa moved forward and abruptly embraced Mallory. "Thank you! The girls are all I have left of my family. I will love them and care for them. They will want for nothing!"

Mallory hugged her back. "Thank you. I've grown very attached to them."

"As have I," Rhemun added, standing beside her.

Jessa looked from one to the other. "A human female among Cehn-Tahr," she said, shaking her head. "I had heard the stories. I did not believe them."

"Mallory is a specialist in Cularian medicine," Rhemun explained. He glanced down at her. "She assumed the post aboard my flagship when her colleague, Dr. Madeline Ruszel, left the military to bond with the son of our emperor."

"Oh, we heard of this, too. I could not believe that, either," Jessa said with a tinkling laugh. "Cehn-Tahr can crush metal. Humans are very fragile."

Her meaning was clear. Rhemun smiled. "Ruszel and Dtimun have a son. So, as you see, the stories of the bonding are quite true."

She smiled. "Will you come in and share tea with us?" she invited.

"It would be an honor," Rhemun told her. "But unfortunately, we have pressing duties. There is no time."

"And you wish to be gone quickly," Jessa said knowingly, perceiving Mallory's sadness. "I understand. But the invitation stands, whenever you come near our space."

"Thank you."

Rado came forward. He proferred a small com-chip. "This will grant you access to our communications web. You can visit the girls whenever you like."

"How kind," Mallory said softly. "Thank you!"

"I have something for them, also." Rhemun reached into his pocket and produced a small green ball. He tossed it to Minat and it suddenly turned into a small turtle. The girls exclaimed with delight.

"It's a virtual techmach," he explained. "A variety of amphibian native to Memcache. It is not quite alive, but it has biological properties. It will learn your language and interact with you. It grows in intelligence as it learns."

"Thank you so much, sir!" Minat exclaimed.

Rhemun bent down and hugged the girls close. "Be well. Be happy. Grow strong."

"Thank you, sir," Marcella said softly. Minat echoed the words.

Mallory also bent and hugged them close. It was harder for her. She'd been with them even more than Rhemun had, and she was sorry to part with them. But they should be with family. It was the right thing to do.

"I'll miss you both very much," she said, fighting tears. She was still weak from her ordeal, and it made her more emotional.

"We will miss you, also." Minat looked as if she might start crying.

"Talk to the techmach," Rhemun said, diverting her. "It looks lonely."

"It does!" Minat turned and ran to it. She and Marcella began to stroke it.

"We must go," Rhemun said. He transformed back into the form that was familiar to outsiders. "Take care of them."

"Certainly we will," Rado said. "Thank you for bringing them to us."

"Thank you very much," Jessa seconded.

Rhemun only smiled. He motioned Mallory back toward the skipper.

"No," he said curtly when her head started to turn. "Do not look back. It will only upset the girls."

She swallowed down the bitter pain. "Yes, sir."

He drew in a short breath. He didn't want to make her uncomfortable, but he wanted an uncomplicated departure. He put Mallory into the skipper, fired it up and made quick time back to the small spaceport.

"Back so soon?" the flight operator asked. He smiled at Mallory.

Rhemun gave him a look that sent him away with a brief apology. He and Mallory walked into the scout ship, and left the planet.

Mallory was too preoccupied to notice that Rhemun had been aggressive with the operator of the spaceport. Her eyes were already threatening tears when they reached the ship.

Rhemun opened the hatch. "Get some rest," he advised. "This has been an ordeal for you."

She nodded. She started to salute.

"Don't be absurd," he muttered. "This is no time for formality." He turned and walked away.

She went back to her quarters and let the tears fall.

CHAPTER TEN

MALLORY TRIED TO SLEEP, but she missed the girls terribly. In the weeks she'd known them, they'd become like family—the family she'd never been allowed to have. The child hunger in her was overwhelming. It was a pity, she thought, that she'd been born into a society where people had to have a license from the state to have a child.

She was also worried about the future. She couldn't stay here. Her stupid hormones were going to get her in trouble with the CO all over again. She remembered how he'd growled at the base flight operator on Tol Shalad and the more she thought about it, the more it worried her. It had finally occurred to her that it was the operator's interest in herself which had provoked the growl. It was a mating behavior. She felt absolute anguish that her body had betrayed her and caused him such difficulties. She didn't know much about the mating cycle, just that it was said to be impossible to stop. But she couldn't mate with a male Cehn-Tahr—she did know that much. Their natural strength, uncontrolled, would make any such encoun-

ter a fatal one for any human female foolish enough
to incite them.

She hadn't meant to cause Rhemun any more
problems than she already had. She must leave the
ship, and soon. She could ask the emperor to give
her reserve status and she could go to work on the
Freespirit. They always needed doctors. Of course,
she was much younger than most of the retirees who
worked aboard her, but perhaps that wouldn't matter. She had skills.

THE DOOR TO the cubicle slid open unexpectedly. Rhemun walked in, dressed in the curious culotte-style
skirt that Cehn-Tahr wore for the Kahn-Bo compe-
titions. It seemed that they also slept in some similar garment, because the one he was wearing was
of a much-softer material. It was black and reached
just below his ankles. His chest, broad and muscular, was uncovered.

He moved to the side of the bed and pursed his
sensual lips. "Still awake?"

"Sorry, sir." She tried to salute lying down.

He caught the saluting arm and drew her gently up. Before she realized his intention, he uncovered her in the straight, soft shift that patients wore,
swung her up in his arms and walked out of the cubicle.

"Uh, sir...?" she faltered.

Hahnson was standing in the outer office with a
laserdisc in one hand.

"If you please," Rhemun asked, cocking his head to make his neck available.

Hahnson shot the dose of dravelzium into the artery there while Mallory, all at sea, tried to understand what was happening.

Hahnson put two small laserdiscs in her hand. "Backups," he said with an amused smile. "In case they're needed. Two ccs," he added.

She grimaced. "So much?"

"Yes," the other physician assured her.

"Thank you," Rhemun told him with twinkling eyes. He turned and carried Edris into the freight elevator.

"But these are forbidden," she tried to protest as the door closed behind them.

"Not to the commander of the vessel," he assured her. The elevator stopped and the door opened into his own quarters.

He placed her gently in the huge round bed and drew the covers over her. "You don't sleep," he explained. "I told you that I had a solution."

"But…"

He sprawled in the bed beside her. "The dravelzium will protect you."

She drew in a painful breath. "It's all my fault. My stupid hormones…!"

He chuckled. "None of us can control such things." He turned his head on the pillow and looked at her with golden eyes. "Not even I."

She bit her lip. "But, even if I wanted to, even if… I mean, we couldn't…"

He lifted an eyebrow.

She flushed. "Sir, humans can't mate with Cehn-Tahr," she said miserably.

"With some Cehn-Tahr," he amended. He stretched hugely. The medicine was making him drowsy. He rolled over toward her, as gracefully as a big cat. "My father was one of our finest military commanders. He rebelled and turned against the emperor when the first genetic manipulations were ordered in our children." His face was solemn. "He said that his child would never be made into a weapon of war." He rolled onto his back. It was painful even now to speak of this. "The emperor and his son made war on my father. He permitted himself to be killed, to lessen the stain on our Clan. His human advisor, the one who urged him to rebellion, died at his side." He shifted on the comfortable bed. "So you see, I had ample reason to hate humans even before my son died."

"I'm so sorry," she said in her soft voice.

He rolled over and put an arm beside her, so that he could lift up enough to see her eyes. "None of this was your fault. You ran headlong into my prejudices." He smiled self-consciously. "It did not help that you were attractive."

She studied his strong face quietly. "You hate me."

He shook his head and smiled. His eyes were an odd, soft shade of gold.

"You growled, at the base operator on Tol Shalad…"

"And at your friend Patch."

"Patch?" she asked, shocked.

"He attempted to smooth your hair before we lifted you to the ship." His eyes went black. "If he had touched you, I would have snapped his neck like a twig."

"Oh…dear…"

"It gets worse, I'm afraid. No male on this vessel is safe if he dares to touch you, not even Hahnson. Cehn-Tahr males are dangerous when they seek a mate. There are few things in the three galaxies more lethal."

"But we can't…" she tried again.

He touched his finger to her mouth, enjoying its softness. "As a result of my father's actions, I have no genetic modification of the sort that Dtimun was given. My great strength comes from tech, which can be temporarily disabled." He nuzzled his cheek against hers. "It will be like mating with a very large human. Difficult, perhaps, but certainly not fatal."

"I…never dreamed…" She swallowed, fascinated with the way he looked at her, drowning at the pleasure his touch gave her.

"I want to make a child with you," he said, lifting his head. His expression was solemn, intent.

SHE CAUGHT HER BREATH. Pleasure flooded her. She felt tears stinging. "But they won't let me," she whispered. "It's illegal…"

He nuzzled his face against hers again. "You are Holconcom. You have Cehn-Tahr citizenship. They cannot touch you on Memcache."

She reached up, very shyly, and touched his hard, warm face. Cehn-Tahr, like cats, had a normal temperature above that of humans. "I'm human," she whispered.

He smiled. "As you might have noticed, my prejudices went away when you were endangered. I risked court-martial, even summary execution, to rescue you—just as Dtimun did, to save Madeline Ruszel's life." His face grew quiet. "I have no life, without you."

She burst into tears. He gathered her close, loving the feel of her small softness against his body, loving the way she melted into him. He was grateful for the dravelzium that kept him from devouring her in passion.

He drew in a shaky breath. "You must bond with me first. We do not mate without the appropriate ceremony."

"Yes," she whispered into his throat.

He smoothed her hair. Impulsively, he loosened the soft fabric that held it on top of her head and let it fall around her shoulders. It was as soft as he'd imagined. He liked tangling his fingers in it, just as she was enjoying the feel of his long, curling hair in her hands.

"You know, I haven't…ever," she stammered.

He lifted his head and looked into her eyes. He smiled. "I can be quite gentle."

She nodded. "O...okay." She hesitated. "When?"

"When you are less damaged," he said softly. "However, in the meantime, you must make certain that you permit no male to touch you. Ever. At all."

She smiled. "Okay."

He chuckled.

She shrugged. "Sorry. I like it, that you're possessive."

"The violence will dissipate after the bonding," he assured her. He rolled onto his back and pulled her to his side, pulling the covers over them. "We must attempt to sleep now. Before the dravelzium wears off."

She curled up next to him. "I have more."

He laughed softly. "So you do." He kissed the top of her head.

She closed her eyes. And to her amazement, she slept peacefully for the first time since Benaski Port.

IT WAS AN open secret that Mallory and the CO were involved. They could hardly hide it. Once, Stern reached out his hand to pat Mallory on the back and before she could warn him, there was a fierce, dangerous growl from behind him.

He stuck both hands behind him. "Sorry, sir!" he exclaimed. "Honest!" He raised both eyebrows. "Please don't kill me. You'll never get to Memcache without an astrogator."

The anger passed quickly and Rhemun burst out laughing. But word got around. None of the male crew members came closer than arm's length to Mallory. Not even the Cehn-Tahr.

But the hunger was growing harder to control by the day.

"We must have the bonding ceremony now," he said to Mallory a few days later. "It will prevent the more dangerous manifestations from escalating."

"On Memcache?" she asked.

"No. Here. I have arranged with Lady Caneese to do the ceremony over a vid channel." He paused. "We might have some of the crew to stand with us. And of course, the mating must be witnessed."

She was visibly horrified. "Witnessed...?!"

He burst out laughing. "A member of my bodyguard must visibly inspect my quarters before we enter them. He must testify that no other male is concealed there. Then he must stand guard outside to witness that no other male has entered. This is the law, where my Clan is concerned. It protects any child we produce from even the hint that some other male could have fathered him."

She didn't understand. "I thought that was only required in royal circles..."

"My Clan is part of the aristocracy," he said, but he averted his eyes briefly. "We must follow protocol."

"Oh. Okay. Do we wear our uniforms?" she added. "I mean, I don't have any garments that aren't military."

He pursed his sensual lips and smiled at her from behind golden eyes. "I have a solution for that."

AND HE DID. It was a beautiful royal blue gown with gold trim. He presented it to her before the ceremony. He was wearing blue-and-gold robes of some silky material that emphasized his muscular body. They were Imperial colors and there were penalties for any Cehn-Tahr who wore them without permission. Rhemun assured her that permission had been given for both of them. Probably, she reasoned, since Rhemun had been captain of the emperor's bodyguard for many years, he was exempted from the taboo.

When she emerged from her quarters in the close-fitting gown with its high, exotic neckline and uncovered nape, with her blond hair around her shoulders, he caught his breath.

"You are quite beautiful," he said huskily.

She stared at him. "Me?"

He smiled. "You."

She flushed. "Thank you, sir. I mean…"

He laughed. "Never mind. We should go."

He stood aside and let her move ahead of him down the deck to the briefing room that was being used, temporarily, as a sort of chapel. On the huge viewscreen, Lady Caneese was visible and, next to her Madeline Ruszel. They both bowed to Caneese.

"Dr. Ruszel!" Edris exclaimed. "It's so good to see you!"

"It's good to see you, too, Edris. I had to be convinced that you were actually marrying him." She indicated Rhemun and grinned. "Honest to goodness, I didn't believe it."

"He hasn't poured a single pot of soup over my head," Edris assured her.

"And she doesn't throw things at me," Rhemun said with a grin.

"It's good to see you, too, your Highness," Edris told Caneese, and made a very formal and graceful bow.

"It is very good to see you, as well, my child," Caneese said in her tender voice. "This bonding is gratifying to me, for reasons I can't really tell you."

"Don't ask," Madeline said, holding up a hand. "It's a secret that we know but can't share with anyone."

Edris looked up at Rhemun with absolute worship. "It doesn't matter. I don't care. I'm so happy!"

He laughed at her expression. "So am I."

Several members of the crew filed in, interrupting the conversation. Among them were Strick Hahnson, Holt Stern, Higgins, Crandall, Jennings, and Jones from Rhemun's bodyguard.

"Thank you for standing with us," Rhemun told them, and Edris nodded.

"Oh, we're very happy to do it, Captain," Stern said with twinkling black eyes. "The sooner you two are bonded, the safer us guys are."

"Especially her physician," Hahnson agreed, tongue in cheek.

Everyone laughed.

"Safer. Not safe," Rhemun added. "It takes much time for the possessive instincts to weaken."

"Not to worry, sir, we're all pretending that Dr. Mallory has some highly contagious virus," Higgins assured him. But he grinned.

Rhemun just shook his head.

"Shall we begin?" Caneese interrupted softly.

THE CEREMONY WAS BRIEF, but poignant. There was a statement spoken by both parties, in the Holy Tongue, only ever used among the highest levels of Cehn-Tahr society and known only to the members of the emperor's bodyguard and the imperial family. But Edris knew it.

She repeated it after Rhemun, translating it in her mind as she spoke: "Heart of my heart, blood of my blood, soul of my soul, until life ends."

He knew that she understood it, but he didn't dare say so. She had no knowledge of his telepathic abilities, and he was going to make sure that she didn't, for the time being. It would raise issues he was not ready to face. On the other hand, she was now his. She belonged to him. It made him feel incredibly possessive. There was also a burst of pleasure inside him, a feeling of warm comfort, of joy, of belonging. His first bonding had been forced. He had been tricked, manipulated into it. This one was of his choosing, and welcome.

He smiled at Edris, who was looking very nervous as Jones was sent off to fulfill the requirements of the bonding by inspecting Rhemun's quarters. "It will be all right," he told her softly. "You must trust me."

Before she could answer, they were surrounded by congratulatory crew. It diverted her from her concerns. But just briefly.

THEY WALKED INTO Rhemun's quarters, and Jones stood at attention at the door, assuring him, when asked, that everything was perfectly in order.

They went inside, and Jones sealed and locked the door from the outside, the only time it had ever been done in the unit's history.

Rhemun turned to Edris and led her into the bedroom, closing the door and activating controls on a virtual panel that appeared when he touched it.

"The cubicle is soundproof," he commented, in answer to a hidden fear of hers that people outside might be able to hear them.

He had morphed into his true form for the bonding, and he retained it even now. He looked down at her with quiet pleasure.

"I'm sorry. I don't know anything," she blurted out. "Well, I know the mechanics. I'm a doctor, after all…"

He put his finger against her soft lips. "I mated once, with a female whom I detested. She tricked me into bonding with her. We mated and a child was produced at the first mating. She went home to her brothers immediately thereafter and I never saw her again, except in vids," he confessed. He made a face. "The…coupling—" he described it discreetly "—was brief and brutal and I took no pleasure from it." He sighed and touched her cheek with his fingertips before he laid his forehead against hers in an intimate caress, used only among family. "So you see, my experience is not much more than yours."

"But you've lived so long," she began.

He laughed. "I am Cehn-Tahr. We do not visit brothels. You must know that, from gossip. And to mate with any female to whom we are not bonded is taboo." He shrugged. "I was captain of the *kehm-atemer*, the emperor's own bodyguard. My duty kept me quite busy, and we were in a constant state of high excitement. Many times we were involved in conflicts during state visits to outlying colonies." He drew in a breath. "I hated females, especially human females, for a very long time." His forehead moved against hers. "Until you came into my life and began to disturb me."

"Disturb you?"

He laughed. "I wanted you, almost from the beginning. And hated myself for it. I spent months making of your life an absolute hell, to protect myself from any involvement with you." His eyes were apologetic. "I cannot begin to apologize for the anguish and pain I caused you. But I will spend the rest of our lives together trying to atone. I promise you that."

She was fascinated with him. "I thought you... I mean, that you had lots of women..."

He shook his head. "We are not mentally neutered, as your military is, but there are very strict rules of conduct that public censure teaches us not to break."

"So," she said hesitantly, "would that mean that you're as nervous about this as I am?"

His chest shook as he chuckled. "Probably even more so."

She was delighted. "I feel better." She hesitated. "Could we, you know, have the lights out?" she blurted.

He drew in a long breath. "I was thinking of asking you the same question."

She grinned.

He smiled back. He went to the panel and suddenly the room was in total darkness, except from the charging lights of the padd. He turned to her, his cat-eyes gleaming like metallic emerald in the darkness.

"You aren't afraid of me, like this?" he asked softly. "Of my eyes?"

"No. Honest, I'm not."

He drew her carefully into his arms. "We are a passionate species," he whispered at her throat. "We don't mate. We devour. We dominate. It is part of our makeup, a part we inherited from the genetics our scientists derived from the galot species."

"I look forward to it," she said, because he sounded torn.

"Do you?" Then his mouth ground down into hers, and she said nothing more.

"How are you feeling?" he whispered later.

Never having mated before, she'd had no idea what to expect. It had been tough, but enjoyable.

"You told me how it would be," she said. "It was nice."

He pulled her to him. "This is very important. Is there a child?"

She used her instrument, with some difficulty, because it was still dark in the room. She swallowed. "No."

He drew in a soft breath. "I am most grateful for that."

"But...you said you wanted a child," she faltered.

"I want a child born of joy and pleasure," he countered. "But first I had to know that a child had not been conceived," he whispered. "Because even a Cehn-Tahr woman cannot carry two at one time. It would be fatal."

"Oh. You mean, we're going to...?" she hesitated.

"We're going to," he replied deeply.

Then his mouth was suddenly all over her, in places she'd honestly never considered he might put it. She was shocked at first, and then pleasured, and then almost insane with a sweet, building tension that made her reach up to him.

The soft cries that passed her lips this time were not sounds of pain. They grew in intensity as his movements quickened, and she felt him in a new way, welcomed his passion, welcomed the hard, heavy weight of him as the tension suddenly snapped and she learned a different definition of mating. It was the purest, sweetest pleasure she had ever imagined in her life. And it continued, again and again, all

night long. The only interruption was her frequent
use of the diagnostics in her wrist scanner to detect
pregnancy. And it wasn't until very, very long after
they began that she was able to tell him that a child
was growing in her womb.

HE WAS FASCINATED. His big hand rested on her flat
belly. "We made a child," he whispered. "I thought…
I was not certain that we could."

"Dtimun and Madeline did," she reminded him.

"Yes, but classified tech was used," he told her.
"Which you must never divulge."

"I already knew." She laughed. "Your mother told
me."

He rolled over on his back and laughed, too.
"Classified information seems to be public information in this family."

"Well, your mother likes me," she pointed out.
She grinned. "I like her, too."

She smoothed her hands over her stomach. "I've
dreamed of being pregnant for so long," she whispered.
Tears stung her eyes. "And to have your child…"

He drew her close, licking away the tears in a
very catlike fashion. "We must take very good care
of you. I hope it isn't too soon, after the ordeal you
suffered on Benaski Port…"

"I'm perfectly all right," she assured him. "I'll
be just…fine…"

She stopped suddenly, pushed herself off the bed,
and ran for the head. She barely made it in time.

Rhemun was two steps behind her. He threw a towel around his lean hips and a robe around her, after which he turned on the light and found a cloth, wetting it in the sink.

"Here," he said, kneeling beside her to mop her brow, and her face.

"Oh, you shouldn't be in here," she choked, throwing up again.

"You're my mate," he said, not understanding. "Why should I not be with you when you need me?"

She was thinking of all the things she'd read, secretly, about rare married couples. Most men, she learned, seemed to avoid any illness like the plague.

He waited until she finished, wiped her face, and her mouth gently. "We must see Hahnson. At once."

"Okay," she whispered weakly.

He laid her on the bed and went to dress. When he came back, she had a gown on under the robe. He picked her up and carried her through the vator to sick bay.

HAHNSON WAS WRITING up a report when the door to his sick bay opened and Rhemun came in, carrying Mallory in his arms.

She was shivering, bruised, a little shaken. Her hair was disheveled. She looked strange.

"Put her down here," Hahnson told Rhemun as he grabbed up a diagnostic tool.

He ran it over her, careful not to touch her, noting

that Rhemun looked extremely apprehensive, odd for their usually impassive commander.

Hahnson went over the readouts. "I think I know what you're hoping for," he told Rhemun. "Yes, she's pregnant."

Edris managed a laugh. "Told you so," she said to Rhemun.

Rhemun smiled at her.

Hahnson tidied up the injuries. "Would you like to know the sex of the child?" he asked Edris.

She smiled and shook her head. "He wouldn't look that arrogant if it was a girl," she said softly.

Rhemun's eyebrows arched. "Actually, I would," he told her. "In four hundred years, only one female has been born into my lineage."

"Really?" she exclaimed. She started to speak and suddenly doubled over and was sick all over the floor.

"Hahnson!" Rhemun exclaimed, horrified.

"It's all right," he assured the alien. He was busy getting something for Mallory to throw up in. Rhemun took it from him and held it under her chin.

"She's been losing her stomach contents since… well, since," Rhemun said, pushing back Mallory's disheveled hair. "This is why I brought her to you. Is this natural?" He was worried.

Hahnson gave her a drug to control the nausea and another to inhibit, just a little, the natural growth of the impatient Cehn-Tahr baby.

"We went through this with Ruszel, if you recall,"

he reminded the alien. "I'm an old hand at human/
Cehn-Tahr children. It's just the initial growth spurt.
She won't die. Honest."

Rhemun's strung-out features relaxed.

"You've been through this before, seen the symptoms of pregnancy, surely," Hahnson said, puzzled
at his reactions.

"I have not," the alien returned curtly. "My first
mate went to her family from the day of conception.
I was not permitted to be with her during the pregnancy, nor at the birth of my son."

Edris looked at him incredulously. "Not...per-
mitted?"

"My mate and I were married for political and
material benefits to her Clan," he said shortly. "Not
for any personal reasons. We despised each other."
He hesitated. The subject was taboo, but Hahnson
knew more about his species than other humans.
He didn't really mind telling Edris in front of him.
He shrugged. "She knew an herb that could initiate the mating cycle. I had no choice. I truly hated
her for that."

"Oh."

"Will you be all right now?" he asked her, still
concerned.

"Of course."

"She will stay in sick bay during my duty hours,"
Rhemun told Hahnson firmly.

"I can stay in my own quarters," Edris tried to
argue.

"No. And you will be with me when you sleep," he said, aware that he was being possessive of a female for the first time. It was only for the safety of the child, he told himself.

"Well, we are bonded…" She tried to find the words.

"Yes we are. Well, it is a temporary bonding," Rhemun replied. "There must be a formal ceremony in the future, but this suffices for purposes of legitimation of our child."

He turned to Hahnson. "I'm going to the bridge, but only if you will swear to inform me if she worsens."

"Of course," Hahnson said easily, having lived through Dtimun's behavior while Ruszel was expecting. He was getting used to it.

Rhemun went back to Mallory and touched her long, disheveled hair. "You must do as the doctor says."

She tried to repress a smile. "All right."

He let go of her hair and seemed less rigid. "I must go." He paused at the doorway and looked back at Edris. He stared for just a second too long for polite interest before he left the room.

Edris touched her stomach with awe. "My goodness."

Hahnson grinned. "Congratulations, Edris. How about a nice comforting cup of herbal tea?"

EDRIS WAS USED to her own company when she was off duty. But life with Rhemun was far different than she'd expected it to be. He was animated in his own quarters, always involved in some sort of research or finding odd sites on the nexus, or even, surprisingly, playing vid games.

He liked to wear a long divided pant, like the Kahn-Bo skirt, and go bare-chested around his quarters. With his long, curly hair down to his waist, he was very attractive. Edris couldn't stop looking at him the first night she spent there, and the subsequent ones.

It amused him. He found himself growing addicted to that wide-eyed stare and that secret little smile of hers. He piled into the bed next to her and pulled up a 360-degree holoweb, his long-fingered hands flying over the colorful virtual controls as he searched out new military weapons and spacecraft that were only in the design stages. There were other features of these virtual toys—she didn't know, and he didn't mention, that the tech could allow people parted at great distances to see, hear and even touch each other with the tactile interface that the Cehn-Tahr had developed at their research labs at Kolmahnkash. The humans thought it was for game development, but it served a much-different purpose.

"I like that one." She pointed to a sleek, wicked-looking attack ship.

"So do I," he replied. "It is the newest design. It has twice the firepower of our best fighters. It can be flown by a pilot or used as a drone for weapons placement."

She rolled over and pillowed her head on his

shoulder. He looked down, startled, and then he smiled as her eyes closed drowsily.

"The child tires you," he said.

"Ummm." She smiled. "He grows at a phenomenal rate. I didn't realize how fast the growth spurts came."

"Ruszel was at Benaski Port with Dtimun during her earliest stages of pregnancy," he recalled. "You did not see her then."

"No. I wish I had. This would be easier if I understood it better."

He hesitated. His hand touched a sensor node, and then withdrew. "How does it feel?"

Her blue eyes opened. "Sir?"

"The pregnancy."

She smiled. "Incredible." She sighed. "Like I hoped it would feel, all those years ago, when I waited and hoped in the breeder camp."

His eyes were on the holo. "I still regret the violence of our first mating," he said quietly. "It is the curse we entailed when we rewrote our genetic code."

"I know about Cehn-Tahr mating rituals," she said. "The court physicians had a new colleague who was nice and didn't mind talking to me, when the rest weren't listening. The first mating is only to prove fertility. It isn't supposed to be pleasant. I didn't expect it to be."

He touched another sensor node. He seemed deep in thought.

She moved suddenly, and grimaced, as a growth spurt caught her unaware.

Rhemun reacted immediately. He had the injection Hahnson had given him for Edris. He used it. Then he held her, gently, and rocked her against him until the pain lessened.

She let out a husky breath and shivered. "Thanks."

He smoothed back her blond hair. She was so fragile, this little blonde human. She had courage, and she was very intelligent. She was gentle. He felt protective of her, more than ever since the child was conceived. He was sorry he'd been so rough. Not that he had a choice. It was his nature, even without the genetic enhancements that made his species so much more ferocious.

He drew in a long breath and curled her gently against him. "At least Hahnson knows what to do. On Memcache, you will live near Ruszel, who also has experience of hybrid babies."

She tilted her head back and looked up at him curiously. "You weren't with your mate when your son was born?"

He shook his head. "She disliked bearing children, but her Clan insisted on a child to strengthen the relationship."

"She was an aristocrat, too, though?"

"Her people were merchants," he said coldly. "As I mentioned before, they knew of a certain herb that could facilitate the mating cycle in males."

"Oh." She began to understand. He hadn't wanted to mate with the female.

He looked down at her solemnly. "The herbs were a necessity. She repulsed me."

"But you loved your son," she said sadly. She smiled gently and touched his long hair. "You were so tender with the little girls we rescued."

"They were sweet. I would not mind having a female child."

"I never thought I would have a child at all. It grieved me." She looked down at his broad, bare chest. "I was ready to go back to Trimerius and let them take away all I had. I didn't think my life was worth much."

Surprisingly, he gathered her up close and buried his face in her soft, warm throat. His big hands bruised her against him involuntarily. "I wanted you the first time I saw you," he murmured roughly, "standing there so insolently when we boarded the *Morcai*, telling the Old One you mistook me for a Rojok." He laughed softly. "So small, to have so much courage."

She smiled against his hair. "I would always need it, with you." She sighed. "You aren't an easy person to get along with."

"That was because I needed my prejudices to ward you off," he murmured, and when he lifted his head, he was smiling.

Her smile faded. "What if the child looks like me,

more than like you?" she asked worriedly. "What if he's blond, instead of dark?"

He traced her eyebrows. "That is unlikely. Komak looks like Dtimun, not like his mother."

"Yes, but we don't know how he may appear when he's older," she returned. "There's a good possibility that his appearance will change, over time. There's so much we don't know about the combination of DNA."

"You worry about shadows," he whispered. "And unnecessarily. I could not hate a child born from your body."

Her fingers reached up and drew down along his cheek, to his chest. "You feel so warm," she mused. The room was chilly, but he was like a heating cloth.

He smiled. "My body temperature is higher than yours."

"I know." She cocked her head. "Why do you still hide from me, even when we're alone?"

He frowned. "Hide?"

She nodded. "You don't morph."

He drew in a long breath. "It is difficult for me. We have old prejudices about revealing ourselves to outworlders."

"Yes, but this outworlder is carrying your child," she reminded him.

"It will not frighten you?"

"Of course it will." She laughed. "I'll be horrified. I'll scream and run and…"

He put his finger over her mouth and smiled. "Very well."

He touched his wrist and pressed. He appeared in his true form, big and muscular, overwhelming at close range. His black mane was still thick and curly around his head, draping over his shoulders and down over his hair-roughened chest. Only his eyes, in that alien face, were familiar. But Edris loved him. He was beautiful to her.

He saw the thought in her mind and reacted to it. Waves of feeling came from her, emanating like rays from the sun, engulfing him in warmth and tenderness. It was not an emotion he connected with females.

She gasped suddenly and stiffened.

At first he thought it was his appearance. But she was looking at the faint swell of her stomach.

"It can't be," she exclaimed, shocked.

"What?"

She looked up into his eyes. "He's moving! He can't be moving! I'm only a week along!"

His big hand slid over hers on her belly and pressed, fascinated. He felt the sudden throb of life inside her, felt his child, felt him move and breathe, felt his mind!

He gasped out loud.

She looked up. "But how?"

"You have forgotten," he said huskily. "Our gestation period is much less than the human one. Our children mature at a quicker rate, as well."

"Then, it's natural?"

He nodded. His eyes went back to his child, under his hand. "I never knew how it felt to touch my child in the womb." His face was solemn, melancholy. "I barely knew my son, Edris. From the night she conceived, she lived with her own Clan. It was not until she died that I was allowed full access to my son, and he did not know me."

It shocked her, that confession. She felt it to the marrow of her bones and felt rage at the unknown female who had treated him in such a fashion. He looked at her suddenly, as if he saw the thought in her mind. Ridiculous, she told herself. He wasn't a telepath.

He drew her up into his arms and stared into her wide, soft eyes. "I will have to be away sometimes, while you are carrying him. But even when I am away, I will stay close to you, through the nexus. I do not want to miss any of this time."

She smiled. "You won't. I promise."

He smoothed back her hair and rubbed his face against hers with tenderness. "We should sleep."

"You don't sleep. You nap," she said, smiling. "You don't have to have the lights out just because I'm sleepy."

"I will 'nap' when you do," he replied with an almost-human grin.

Abruptly, he moved and unfastened her jacket, sliding it off her arms. He drew her to him, so that bare skin touched bare skin.

She caught her breath. "Is it a custom?" she asked when he eased down with her and waved his hand to extinguish both the hologram and the lights.

"No," he replied, stretching. "It is because I like the feel of your skin against mine."

"Oh."

He laughed. "You will not exploit this weakness," he said firmly.

She rolled over against him and slid her arms around his neck. "You don't have any weaknesses," she murmured.

But he had one. And it was lying against him, soft and sweet and loving, in the comfort of his arms.

CHAPTER ELEVEN

EDRIS'S PREGNANCY ADVANCED so quickly that Rhemun
refused to allow her to remain on the ship.

"Tellas can handle any Cularian patients we encounter," he assured her. "You trained him well."

"But this is my job," she protested weakly.

He put his finger against her soft lips and smiled.
"Your job is to bear our firstborn," he whispered.

The radiance in his face, the soft golden color of
his eyes entranced her. "Yes," she conceded gently. "It is."

"To that end, you must be safe. I can't run the ship
if I worry all the time about you," he added. "You
will live on my estate near the Imperial compound.
My houseman, Devroshe, will make sure that you
have access to medical care and anything you require. We can keep in touch on the nexus."

She drew in a long breath. "It will be lonely without you."

"Yes," he said solemnly. "For me, as well. But we
must think about what is best for you and the child.
Ruszel is nearby if you need her. She has experience
with Cehn-Tahr children," he added with a smile.

"So she does. Okay. I'll go." She bit her lip. "This houseman, Dev…"

"Devroshe."

"Devroshe. He doesn't hate humans, does he?"

He was a little hesitant. "It should not be an issue. He loved my father. He thought of him as his own child. He was a broken man when my father was killed. It has taken many years for him to recover from the grief. But he has no reason to take out his prejudices on you."

She could have replied to that, but she didn't.

Rhemun touched her cheek with his fingertips and laid his forehead against hers. "If there are problems, I will handle them."

She drew in a long breath. She hated the whole idea of going to some strange place to wait for the birth of her child, but she wasn't going to say that to Rhemun. She'd cope.

He bent and kissed her softly. "It will be all right."

SHE HAD CAUSE to remember those words during her first week in Rhemun's enormous house. It had classical lines, like vids of ancient Earth, a land called Greece, ruins with columns of marble. Except that Rhemun's home was more like a palace, with marble floors and exquisite paintings, and everything clean and bright. There were no ruins here.

Devroshe was old, bald, fat and efficient. He did not like Mallory and made it apparent the minute Rhemun left for his command. He was careful to hide it in front of the two housemaidens, Ledache and Kresene. They liked Edris from the beginning and did all they could for her comfort. But Devroshe assigned them to duties that kept them away from her.

One morning, very early, she found bleeding. She tried to send a vid to Madeline Ruszel, but Madeline and Dtimun had gone off-planet to a diplomatic conference on Trimerius and were out of contact, even to Edris. She tried to call Rhemun as well, but the *Morcai* was on a mission and radio silence was being observed. She had to resort to the houseman, which made her uneasy.

She cleaned up and, very sick, went to speak to Devroshe.

"I'm sorry," she said softly, "but I'm very ill. I think something is wrong. I can't use my medscanner because of the interference. Can you disable it just briefly, please?"

He looked down his wide nose at her. He didn't morph in her presence, another indication that he didn't trust or like her.

"That will not be possible," he said haughtily. "The master left strict orders that the protections be left in place."

"But this is an emergency." She tried to convince him.

He shrugged. "I must do as I am told."

"Then will you summon a physician, please."

He gave her an indignant look. "You are a physician, madam. Or so I am told," he added with sarcasm.

She drew herself up and glared at him. "Since my instruments will not work here, I am forced to resort to a Cehn-Tahr physician."

He gave her a dismissive look. "Very well. I will see if one is available."

"Thank you." She started to turn, then hesitated. "I know you don't like me," she said. "I know you don't like humans. But I am bonded to your master. If anything happens to me, he will hold you responsible." She managed a cold smile. "I promise you that."

For just an instant, an expression of unease claimed his features. "I will summon a physician."

She nodded, turned and left him.

BUT BACK IN her room, the pain became terrible, and there was more spotting. She was afraid she might lose her child. Was that what Devroshe wanted?

She used the house intercom switch. "The physician, is there any word of when he may arrive?" she asked weakly.

But it wasn't Devroshe who answered, it was Kresene, the elder of the housemaidens.

"A physician, madam?" she asked. "Are you ill?"

"Something is wrong...with the baby, I think," she said faintly. "My instruments won't work. I asked Devroshe to summon a physician..."

"I will see to it at once, madam," she said abruptly.

AN HOUR LATER, a physician, a female physician, arrived. She fussed over Edris and muttered in the

Holy Tongue. Her comments, which she didn't realize Edris could understand, were quite full of venom for Rhemun's houseman.

"It will be all right," she assured Edris, and discussed the condition, which was a result of the hybrid pregnancy.

"You're quite knowledgeable," Edris said with a smile and praise. "I hold a degree in Cularian medicine," she added.

The doctor was surprised. "Yet you could not treat this?"

"I'm afraid jammers are being used in the house," she said heavily. "Devroshe said that he had strict orders not to disable them, by my mate."

There was an even more shocked look, from the doctor and from Kresene.

"This is the first I have heard of such a thing," the handmaiden said curtly.

"Perhaps you might speak to Devroshe," the physician suggested.

Kresene was hesitant. "He has absolute power here, in Lord Rhemun's absence," she said in a subdued but angry tone.

The physician turned to Edris. "Perhaps it would be wise for you to speak with your mate," she said.

Edris nodded. "I intend to. But right now, he's observing radio silence. I can't contact him."

"That is unfortunate. You must take great care of yourself. It delights me that he has finally selected a mate of his own choosing. And a lovely one," she added gently. "The child will be beautiful."

"Thank you," Edris said, surprised.

"You may call me yourself if you have need of me," the physician added, and handed her a comm chip. "I am Dr. Meracache. This will give you access anytime, even through the interference in this house," she added.

"I am in your debt."

The physician smiled. "I have known Rhemun since he was a child. It is my joy to do anything I can to help him."

Kresene showed the doctor out. On the way back, she paused in front of Devroshe, who was looking angry.

"Lord Rhemun told us to take great care of the little human," she said with her eyes lowered. "I do not wish to find myself on the wrong side of Lord Rhemun's temper. And even you, my master, would do well to remember just how angry he can be when provoked."

"I have been here for many years," Devroshe said haughtily. "I have no need to fear that I might lose my position."

Kresene raised her eyes. "For many things, there is a first time. My master."

She nodded politely and left him.

Devroshe glared after her. He had no intention of permitting himself to be shown the door by a human. He recalled with grief Rhemun's father, who had gone to war with the empire because of a human's influence. Rhemun must be out of his mind to wish to ally his great house with one of the inferior race. And to produce a child with her! It was an abomination. He had to do something to prevent the child's birth. Since the herbs had not worked, he must look to other means. If only Kresene had not taken it upon herself to summon a physician! Well, it was a setback. But, still, he would find a way to save his master from such disgrace.

BUT BEFORE HE could do more mischief the child grew so large that Edris could no longer carry it. The physician made a decision to go ahead with the birth, even though the child was slightly premature.

"It is a question of saving both of you," she told Edris gently. "Believe me, I know what I am doing. I had a consultation with Dr. Ruszel while she was carrying Komak."

Edris nodded. "It's all right. Do what you must. But Rhemun… Can someone contact him? I want him to be here, if he can…"

Kresene patted her on the arm. "I will do it myself, Lady Edris. At once."

SHE WENT OUT into the hallway, where Devroshe was standing, sour-faced as always. "She wants Rhemun to be present at the birth," she said worriedly.

"He is on the other side of the galaxy," he replied.

"Yes, but the holon can be used, can it not?"

He pursed his lips. Wheels were turning in his head. "She has no knowledge of its existence?"

"I think not. I certainly have not told her. Even though she is bonded to our lord, it is not permitted for anyone except Cehn-Tahr to know of it."

He nodded. "Good. Good. I shall contact him, so that he can be present." He shrugged. "We must hope that the child has at least the appearance of a Cehn-Tahr," he said coldly.

"I think she is quite beautiful," Kresene began.

"You have duties. Attend them!"

She swallowed. "At once, sir." She would have continued, but he had the power to fire her. If he did, poor Lady Edris would have no one to help her at all. The other housemaiden was very young and terrified of Devroshe. She would do whatever he said, even if it was to the detriment of the lady.

THE FEMALE PHYSICIAN, Meracache, did a caesarean section, very efficiently, and delivered the child. Edris was overjoyed to have Rhemun at her side for the procedure. He stood by the bedside and held her hand in his, very tightly. Even though she felt no pain, it was obvious that he was concerned for her.

When the child was laid on her belly while the umbilical card was cut, she saw tears welling in his eyes.

She felt teary, also. She smiled up at him. "Our son," she whispered.

He smiled back. "Our son, Edris. Our firstborn."

He bent and kissed her very softly on the lips. "Thank you."

She touched his cheek with her fingertips and coaxed his forehead against hers. "He's perfect. Just perfect."

Perfect. And very human looking. There wasn't one thing about him that indicated he had a Cehn-Tahr parent at all. It disturbed Edris. She hoped it didn't disturb Rhemun, but he was holding the child and marveling at him, so perhaps it didn't matter.

"Why didn't the others come with you?" she asked. "I thought Dr. Hahnson might, at least."

He looked at her with faint consternation. "We had some casualties from our last conflict," he said quickly. "Nothing that he can't handle, but he was afraid to leave the wounded. The others also had duties not easily put aside, even for something so important as this," he added, and softened the words with a smile.

She might have questioned that, but she was very tired and happy. She only smiled.

RHEMUN COULDN'T STAY LONG. He bent and kissed her gently.

"You aren't concerned, that he looks more like me?" she worried.

"He is quite beautiful," he said. "And I will be proud of him."

"We haven't discussed names," she began.

He held up a hand. "There will be time for that

later," he said. He looked at the child again, frowning. He was sorry that he couldn't be there in person, to hold his son, to be physically with his family.

Edris didn't know that. She only saw the frown. Later, it would have more significance than he realized.

"What's wrong?" she asked.

"Nothing." He tried to sound convincing. "I must go. But I will come again as soon as I can. Be well. Take care of our child."

She smiled.

"And yourself," he added. He smiled. "Farewell." He walked out of the room.

SOMETHING DIDN'T FEEL right about the visit. Edris was worried. He didn't mention naming the child. Perhaps the birth had been a shock. Perhaps he'd expected the boy to look like him and he was disappointed. He'd frowned as if he was uncomfortable.

"The child looks very human," Devroshe commented as he entered the room later. "A shame."

"Why?"

He lifted a shoulder. "It was a human who took Rhemun's father in conflict with the empire." His face hardened. "There were other avenues of protest, but the human convinced him that only war would suffice." His eyes had a faraway look. "He was a beautiful man. Very much like Rhemun, strong and capable, a great military leader. He was...like my own child. I tutored him, taught him things, spent most of my day with him for decades. I...loved him."

She grimaced. "I'm so sorry," she said, with genuine feeling.

He looked at her and went cold. "I do not need pity from the species that took him from us."

"I meant no offense," she began.

He put his hands behind him. "Lord Rhemun was disappointed, did you not notice?" he asked, having spied on the meeting through his private vid channel. "He told me. He did not expect the child to appear so human. He said that it would disgrace us, to have a hybrid child who would be out of place here."

Her heart fell. "He wouldn't…couldn't…have said such a thing about his own son!"

"His son died, because of a human's treachery." His face was cold. "He loved the child, even if its mother was disgusting. At least it was a pure-blood child." He gave the child in the crib a distasteful glance. "He is right. It will disgrace our house, our Clan, when people see this…this hybrid."

She swallowed. "I don't believe that."

"No? You will see. Lord Rhemun told me that he will return soon. It is distasteful to him to have to say such things to you, but he knows that you will not believe unless you hear it from his own lips. He made a terrible mistake, out of pity for your traumatic experiences. It is a gesture he greatly regrets."

She was sick all the way to her soul. Surely he couldn't have hidden such distaste from her all this time? But he'd confessed that he felt guilty for his treatment of her, hadn't he? And that frown, when he'd looked at the child. Had he been disappointed? Had he regretted his attraction to Edris? Once the mating behaviors began, only mating could stop them. But he'd said he wanted a child. Yes, but he hadn't known the child would look so human, had he? Komak didn't. Komak looked Cehn-Tahr...

"You will see," Devroshe said. He turned and left the room.

EDRIS WAS CERTAIN that Rhemun would come and deny everything Devroshe had said to her. She was going to tell him about the man's rudeness, as well. She hated to, but it was making life very hard for her.

It was so hard, in fact, that she'd moved into a small summerhouse on the property, where she could tend to her child and not have Devroshe watching her every move. He said that it was inconvenient for food to be sent down to her, but she had a replicator of her own and she made food for herself and the baby just to spite him.

He came into the house only once, to place some sort of apparatus in the small sitting room.

"Since you will not live in the house, you must have the same protections that we have. It is our lord's order."

"Very well," she said quietly.

He activated the unit, glared at her and left.

SHE WAS GETTING sleepy when the door suddenly opened and Rhemun walked in.

She jumped up and ran to him, to embrace him, but he put his arms out and prevented her. He looked angry and uncomfortable.

"I'm so happy to see you!" she exclaimed. "Do you want to see the baby?"

He folded his hands behind him. "I have come to speak with you," he said in a cold monotone. "This will not be pleasant, I'm afraid."

"Speak…with me," she flustered. "About what?"

"About the child. Please sit down."

SHE DID, BUT her face was taut. "You said you wanted a child with me," she began defensively.

He drew in a curt breath. "You must know that I felt much guilt for the pain and suffering you endured because of my behavior toward you."

"Yes. You said so."

His chin lifted. She noticed that he hadn't morphed into his true form. It was another indication that his feelings toward her were changing. "The child looks very human," he began sadly. "Far more human than I anticipated. And my…feelings…for you were a result of the mating hunger. Now that it has been assuaged, I… I feel differently toward you."

She just stared at him, with pieces of her life falling, shattering around her. "Differently?" she parroted numbly.

"Our bonding was a mistake," he said heavily. "And there is no way to undo it, as we bond for life.

But I cannot come back here, ever again, as long as you and the...child...are in residence."

"You want me to leave?" she exclaimed, fighting tears.

"You, and the child," he said. "I am very sorry. I can't...live with this. You are a disgrace to my Clan, to me. You are a living memory of all that I have lost. I should never have let my instincts lead me to bond with you."

"You want me to leave." She felt numb all over. She sat down on the edge of a chair.

"Yes," he said flatly. "Devroshe will make arrangements for you, on a passenger ship, to the Rim. You must not speak to Ruszel or the emperor... It would disgrace me even more, especially because Ruszel is your friend."

So she wouldn't even be able to say goodbye. This was wrenching.

"Mems will be provided. You can live quite well with your...the child. But you must never contact me again."

"Don't worry," she said heavily. "I won't."

"I am very sorry."

"You said that."

"This is for the best," he said in that same odd monotone. "You will be happier away from Memcache. So will I."

She just nodded.

"Speak to Devroshe when you are ready to leave. Please make it quick, for both our sakes."

She nodded again.

He paused at the door. "Farewell."

He went out, closing the door on her, their child and their life together.

She couldn't believe it. She thought maybe it was a joke. She even tried to raise Rhemun on the private comm channel, but the call wouldn't go through. The message said that he refused the call. That was when realization hit. He wasn't kidding. He meant it. He didn't want her. He didn't want a hybrid child. He wanted her to leave.

She got to her feet, numbly, and went to the comm panel. "Devroshe, will you come down here, please?"

"At once, my lady."

At least he sounded joyful, she thought miserably.

IT DIDN'T EVEN take long to arrange. The following day, she was on a passenger ship with the baby. She'd wanted to say goodbye to the handmaidens, but they hadn't been at the house when she left. She did leave a note for them, and one for Rhemun, in the small summerhouse she'd occupied. If he found the note, perhaps he might read it. Perhaps he might have a change of heart, because she'd poured hers out in the communication. It was still so hard to believe that he'd asked her to leave.

Devroshe had given her a white noise ball from Rhemun, one that would block telepathic communication. In case the emperor sought her on behalf of Ruszel, Devroshe said. He gave her a voucher for enough mems to get her on her way to a new life. A surprisingly small amount at that. Rhemun apparently didn't feel generous in any way.

She lay down on the bed with her child and tears fell from her eyes. She pulled the baby close. "Well, I want you, my darling." She smiled as she brushed back his hair. He was newly born, but already the size of a six-month-old child. His hair was going to be blond like hers, and his eyes were green. She smiled. "Kipling," she said. "I'm going to call you Kipling. He was a soldier and a poet. I think when you grow up, you'll like your name. And nobody will ever know who your father was," she added heavily.

THE QUARTERS ON the passenger ship were cramped, but she was used to living in a small space, having been on the *Morcai* for such a long time. There was a bed and a closet of sorts, a toilet and a small sink. Besides, she told herself, it was only for a few weeks, until they reached the Rim.

She worried about how she would find work there. A doctor's services were always needed, but the Rim was a lawless place. Without guidance, she could become the slave of some entrepreneur with a criminal empire. She shuddered at the thought. Her whole life, she'd been sheltered in the military. Now, for the first time, she was a civilian, alone. It was disconcerting. But then, she'd survived on Benaski Port until Cartha's brutal assault and the aftermath. She could survive the Rim, too.

There was a faint noise and when she turned, there was a giant galot sitting on the bed with her son.

She cried out and ran toward him. Then, when the great cat's head turned, she stopped and tears began to fall. "Kanthor?" she exclaimed.

"Yes," he said, in his raspy voice, "it is I. The cub is quite beautiful."

The tears fell harder.

"Why are you here?" he asked, padding softly onto the floor. He sat down again, so tall that his pale green eyes looked directly into hers.

She lowered her face. "Rhemun…asked me to leave," she said heavily. "He said that the pity he felt for me, the guilt he felt at his treatment of me, led him to the bonding. He said it was a terrible mistake and he…didn't want me anymore."

There was an intake of breath. "I shall go and speak with him," he said sternly.

"No. Please. Don't interfere. He said it to my face, in person. At least he didn't just leave a message…"

He was disconcerted. It disturbed him that he couldn't see into her mind. He couldn't reach Rhemun's, either. Odd. That had rarely happened. Perhaps he was growing old.

He sighed. "You know, researchers are constantly pleading for access to my homeworld, Eridanus Three. In fact, I believe a representative of the corporation is even now having a meal in the canteen." His green eyes gleamed. "Perhaps you might volunteer to do this work."

She gave him a wary look. "Kanthor, researchers don't go to Eridanus Three because they become lunch rather quickly."

He chuckled. "That is true. However, if I go with you, none of my people will harm you. I give you my word. You and Rhemun's cub will be safe."

She felt hopeful for the first time in days. "In that case," she said, "if you don't mind watching the baby, I'll go and find him."

He nodded. "The cub will be safe with me."

She smiled. "I know that."

Considering the fierce, and mostly warranted, reputation of the galot species for ravenous behavior, it was a demonstration of her utter trust in him.

"What does he look like?" she asked at the door.

He described the representative. "Also, do you carry a restorative in the drug banks of your wrist scanner?" he mused.

"A res...well, yes."

"You may need to revive him after you ask for the work." He chuckled.

She rolled her eyes, grinned and went to find the man.

IT WAS A hard life. The supply ship only ran every two months. Sometimes Kanthor had to hunt game for them to stretch out their rations.

The child, Kipling, grew at an astonishing rate. Only four years had passed, but Kipling had already the size and intellect of a child of eight. He was very mature for his age, as well. He lived on the nexus, studying, learning, questioning. He was fascinated with military things. He had a passion for any information about the famous Holconcom.

Edris pretended to know nothing about it. Her past was carefully hidden from anyone who might represent a threat to Rhemun's peace of mind. She had few visitors, but she didn't want to slip up and mention her service with the Cehn-Tahr. In fact, she pretended that she had no knowledge of anything about Memcache.

Kipling was frustrated. Such secrecy was maintained that not even the name of the Holconcom commander was published. Only Cehn-Tahr were privileged to know anything about it, and their AI skills were so advanced that they easily blocked any information about it that might reach the nexus.

"I just want to know a few things," Kipling muttered. "I can't even find out what weaponry the *Morcai* carries."

"Eat your *mocrat*," she instructed. "Kanthor went to a lot of trouble to find these. They're rare on this continent."

Kipling tasted it and nodded. "It's very good." He grinned at her. "You're not a bad cook, Mom."

"Thank you." She smiled. He still looked completely human. He had long, blond hair that curled madly over his shoulders. It was like Rhemun's except for the color. His eyes were green, and his complexion was a nice soft tan. Nothing about him could be detected that looked in any way Cehn-Tahr. It grieved her, because if he had looked more like Rhemun, probably they'd still be living on Memcache. That would have been unfortunate, however, because she now knew how Rhemun really felt. She knew that he'd never loved her. It had only been physical hunger and guilt that drove him to bond with her.

If she'd thought about it very much, she would have realized how he felt because he'd never marked her. She knew that Madeline Ruszel carried a small scar that Dtimun had given her at their first mating. Each mark embraced a character of the Cehn-Tahr alphabet, and had meaning far beyond the letter itself. It was a tradition thousands of years old. If Rhemun had truly cared for her, he would have marked her. But he never had.

The pain was still fresh, after four years. She wondered if he'd ever had second thoughts, if he'd missed her at all. She hoped, still, that he might show up one day and say he'd made a mistake, that he wanted her and the child. But that was a dream. A sad and hopeless dream.

She'd made up a story, that Kipling's father had been a fighter pilot for the Terravegan military and had been killed in action. It had the advantage of also explaining her reluctance to discuss anything about the military. Kipling obliged her. He was curious about his other parent, but he refrained from questions most of the time.

She wondered about the future. But she forced herself to live from day to day. It was best.

CHAPTER TWELVE

THE MEMORIAL SERVICE for Edris Mallory and her baby was solemn and private. Only Rhemun and his mother, Madeline Ruszel and Dtimun, the emperor and Lady Caneese, Chacon and Lyceria were present. It was brief and poignant.

The news of the fire had reached Rhemun just after an exhaustive battle on a front in the New Territory, where renegade Rojoks were making progress at appropriating a mineral-rich moon for their cause.

Devroshe had been apologetic. The fire had started mysteriously. The young human had insisted on living in the summerhouse, despite Devroshe's misgivings. She would not even allow him to supply her with food. She had been secretive, quiet.

Even as he digested the loss of his family, Rhemun thought how unlike Edris Mallory that description sounded. But grief overshadowed suspicion for the moment. He called the emperor, who broke the news to Madeline. It hit her hard. Edris was the only female friend she'd ever had. She took the loss badly.

So did Kresene of Rhemun's household. She dissolved into tears and would speak to no one. The other housemaid was equally distraught. Devroshe, while he displayed the appropriate solemnity, was pretending. Rhemun knew.

After the service, he went straight to his house-man.

"I am so deeply sorry," he told Rhemun, bowing. "It is my fault…"

Rhemun glared at him. He couldn't penetrate the other man's mind. Devroshe had been taught by Rhemun's father to block telepaths, so that he couldn't impart any incriminating information. The very fact that Rhemun couldn't see into the other man's mind was an indication that there was something to hide.

"How did the fire start?" Rhemun asked coldly.

"We do not know, but the authorities were called. They believe that it was…set." His eyes remained lowered. "They questioned us all and we were checked for chemical residue. They found nothing, of course."

"Nothing."

Devroshe was bustling around. He looked strangely happy for a man whose mistress had recently deceased. "I will make supper, yes? Something nice…"

Rhemun turned, imposing in the white robes of mourning he wore for Edris. "You will close up the house."

"W…what?"

"You will close up the house. Dismiss the handmaids and make certain they have provision and pensions."

"But, you will come here when you are on liberty." Devroshe became flustered.

"I will go to my mother's house, in such case." He looked around with cold, pain-laden eyes. "I can never live here again, with the memory of how she died."

Devroshe was shell-shocked. "But...but it has always been your home."

"Not anymore." He turned to the other man. "You will have a pension, as well. You can go home to your brother."

Devroshe swallowed, hard, and colored faintly. "My younger brother has...gone to live on the Rim," he faltered. "I will not see him again, I imagine."

He frowned. "Anglos has left Memcache? Why?"

Devroshe could never reveal that. "He was...he had a relationship that failed," he lied. "He said that he could no longer live here."

Rhemun sighed. "That is unfortunate."

"I could remain here," Devroshe suggested urgently. "I could keep the property in good repair, I could..."

"You will close the house," Rhemun reiterated. "Now."

Devroshe wrung his hands. "It is the only home I have known since my youth," he groaned.

"Devroshe, you cannot seem to understand what I am telling you," Rhemun said with growing irritation. "This house and its memories are unbearable to me! I cannot look at it without seeing her here, in every room. Without remembering...her loss." He turned away, his teeth grinding together.

"If we could discuss…" Devroshe pleaded.

"There is nothing to discuss."

Devroshe saw his life going down an imaginary drain. Little had he considered this outcome of his treachery. He had rid his master of an inconvenient mate, of a hybrid child, and it should have had a rewarding outcome. But he had not foreseen this result. Rhemun was not pleased. He was heartbroken. He was mourning the female, for whom he had feelings that Devroshe had not imagined.

Guilt racked him. He should tell the truth. He should tell his master that he had lied, that he had rigged the holon to show Rhemun asking Mallory to leave. He should tell him about the white noise ball that would make finding her now impossible. He should confess that his younger brother had set the fire undetected, and planted evidence of a woman and child consumed in the white-hot blaze. But if he did that, Rhemun would hate him forever. He had lost Rhemun's father. Now he was going to lose Rhemun, as well. He had caused the younger alien untold misery out of jealousy and misplaced hatred.

"I am…sorry," he choked.

Rhemun waved his words away. "I must return to my command. My mother will answer any questions or concerns you may have about the future of the property." He looked around with eyes that barely registered the ancient structure. "I may sell it."

"No!" Devroshe dropped to his knees. "No! I beg

you! Please! Not such a result for such an unworthy human!"

Rhemun was very still. His eyes went dark brown. "What did you say?"

Devroshe was horrified at his outburst. He covered his mouth. His eyes were wide with fear. "I did not mean it! I did not... Forgive me!"

Rhemun was contemptuous. "I thought you would respect me enough to treat my mate with every care. Apparently her treatment was far worse than any I could have imagined."

"I did not kill her!"

"Did I accuse you of setting the fire, Devroshe?"

The words were honeyed. Soft. Silky. Devroshe swallowed hard and lowered his eyes. "I have...failed you in many ways," he said finally, with quiet resignation. "I shall go back to my province when the household is dissolved. I am...deeply sorry, for the loss of your mate. And your child," he added heavily. "Deeply sorry."

Rhemun looked around at the emptiness of the house, and his life. He turned and left without another word to his houseman.

Devroshe watched him go with anguish. He should have told the truth. He should have confessed his fault. He could not. His brother was safely hidden; he would never tell what he knew. But as long as he lived, Devroshe would remember the look of horror and pain and loss on Rhemun's face. He had lied and cheated and caused untold misery to his master's son, whom he had tutored and cared for, as he had cared for Rhemun's father. His hatred of humans had brought him to this. The woman was out there, somewhere, with Rhemun's child, his son, whom he would never know. Devroshe knew, and kept his silence. But he could not bear to confess it. There was still a chance, a very small chance, that Rhemun would relent one day and open the great house again and invite Devroshe back to run it for him. A chance worth any risk.

IT WAS FOUR years later that a chance encounter brought Rhemun face-to-face with Devroshe's younger brother. The man came to see him in his office at the Dectat during a conference with military leaders.

"Anglos, is it not?" Rhemun asked. He had changed over the years, grown cold and hard. His loss haunted him still.

"Yes, Lord," the man replied. He was gaunt and pale, walking with a stick. Odd for such a young Cehn-Tahr.

"I am sorry for the loss of your brother," Rhemun said. Devroshe had committed suicide not very long after he left Rhemun's employ, driven mad, some said by unknown forces.

"My brother did an evil thing," Anglos said quietly. "I never spoke of it, for fear of retribution. But I am dying," he said with a pale smile. "And I wish to clear my conscience before I step into the unknown."

Rhemun frowned. "I don't understand."

"The fire, the one that consumed the house on your land, where your mate and her child were staying. I set it..."

He stopped because Rhemun had him suspended by the throat. He could feel the claws digging into the flesh. Rhemun's eyes were black, like death, like the unknown.

"Not...dead," he managed to get out with what he feared would be his last breath.

Rhemun had to fight the blood madness. He wanted to kill the man who had robbed him of Edris and his son. He drew in deep breaths until he could control the rage, the horrible rage. He slowly eased the sickly man to his feet and abruptly let him go.

"Explain."

Anglos swallowed, rubbing his throat. "Your mate and the child," he rasped, "are not dead."

"They were consumed in the fire!" Rhemun raged.

"No."

Rhemun's face paled. He waited, his fists clenched at his side, his eyes burning with hope.

"Devroshe...used the holon...made her think you did not want her or the child...who looked so human. She did not know...about the holon. She thought it was you. She left. Devroshe gave her a few mems and a ticket to the Rim. He had me set the fire...so that you would not go after her."

Rhemun cursed. He cursed violently. No wonder the man had begged forgiveness. Four long years...!

"The emperor could not touch her mind, nor could I!" he exclaimed.

"Yes. Devroshe said…it would dishonor you if she told anyone. He gave her the white noise ball, to carry. She was told it would block a telepath."

Rhemun was absolutely stunned. "She is not dead."

"No. She is not. I cannot tell you where she is. I am most sorry." Tears ran down the other man's face. "Your life was shattered because my brother was jealous of your mate, of your child. He tried to poison her, but Kresene called the physician in time…"

Rhemun cursed again, putting his face in his hands. This was monstrous. He left Edris with a man he trusted with his own life, and it had almost cost her her own.

"Kresene went to her people and said nothing because Devroshe threatened her with a secret about her mother," he continued. "She would have told, but for that."

Rhemun closed his eyes. A conspiracy of silence.

"My life is almost done, Lord," Anglos said softly. "I could not die without telling you what was done, and my part in it. I know that words will not erase the misery you were caused. I wish I could do more. I beg forgiveness, so that my soul will not suffer in the afterworld for this tragedy I have caused you."

Rhemun opened his eyes. The rage was gone now, replaced by hope. Edris was not dead. She was alive, somewhere in the three galaxies, with his son. His son! He stood erect, turned to his desk, and activated the communicator. He spoke into it quickly.

Anglos, understanding the commands, was so stunned that he sat down without asking permission.

Rhemun cut the connection. "A skimmer will come for you, here. You will be taken to the medical center and anything that can be done for you will be done."

Anglos wept. "But I have nothing…"

Rhemun went closer. He put his hand on the man's trembling shoulder. "You have given me back my life," he said quietly. "You did not seek treatment because you had no financial means. I do not pry, but your thoughts lie on the edge of your mind."

Anglos only nodded.

"Your condition can be treated. I will make certain that you have everything you need for the rest of your life."

"But I set the fire," Anglos sobbed.

"Yes. But if you had not come to me, I would never know that Edris was alive," he replied. "For that, I owe you a great debt. Which I will gladly pay."

"I will do anything for you, Lord. Anything!"

"The skimmer will be waiting at the door. Anglos…thank you."

"It is I, who thank you, Lord. With all my heart. I am so sorry for what Devroshe did."

"He paid for it," Rhemun replied. "At his own hand."

"Yes."

Now there was the business of trying to track down where Edris had gone. The obvious person to manage that was his mother. Sfilla was overjoyed when he told her what Anglos had said.

"I will find her. I promise you that I will," Sfilla said. "You must tell Ruszel at once."

He smiled. "That will be a pleasure."

HE CALLED HER on the family vidchannel immediately.

"She's alive? Where is she?" Madeline exclaimed, laughing and crying all at once.

"That, we do not yet know," Rhemun said, after he explained how this had come about.

"You should have had Devroshe skinned alive and eaten at a family banquet," Madeline said harshly. "And don't remind me that I'm a doctor. I'm not above vengeance."

"Devroshe died by his own hand. He left a message for me, only saying that he was sorry. I had no idea what he was apologizing for until Anglos came to see me and told me what had happened."

"Just as well, and good riddance," Madeline said coldly. "But how will we find Edris? It's been four years!"

Rhemun smiled. "My mother can find anyone."

Madeline laughed. "Yes. She can. I'm very happy for you."

"How is Komak?" he asked.

"See for yourself." She beckoned to a young man of six years, who looked twelve. He was on the verge of adolescence. His eyes were green like his mother's, but they were beginning to undergo the mood color changes of his father's race. He had dark hair, but it had auburn highlights, and his skin color was more human than Cehn-Tahr.

"Hi, Commander!" Komak greeted him with a big smile. "When can I come and be your executive officer?"

Rhemun laughed. "When you grow another foot."

"I'll eat more," Komak promised.

Madeline ruffled her son's hair with pure affection. "Don't be pert with your elders."

Komak made a face. "Yes, Mother."

"Back to work," she teased.

He rolled his eyes. "Theoretical physics," he muttered. "I'd rather practice with the Kahn-Bo. Can't Mekashe come over and give me some more pointers? I'll study hard."

Madeline looked at Rhemun with raised eyebrows.

"I'll ask him," Rhemun said. He smiled at Komak. "Study hard."

"I promise! Thanks!" He ran out of the room.

"I'm very happy for you," Madeline told Rhemun. "I know these years have been hard to live through. I've missed her, too."

He nodded. "Her life cannot have been an easy one," he said sadly. "Living off the nexus, she will have had to take jobs in dangerous places. I hope that I find her well."

"As do I. Please keep us informed."

"Certainly, Lady Maltiche."

She smiled. "Farewell."

"And you."

IT TOOK SFILLA all of two days to locate Edris. She was laughing outrageously when she told Rhemun.

"Why are you amused?" he asked.

"Because of her job," Sfilla said, eyes brimming with green laughter. "She is living on Eridanus Three, researching galots for the Vega Corporation."

"The genetic patent firm?" he exclaimed. "And she hasn't been eaten?!"

"Kanthor is with her."

He let out a breath. "He did not tell me." He was saddened by the thought that his friend had kept that knowledge from him. He had actually seen Kanthor recently, too, although their conversation had been limited to polite pleasantries and without any personal discussions. Presumably Kanthor had been told that Rhemun had asked Edris to leave, and he had believed that his friend had no interest in his abandoned mate.

"Devroshe was an animal," Sfilla said coldly. "I cannot believe he would betray you in such a manner."

"He was never the same after my father was killed," Rhemun said heavily. "He hated humans even more than I did."

"You hated them as much because he taught you to, and because of what happened to your first son," he was reminded. "He filled you up with prejudices. I was away far too much on jobs for the emperor, and I trusted him."

"So did I," Rhemun said. "I should have been suspicious about the fire. The only reason the authorities believed Edris and our son died in it was because Devroshe claimed he saw them in the house. The fire would have consumed every trace of DNA, it was so hot."

"Yes. None of us had reason to doubt his eyewitness testimony," Sfilla said. She smiled. "So your mate and your son are still alive. And you know where they are. Why are you still standing here?"

He burst out laughing. "Why, indeed." He sobered. "She will not be forgiving when she learns the truth."

"It was not your fault. She will understand."

"I can only hope that she will." He touched her cheek and laid his forehead against hers. "I will call you the minute I find her."

"I will call Kresene and have her open the house again," Sfilla offered.

He laughed with delight. "I think that would be appropriate. You might also inform her that any attempts to blackmail her because of her mother's past actions will be met with deadly force."

"That I will enjoy telling her. Farewell, my son."

He smiled. "And you."

RHEMUN LANDED THE skimmer close to the station where Mallory and Kipling lived on Eridanus Three. As he opened the door, a small group of galots surrounded him, sniffing and watching.

He laughed and morphed and was welcomed as a member of the pack. He spoke to them in their own odd tongue of hisses and sibilants, assuring them that he was only here to see their human visitors, one of whom was his son. They were joyous for him when they read in his mind that he had thought his mate and child dead for many years, only to discover them alive and living here. Kanthor lived with them, they told him with some small contempt, for galots never lived with any but their own kind. Still, Kanthor was very fond of Rhemun's cub and had become his protector against the few forms of native predatory life.

They followed him to the prefab dome, leaving him to approach it alone. He changed back into his human form and scratched gently on the door column. There was a small hesitation, then the door suddenly opened and there was Edris Mallory, even more beautiful than he remembered her.

She caught her breath audibly and color rushed into her face. "Rhemun!"

He read in her mind a thousand thoughts, most of which dealt with his supposed rejection of her and the child, the loss she felt when she had to leave Memcache. She had left him a vid, inside the small summerhouse. Of course, he never received it, because the house was burned. He read something far more disturbing in those few seconds, of how Devroshe had treated her, with disgust and unkindness, that he had said her presence in the compound was shaming to Rhemun. He also saw himself, in the altered holon, telling her that he didn't want her anymore, that she was an embarrassment to him. He was furious and horrified, and had to hide both emotions from her. She could not know, even now, that he was a telepath. It would raise too many questions.

"Edris," he said softly. His eyes were displaying a rainbow of colors as he assimilated her thoughts, and he could see the puzzlement in her own odd eyes that did not change color to mirror moods.

"Why are you here now, after so many years?" she asked, and her face tightened. "You didn't even try to contact…"

"The house where you were living was burned to the ground," he said quietly, his eyes still locked to her face, as if he couldn't bear to turn them from her for an instant. "I thought you and the child were dead. I was told so, by Devroshe, who swore that he saw you and the child burned. Until his brother confessed to setting the fire, when he thought he was dying, I had no idea you were still alive." He drew in a long breath, watching the anger in her face turn to anguish. "There was a memorial service. Ruszel and Dtimun, the emperor and Lady Caneese, my mother…" He swallowed, hard. His face showed the terrible strain of the past few years.

Edris was speechless. "Devroshe...he actually told you I was dead?"

He nodded solemnly. "He committed suicide, soon after I made him close up the house and leave. Apparently he thought everything would be as it was before you came to live there with our child." His eyes flashed. "If he were still alive, I would have killed him with my own hands!" he said shortly.

She just stared at him. "But...but you came home. You told me to leave..."

He moved closer. "I kept secrets from you. We have technology of a sort we never share. It permits touch and smell and taste through an avatar. Devroshe must have programmed it." His eyes searched hers. "I thought you were dead, you and my son." His chest rose and fell a little unsteadily. "You cannot know the anguish I felt, that the others felt, when we were told of the fire."

Her face softened. She had aged, too. The years had been kind, though. She looked stronger, more confident than she had been at their bonding.

"Did you tell the others that you found me?"

He nodded. He managed a smile. "There were celebrations. I left them going. I came here as quickly as I could." He studied her face intently. "It is...so good to see you. The child...?"

There was a human curse from the back of the building. Edris let Rhemun inside just as a small boy with long, curly blond hair, burst into the room.

"That *frasmach* machine!" he was raging. "It

consumed my essay for schoolwork…!" He stopped dead, gaping at their visitor. Rhemun was still in his human form, but his hair was very like the boy's, long and curly, almost to his waist. Black, not blond.

"We'll discuss your language later," Edris told him firmly. "We have a visitor."

The boy moved a little closer. He wore the conventional garb for a child, soft fabric in a tan color, pants and shirt with a leather vest that flared over his small hips. He was going to be tall. He had long legs. His face was pleasant to look at, like Mallory's. He had her coloring, but his eyes did not change color. He looked completely human. Rhemun was sad to see it.

The boy frowned. *Why does my appearance disturb you?* he asked the tall man mentally. His lips did not move.

The tall man's expression didn't change, but his eyes abruptly changed color, to a dancing green. *Do not tell your mother that you can read my thoughts*, he said sternly.

He frowned. *Why not?*

We will discuss this later.

"Is he trying to see what you're thinking?" Edris laughed. "He has these flashes of insight. I'm afraid he's trying to be a telepath, but he isn't."

The boy glared at her.

For shame, Rhemun thought to him. *Such language!*

"Sorry," the boy said contritely.

"All right," both adults said at the same time.

Edris gave Rhemun an odd look. The boy grinned.

"Who are you?" the boy asked.

"I didn't think…this is Rhemun," Edris told the boy. "He worked with me in…in biological weapons research, many years ago," she fabricated. "And this is my son, Kipling." Her tone made it evident that she was warning Rhemun not to reveal anything of her past, even though, unknown to her, he read it in her mind.

"Kipling?" He was puzzled. They had not discussed names. A child on Memcache customarily was not named until his second week of life. By then, the house had been gone. He was careful to compartment those thoughts, so that the boy couldn't read them.

"For an ancient human, who was a great poet and soldier," Edris confessed.

He was impressed. An odd name, but quite appropriate.

"Your eyes change color," Kipling said to the visitor.

"Yes," Rhemun told him. "I am Cehn-Tahr."

Kipling caught his breath. "I've read about the Cehn-Tahr, and the Holconcom," he said excitedly. "They're the greatest fighters in the galaxies! Do you know any of them? Have you ever met Commander Dtimun? He married, excuse me, bonded with, a human, Dr. Madeline Ruszel!"

Rhemun made the sound that, in a Cehn-Tahr, passed for laughter. "Yes. I do know him."

"I'd love to see a real, live Holconcom," he said. "She—" he indicated his mother "—thinks that war is terrible and she won't even talk to me about studying in a military academy when I'm older."

Rhemun carefully hid the thought, shameful to him, that Kipling would never be admitted to the Cehn-Tahr academy because he had no idea who his father was—and his mother apparently didn't want him to know.

"We're moving soon to the Rim colonies," Edris told Rhemun. "My research job here is completed, and I have a job with the medical facility on Araman," she added. "Kipling will apprentice with a tradesman there."

"Learning to make shoes or harnesses for yomuth," the boy said disgustedly.

Rhemun had to hide his own disgust. Generations of his Clan had commanded armies.

"Hey, it's a trade," she told him firmly.

The boy, like most Cehn-Tahr children, grew at an advanced rate. He would be, in human years, the equivalent of a ten-year-old.

Kipling was studying their visitor and frowning. "You look just like me," he said.

Edris froze.

"I mean," Kipling continued, "like a human. But there are stories that say the Cehn-Tahr are really very different from humans."

"We are," Rhemun told him. "We assume this shape among other races so that we do not frighten them. We reveal our true faces only to members of our own race, or to those for whom we have great affection." Or, he didn't add, to those whom they were about to kill.

"I see," Kipling replied sadly.

Rhemun was tempted to show himself to the boy, but he did not. The fears the Cehn-Tahr entertained about morphing in front of humans were still inhibiting. Rhemun had reason not to care, but this was his son. His child. He did not want to frighten him.

He looked down at Edris. "How did you come to this place, to this work?"

"When we left—" she bit her tongue before she let *Memcache* slip out "—the planet where Kipling was born, there was a man on the starliner we took who was complaining that he couldn't find anybody who wanted to study galots for his company, because the galots tended to eat researchers who went there." She laughed. "Because of Kanthor, I knew I would be welcome, and Kip would be safe. So I asked for the job. The company provided me with a small civilian skimmer, pretty used but serviceable." She gave him a strange look. "When we got here, Kanthor was waiting for us. I have no idea how he managed it."

Rhemun only smiled. He knew things about the galots that Mallory still didn't.

"I don't guess you have any vids on your ship about the Holconcom or anything?" Kipling asked plaintively.

"Surely you have access to the galactic signal nexus here?" Rhemun asked him.

"Well, of course, but if you know the former commander of the Holconcom, I thought you might have something that isn't on the nexus," he replied hopefully.

"No," Rhemun said with quiet affection. "No one is permitted to film the unit. Or to know even the names of its command crew."

"I guess I knew that," Kipling returned with a sigh.

"Why don't you finish your homework?" Edris suggested.

"But we have a real visitor, and he isn't a trader, and he knows…!"

"He'll still be here when you're through," she promised.

He grimaced. "Promise?"

She nodded.

"Okay." He gave the visitor a grin and romped off back to his room.

"He is quite remarkable," Rhemun told her as they moved into the kitchen, where she prepared the java drink that both enjoyed.

She glanced at him. "Do you think so? He doesn't look… I mean, he looks just like a…oh, wait…!" She grabbed up the white noise sphere sitting on the counter and abruptly activated it. "I forgot all about that." She gave him a worried glance. "You see, I know that there are telepaths who might listen in on

Kip. If Rojok agents ever found out who he was…
well, you know."

"Yes, I do," he said solemnly. Now he understood why Kip had been able to communicate with
him mentally when he first arrived, and also why he
hadn't accidentally found Mallory with his mind in
the interim. "Do you keep it activated?"

"All the time," she said. "Except today, because
its solar battery finally ran out and I just replaced it.
It's been charging, but I forgot to turn it back on. I
must remember not to make that mistake again." She
hesitated. "Devroshe gave it to me," she confessed.
"He said that it would disgrace you if the emperor or
Dr. Ruszel knew that you'd sent me away."

"He lied."

Her expression was haunted. "I didn't know about
the secret technology. You stood in front of me in
person and told me to go." She lowered her eyes. "I
had no reason to believe it wasn't you." She hesitated.
"It wasn't really you when Kip was born, either, was
it?" she asked with keen perception.

"No," he said quietly. "We were at the other end
of the galaxy. But I had to be there when you gave
birth," he added softly. "I couldn't bear the thought
of you alone at such a time." His face hardened. "If
I had told you the truth, Devroshe would never have
convinced you to leave."

He sat down at the table with her, accepting the
java. He sipped it and smiled. "Just like the, what do
you humans call it, coffee, that we had on the ship."

She glanced past him to make sure Kip wasn't in hearing range. "Yes," she said, laughing. "I remember when Dr. Ruszel used to hide real contraband java beans in the med unit and make it for us. The commander used it as a threat when she did something he didn't like." Her eyes were sad. "Are they both all right?"

He nodded. "Dtimun sits in the Dectat with his father now, as heir apparent, and Dr. Ruszel continues her bioweapons research with Lady Caneese." He smiled. "Their son, Komak, is a little older than Kipling."

"Does he look like his father?" she asked quickly.

He smiled. "No. Like our child, he has the appearance of a human, although his hair is darker now, with an auburn tint, and his eyes have just begun to change color to mirror his moods. However, the doctors begin to think that the boys will start to morph when they achieve adolescence."

"In a Cehn-Tahr child, that will be in about a year or two," she said worriedly. "In human years, Kip is five, but in Cehn-Tahr years, he's ten," she added, reminding him that Kip had had a birthday recently. "They mature very rapidly."

"Yes." He hesitated, sipping coffee. "He does not know who his father is?"

She closed her eyes. "No. When you didn't contact me, I thought it was because you meant what you said—rather what your image said—that you were ashamed of him, because he was half human. So I made up a story, that his father was a human pilot who died bravely in the war." Her eyes made the apology. "I'm so sorry. I didn't realize you thought we were dead."

He looked at the java, instead of her. "I made many mistakes with you. I did not realize how great the consequences might be." His large eyes stared into hers, a solemn blue. "If we could begin again, I would have bonded with you long before the physical need became violent."

She flushed. "Perhaps it's just as well," she said, averting her eyes. "Kip is much safer if people think he's just another human child, while the rebel war is still ongoing."

"I told you that there must be a formal bonding, a public one, in addition to the private one we had aboard the *Morcai*," he said, and she nodded. "But the public bonding must be approved by the Dectat. I had planned this just after we mated, but there was much dissension in the council of politicians because Dtimun had mated with Ruszel. The infusion of human blood still had opponents then." He smiled sadly. "That is no longer the case. Komak has been with his father to the Dectat and has impressed even the most hardened opponents of interspecies bonding. However, at the time Kipling was created, the permission was in stasis."

"Why can't you bond without permission?" she asked.

He couldn't tell her the real reason. "I am an aristocrat among my people," he said instead.

"Oh, I understand. The inheritance laws."

He smiled. "Yes." The smile faded. "But we can have a public bonding now. You and the boy can come to Memcache to live."

She was remembering, hurting with the memory, what Devroshe had told her, about the shame Rhemun would suffer for mating with a human, the stigma of a half-human child. Unlike Dr. Ruszel, who commanded the respect of all Cehn-Tahr, Edris was just a normal human female with no claim to fame, and that would make her position, and Kip's, precarious among Cehn-Tahr aristocrats. Kip didn't know of his dual heritage, and she was reluctant to reveal it to him. Also, there was the danger he would be in, once his true identity was known.

Rhemun watched the expressions flit across her face and was sorry that she'd activated the white noise. He wanted to know what she was really thinking.

"I would rather not," she said at last, and she didn't look at him. "Kip and I will go to Araman for the time being, at least until the war ends. If it ever ends." She sighed. "I thought it would be over long before now. Commander Chacon," she said suddenly. "Is he still in command of the Rojok forces?"

"Yes. He and Princess Lyceria live on Enmehkmehk now. There is a strained relationship between Chacon and the rebel forces, which they hope one day to close with negotiations. For the moment," he replied. "There have been a few kidnapping attempts, but Chacon has foiled them all." He smiled. "The only attempt that might have succeeded was the one at Benaski Port, before Dtimun bonded with Ruszel, and only then because Chacon's attention was on the Cehn-Tahr princess instead of his own safety."

"It's going to be a stalemate, as long as Chacon leads the Rojoks and, you, the Holconcom," she replied.

He laughed softly. "Thank you."

She glanced at him and smiled sheepishly. "Well, you led the *kehmatemer* for many years before you led the Holconcom. You're very good in the field."

He sighed, studying her pretty face. "You have grown more beautiful."

She blinked, and a surprised laugh escaped her lips. "Thank YOU."

"It was all wrong with us, the way it happened," he said softly. "I was cold with you because you touched my heart. I did not want it to be touched, least of all by a human."

She couldn't admit that she thought his prejudice of humans might extend even to his own son. "I wish I were Cehn-Tahr."

His fingers went across the table and touched hers, very lightly, sending a soft pulse of pleasure through her body. "It was a long time ago. I no longer have those prejudices."

She didn't believe it, but she pretended that she

did. She couldn't take the chance that, if they went to live with him, Kip might pay for that human's tragic mistake.

He finished his coffee. "I must go. We are massing for a new offensive. I should be on Trimerius with my men, but when I knew you and…Kipling… were here, I had to come at once and see for myself."

"I named him for a human who was a soldier and a poet. But he should have had a Cehn-Tahr name," she said sadly.

"No! I like it," he said, surprising her. "A poet and a soldier. In my own culture, we are expected to combine the finer arts with the militant ones. It is a good name."

Her cheeks colored with pleasure.

He got up. "You must keep in touch with me."

"That would be very dangerous," she replied sensibly. "Especially for Kip."

He hesitated. He could talk to the boy mentally. She didn't know. But that white noise masker would be an obstacle. No. He could tell the boy. But not here. "Let Kip walk me to my ship. It is the newest military design. He will enjoy seeing it."

"All right."

"He cannot be admitted to either military academy, yours or mine, in his present circumstance. It is this which makes you sad."

She winced. "The Terravegans would kill him, because he wasn't government-bred. Your people would admit him, but he'd have to know who his father is, and that would be more dangerous. That's why I've tried to make sure he has a profession to support him, even if it's not the one he wants."

His eyes were quiet. "That can change. It will change one day. Perhaps sooner than you think."

She didn't reply. If Kip's true parentage were known, he wouldn't be safe anywhere in the three galaxies. "Perhaps." She went out of the room ahead of him. "Kip!"

He came running.

"Rhemun says you can see his ship. It's a new fighter class." She could have bitten her tongue when she made the slip.

"Like you know," he teased. "Been watching my vids when I've been out playing with Kanthor, huh, Mom?"

"Caught me." She jumped on the excuse.

"Where is Kanthor?" Rhemun asked.

"He went hunting. But he might be back, especially if he heard the ship," Kip said. "Sometimes the supply ship is late, but Kanthor keeps us in fresh meat. Sometimes I hunt with him!"

Edris wanted to die. She saw the brief flash of guilt on Rhemun's face when he knew what her life now was truly like. But it couldn't be helped.

"We should go," Rhemun told the boy. He looked at Edris with hunger and guilt. "I will see you again," he said, and it was a promise.

"I'm glad you came by."

"I'll be right back, Mom," Kip assured her.

They went out the door, closing it behind them. Suddenly, there was a loud cat cry, and Kanthor dropped the small rodent he was carrying and made a rush at Rhemun.

Kip cried out, afraid that the big cat was going to attack their unexpected visitor. But Rhemun ran to meet Kanthor, laughed, and he and the galot rolled over and over on the ground, playing together. They ran like blurs, chasing each other. The boy was fascinated by the feline behavior that was only hinted at in Rhemun's eyes. It touched him, seeing the dignified alien in a playful mood with Kanthor. He'd have given a lot to know how the big man inherited the cat characteristics, because Kip was certain it had to do with genetics. He was just now studying it in his homeschooling.

Rhemun and Kanthor stopped finally, panted a bit, embraced, and then the Cehn-Tahr brushed himself down.

"It has been many years," the big cat said in his own tongue. "I have missed you."

"I have missed you," Rhemun replied in the same language. "Thank you for taking care of these two."

"It has been my greatest joy. Can you stay?"

"I cannot. I have duties pressing. But I will see you again."

"I will protect the woman and your cub."

"I know that." He hesitated. "You came to see me. You knew they were here, yet you said nothing."

Kanthor nodded sadly. "She told me that you asked her to leave. She did not wish to see you. I am sorry."

Rhemun put a hand on the big cat's shoulder. "There is much blame, but none of it is yours. It was Devroshe's jealousy of her that caused this misery."

"I am truly sorry that he is dead," Kanthor said coldly. "I would have eaten him slowly."

Rhemun nodded. His eyes flashed. "So would I."

He turned and started back toward the ship. Kip fell into step beside him.

"You can speak galot," Kip noted. "I only speak a few words. It's so complex!"

"Yes."

"Do you speak other tongues?"

"About sixty," Rhemun confessed. It was a requirement in the Cehn-Tahr military. He would have to block those thoughts from his mind when he spoke telepathically to Kip, so that the boy couldn't read them. It was unwise to permit the child to know a lot about him. It might put him in danger if he let anything slip over the nexus.

"Mom said that you worked with her in weapons research, but she never said how. What do you do for a living?"

"I am a weapons expert," he said, which wasn't a total lie. He knew the use of every offensive and defensive weapon known to military science. "I am a consultant." True, because he told his men how and when to use them.

"Wow. So that's how you know the Holconcom."

"Yes."

"I want to be a soldier more than anything," Kip said sadly. "Mom won't even talk about it to me. I don't know why she hates the military so much. I can't learn fighting styles from vids on the nexus," he said miserably.

Rhemun turned to him. "On Araman, in the trade district of the desert continent, lives an exiled Cehn-Tahr named Cotashe," he said. "He is a master of the Kahn-Bo, the fighting stick. I will arrange lessons for you with him, if you like. But you must promise that your mother will not learn of this. She would not approve."

"You would do that, for me?" Kip faltered, his expression joyous. "But you hardly know me!"

"I will contact you when you arrive on Araman. You must make sure that you covertly disable the white noise sphere in your mother's possession when you arrive there. It makes telepathy impossible, even at long range, except for exceptionally gifted telepaths like our emperor."

"So that's how you could read my mind, at the house," Kip said, nodding. "Okay. I can do that." He frowned. "Why don't you want Mom to know that I can read minds, or that you can?"

"It is a secret I dare not share with you," Rhemun said. "You must promise."

"Okay. I promise. Then you won't mind if I talk to you sometimes?"

"Anytime you like," he replied.

"I'd really like that. There are no men here," he said. "Mom doesn't like men. I guess she's still crazy about my father. He was a soldier," he said proudly. "He died in the war, fighting. He was a combat pilot."

Rhemun felt the sting of those words all the way to his soul. But he didn't let it show. "You must look like him."

"Yes. Mom wanted me to cut my hair, but I won't. Most warrior cultures favor long hair in men."

The warriors in Kipling's bloodline would have approved.

They were at the ship. "Oh, gosh," Kip exclaimed when he saw the long, sleek fluid lines of the copper-colored skimmer. "Oh, what a beauty!"

Rhemun smiled. "The latest of the Casham-class fighters."

"It's a military ship."

The statement was a question. "Because I do consulting work for the military," he said smoothly, "they permit me the use of it. Would you like to see inside?"

"I'd love that."

"Come along."

WHEN KIP GOT back home, his eyes were dreamy with memories of the things he'd seen and the delight of having a master train him in Kahn-Bo fighting. If only he could tell his mother. But he didn't dare.

"Have fun?" she asked.

"It was great! You should see that ship. It has a

camouflage shield and emerillium pulse technology, plasma weaponry…" He hesitated, and frowned. "How did you meet Rhemun?"

"We were both working at a research facility," she said blandly. "I was interning in the hospital there. He was working on a design for military application."

"Oh. Well, I'll get back to my schoolwork. I can't wait until we move to Araman!" he added.

She blinked. He'd been morose and angry about the move. "You can't?"

"Like you always say, Mom, most moves are for the best. I will miss Kanthor, though." He hesitated again. "That big man rolled over and played with Kanthor, like they were old friends."

"I'm sure Rhemun visited Commander Dtimun at the fortress where he lives on Memcache," she said, making it up as she went. "Kanthor lived there for many years."

"Of course."

He went back to his room and Edris began, once more, to try and get over Rhemun. It was gratifying to know that he hadn't written her off when she left Memcache. Hating him had, however, helped her get him off her mind. Now he was back, just the same as before, and she wanted to be with him forever. She resigned herself to living her whole life outside his reach, raising a child who would never know his true heritage. Well, hopefully, Kip wouldn't start to morph into a Cehn-Tahr form too soon. Maybe by the time he did, she'd work up enough nerve to tell him that his father was Cehn-Tahr. But she'd never be able to tell him who his father really was.

It was disconcerting to find that her own feelings for Rhemun hadn't changed over the long years, despite the misery she'd felt when he told her to leave Memcache. Now that she knew the truth, she dared to hope, a little, about the future. She would see him again one day, she knew. Perhaps they could regain some of the emotion they'd once felt for each other. At least, there was hope. But for now, it was Kipling who claimed her thoughts. She had to protect him from his own identity. On the Rim, he would be safe.

CHAPTER THIRTEEN

So Edris and Kipling went to Araman to live. She had a job at a medical clinic for one of the larger galactic corporations, and Kip worked, not very enthusiastically, at his apprenticeship. He'd made friends with a young boy from one of the outer districts, whom he visited quite often. What Edris didn't know was that the child was the son of Master Cotashe, the Kahn-Bo master, and that it was a subterfuge so that he could begin his lessons without his mother's knowledge.

Over the months that followed, Rhemun and his son continued an affectionate relationship. Kip would deactivate the white noise ball and he and the mysterious Cehn-Tahr would speak on many subjects. His friend seemed to know a lot about the military, which was Kip's passion. He learned about the Great Galaxy War and the attack on Terramer that had led to the inclusion of a human unit with the famous Holconcom.

Kip had an odd feeling that the big man knew a lot more about the Holconcom than he let on, but he discovered early that Rhemun could block his thoughts with ease when he didn't want Kip to know something.

He queried his mother, covertly, about the visitor who had come unexpectedly to Eridanus Three, but she was as reticent as Rhemun. He did perceive some odd images from her mind that he couldn't explain. A uniform, a confrontation with Rhemun in what looked like a military vessel and a painful episode on Benaski Port. He didn't dare ask her about those images, because she might guess then that he really could read minds. She kept secrets, he surmised. He wondered what they were. But except for rare occasions when he could disable the white noise ball, he didn't have access to her thoughts. His Cehn-Tahr friend had also cautioned him about probing other minds. It was considered impolite, to say the least. So Kip didn't pursue his mother's secrets.

There was a new problem on Araman, though—a human adventurer who fixated on Edris and wouldn't believe that she didn't find him fascinating. He pursued her at the corporation where she worked and started coming to her apartment, which irritated her no end.

He was persistent, Edris thought angrily as the human adventurer, Dan Smith, went right in past her to the apartment. Kip, sitting at the vidplayer in the big room, glared at the newcomer.

"Nice place," the man said, nodding as he looked around. "I could be quite comfortable here."

"We aren't taking in boarders," Edris said irritably. "Will you please leave?"

"Oh, now, you don't really want me to go. Nice-looking woman like you, all alone."

"I'm here," Kip said angrily.

"Yeah. Not for long, though. Go play in your room, kid. Your mother and I want to talk."

Kip ignored him.

"Don't tell my boy what to do," Edris said.

"I said, get out!" the man yelled at Kip.

Kip stood up and glared at him. "I will not," he said firmly.

"That's what you think!" The man grabbed him by the collar and dragged him to the door, while Edris ran after him, hoping she could remember enough of her Holconcom training to stop the adventurer before he hurt Kip.

They were on the sidewalk now, with Kip swinging away, furiously trying to connect with the big man.

"You'll never hit me," the man drawled with contempt. "Little bugger like you."

"Want to bet?" Kip dipped and kicked the man in the shin as hard as he could.

The adventurer roared with pain, drew back his hand and hit Kip so hard that he flew backward to the ground.

Just as Edris approached furiously, a loud, angry growl broke the silence. There was a blur of red, and then a huge Cehn-Tahr morphed into his true form, stood with the adventurer clasped by the throat, suspended in one big hand several inches off the ground.

"Kipling, are you hurt?" the creature asked the child.

Kip was intimidated, not only by the size of the visitor, but by his appearance. "N-no," he stammered.

"Lucky," the Cehn-Tahr hissed at the adventurer, "for you!"

He flexed his hand and threw the big man several feet away to land on his back, shaking. "Run," Rhemun hissed as he crouched in a threatening position. "You might survive."

The adventurer didn't need a second warning. He pulled himself up and ran away as fast as he could, casting worried glances behind him.

Rhemun stood watching him, vibrating with anger, on the verge of going after the man and killing him for having the nerve to manhandle his child.

Edris helped Kip to his feet. "Are you sure you aren't hurt?" she asked worriedly, touching his bruised face.

"I'm fine," Kip whispered. "Who *is* he?" he asked worriedly, nodding at the Cehn-Tahr.

"It's Rhemun," she whispered back.

"But what is he?" he persisted.

"He's Cehn-Tahr," she told him gently. "That's their true form."

"He's so big!"

She was watching Rhemun struggle with his rage. If he pursued Smith and killed him…

"Kip, you have to go and reassure him that you're all right. Do it quickly, before he goes after Smith and kills him for touching you," she whispered. "The authorities would get involved. It would mean big trouble if they try to apprehend Rhemun."

That was all it took to prod Kip into motion. But he still approached the huge creature cautiously, moving in front of him very slowly. He was huge! Tall, and muscular, with a curling black mane that surrounded his face and fell over his shoulders, almost to his waist. His eyes were larger than they appeared in his humanoid form, and his nose was wider and more flattened. But he was still Rhemun.

Kip was touched that the alien cared so much that he would attack a man who threatened his young human friend. He went to him, reached out and gently took the alien's big hand. The creature looked down at him. It dragged in deep breaths, fighting the blood-thirst, fighting the urge to kill. After a minute, he morphed back into the comfortable form that Kip was used to.

"I'm okay," he told Rhemun. "Really. Thanks," he added with a shy smile.

Rhemun smiled back. He dropped to one knee and touched the child's face gently, wincing as he saw the bruise, and his eyes went from a warm brown to a threatening darkness. "I should have killed him," he said icily.

Kip's heart lifted. His friend did care for his welfare. It meant a lot. Rhemun was the only male in his life, in any real way. He smiled. "Just a bruise," he assured Rhemun. "I've had worse from Master Co-tashe," he added in a whisper, "when I didn't duck in time."

Rhemun laughed. "Brave boy."

"Thank you," Edris said as she joined them. "I've forgotten most of my hand-to-hand moves," she added. Kip thought that was a joke, and he chuckled.

But Kip was suddenly noticing things he'd been too unsettled to see. Rhemun was wearing a famil-iar red uniform, and he wasn't alone. Several other red-uniformed men, mostly humans, were standing by a transport at the curb. They had gone tense and crouched when Rhemun attacked the human male, but they were relaxed now.

Kip's lips fell open. "You're Holconcom," he ex-claimed.

"More precisely," Edris said with pride in her voice, "he commands the Holconcom."

"You do? Really? You never told me!" Kip ex-claimed.

Rhemun laid a gentle hand on the boy's shoul-der. "There was no need, until now." He looked over Kip's head at Edris, and his eyes became a solemn blue. "You and Kip are in grave danger. We must act quickly."

He looked at his son, who was still watching him with faint apprehension. "I would never harm you or your mother, Kipling," he said in a quiet tone.

Kip lost his rigid posture. "I know that. It's just,

well, you look sort of scary like that." He laughed
self-consciously. "I'll bet Dan Smith is still running!"
he added suddenly.

"I hope he runs off the flight deck," Edris said
under her breath.

Before Rhemun could speak, he was joined by
four men in Holconcom uniform. One of them was
Jones.

Edris looked past Rhemun to the Holconcom,
while Kip stood silently, fascinated. "Hi, Jones!
Good to see you again!"

"Dr. Mallory," Jones acknowledged, with a careful glance at Rhemun. "Good to see you, too."

That telling comment went right over Kip's head
as he was introduced to the men. He was so excited
that he could barely stand still. This Cehn-Tahr
that he knew so well, who had listened to his woes,
helped him train for combat, who was his friend, was
the commander of the Holconcom! It was a boy's
dream come true.

"I didn't expect you to be here so soon," Kip told
Rhemun. "You said it might be another day."

"You knew he was coming?" Edris said to her son.

He grimaced. "Well, yes, he told me this morning
that he'd be here soon, but not why."

"Told you, how?" she asked.

Rhemun sighed. "That is not a question we have
time to discuss," he told her. "We must move you,
and immediately. Things have happened that threaten
both your lives."

"Move me? Threaten us? My job!" Edris blurted out.

"Our ambassador will notify your employer and help replace you. He will also close out your apartment here and do all that is necessary. The Holconcom will pack your things. Show them what you must take with you, but only necessities," he cautioned. "We still travel light in the *Morcai*."

"The *Morcai*?" Kip burst out. "I'm going to get to see her?"

"You will travel to Memcache in her," Rhemun said gently.

"The home planet of the Cehn-Tahr," Kip said with reverence.

"How did you know that?" Edris asked.

The boy looked stunned. "I don't know."

Rhemun was beaming. He knew. "Hurry," he said.

Edris and Kip went to their respective rooms, with the Holconcom in tow, and started packing.

THE *MORCAI*, A huge copper-colored saucer ship, sat in her berth in the spaceport, waiting. Rhemun and Edris, Kip and the rest, alighted from the city transport and moved quickly to the berth.

"Hahnson and Stern will be waiting inside, and I am certain the reunion will be emotional," Rhemun said with resignation. "It will be necessary for me to be elsewhere during it, but please be brief."

Edris laughed self-consciously. "Okay. Come on, Kip."

"Reunion?" Kip asked. "And he'll have to wait outside…?"

"It's a long story," she said. "Later."

They marched onto the deck. And there was Hahnson, big and husky, and Holt Stern, dark and smiling. She ran to them, hugging them both with enthusiasm.

"It's so good to see you reprobates!" she exclaimed, laughing. "It's been so long!"

"Years," Stern agreed, grinning. "Good to see you, too, Mallory."

"Very good. And that's the boy?" Hahnson added, looking past her to Kip. "My gosh, he's almost grown!"

"This is my son, Kipling," she said. "I told him that his father was a human fighter pilot who died in the war, so you don't need to pretend you don't know." She said it with deliberation, and they nodded, but their faces showed the surprise. "You might, uh, pass that on to Jones and the others."

"I'll do that," Hahnson assured her. "Nice to meet you, Kip," he told the boy, and shook hands. So did Stern.

Kip was looking around, fascinated. "It's cold in here," he remarked.

"Cehn-Tahr metabolism." Hahnson chuckled. "Their body temp is three degrees higher than ours, so they cool the ship to make themselves more comfortable. You'll adapt."

"It's so big!"

"Not when we bring battle casualties aboard."
Hahnson sighed. "Med bay is full. Edris, I could
use some help, if you don't mind."

"Not at all," she assured him, which would also
get her out of Kip's way before he started asking
questions about how she knew these men.

Rhemun came down the deck and joined them.
"Kip, would you like to see the ship?"

"Oh, yes!" he exclaimed.

"I have to be on the bridge, but Stern can take
you to Btnu, and Btnu will show you around. Stern
is my AG."

"AG?"

"Astrogator," Stern translated, grinning. "I was
captain of my own ship, but now I'm the *Morcai*'s
astrogator."

"And necessary to liftoff, which is why he must
delegate your tour to my executive officer, Btnu,"
Rhemun explained. "I will see you later."

"Okay!"

Stern led him down the corridor, running. "We
always run from post to post," Stern explained. "It's
how we keep fit."

"This officer, Btnu, is he Cehn-Tahr?"

"He sure is. He's been with the ship ever since
it was commissioned, so he knows every nook and
cranny."

"Think I might get to see the *kelekom* unit?" Kip
asked hopefully.

Stern laughed. "I'm sure you will."

"I can't believe it. I've read about the *Morcai*. I never thought I'd actually even get to see it, much less get aboard it!"

"Here's Btnu." Stern stopped, with the boy. "Btnu, this is Kipling Mallory. Could you show him the ship, please? Rhemun said it would be all right."

"Of course!" Btnu bowed. "It is an honor, *Dakaashe*," he told the puzzled youth.

Stern caught the officer's eye. "And he knows that his human father was killed in the war serving as a fighter pilot," he added slowly. "So you don't need to worry about it slipping out."

Btnu was quick. "Certainly." He smiled at Kip. "Would you like to see weaponry or the comm unit or the *kelekom* unit first?"

"The *kelekom* unit. Please." The boy was all eyes.

"I'll see you later," Stern said. "I have to get to the bridge. See you, Btnu."

The alien smiled and nodded. He turned to Kipling. "Shall we get started?"

"Yes!"

THE *KELEKOM* UNIT had four operators. The intelligent machine race had been adapted to the Cehn-Tahr centuries past and now comprised the eyes and other senses of the *Morcai*. The machines, sentient, were bound to four operators. One of them Kip was surprised to see, was human.

"This is Jefferson Colby." Btnu introduced the dark-haired, smiling young man. "He came aboard just before Dtimun and Ruszel were bonded. He is the newest of the operators and a fine addition to the Holconcom. Colby, this is Kipling Mallory."

"Dr. Mallory's son?" Colby asked. "Nice to meet you!"

"Nice to meet you, too," Kip said, shaking hands.

He was introduced to the other operators. They also bowed, as Btnu had. Kip, lost for a reason, bowed back.

"The *kelekoms* are able to read star patterns and discern information that even our commanders cannot. They have senses which are developed far more sharply than ours. They bond to their operators for life." His eyes twinkled green as they met Colby's. "Colby's unit is female. She is very jealous of him."

"Thanks a lot." Colby laughed good-naturedly.

"Wow," Kip said. "That must be a fascinating job."

"Fascinating, and very rare. There are only four *kelekoms* in the three galaxies," Btnu explained. "Their race comes from Outside, from the Netherworlds."

He went on to elaborate about the nature of the creatures, how the big units could compact themselves to small glowing ovals that affixed to the operator's clothing and were portable.

Next was the communications center, where he was introduced to Lieutenant Commander Jennings, and then on to engineering, where Lieutenant Commander Higgins showed them around. Last, but not least, was weaponry. Kip got to know the operators of the huge emerillium plasma units that could wipe out an entire fleet.

They went into the ship's gym, where two Cehn-Tahr members of the Holconcom were practicing with the Kahn-Bo.

"Could I spar with them, do you think?" Kip asked.

"You know the Kahn-Bo?" Btnu asked.

"Yes. I trained with Master Cotashe on Araman."

Btnu was impressed. He moved toward the Holconcom and interrupted. "Pardon, please, but would one of you spar with Dr. Mallory's son?"

The taller of the two moved forward. He bowed to Kip. "It would be an honor, *Dakaashe*."

Kip was disconcerted that people kept bowing to him and treating him with so much respect. How did his mother know so many members of the crew? And that word, *Dakaashe*, what did it mean? Perhaps, he thought, it was a Cehn-Tahr custom. He bowed back. "Thanks!"

"We will not have Kahn-Bo clothing that will fit you," Btnu began.

"My kit is in my quarters, wherever they are," Kip volunteered.

Btnu smiled. "I will send for them."

A LITTLE LATER, garbed in his own covert garments, which his mother didn't know he had, and with his own prized Kahn-Bo staff, he walked onto the mat and bowed to his opponent, who returned the bow, but much lower.

They began.

The alien was a master, too. Kip recognized his ability, and fought to the best of his own. The match went on for minutes, during which the combatant and Btnu exchanged surprised glances. The alien made a sweep with his Kahn-Bo. Kip met it, whirled, went to the mat, swung his Kahn-Bo and felled his opponent. Quick as a light blast, he was standing over his opponent with the blunted end of the Kahn-Bo flush against the Holconcom soldier's throat.

"I yield, and gladly, to a master," the alien said at once, smiling.

Kip grinned back, and offered him a hand up. "Thanks, but I'm just a student."

The two aliens exchanged another glance. If they had spoken, they would have said, like father like son. But they didn't dare. Rhemun's instructions had been quite specific.

WHILE KIP WAS felling Holconcom in the gym, once the ship lifted, Rhemun went in search of Mallory. He called her aside when she finished treatment on the last wounded officer.

"You are wondering why I had to make you leave Araman," he told her in the small medical office, with the door closed. "You will not like the answer. One of my household, the newest member, has accidentally leaked information to a Rojok spymaster," he added. "He was horrified when he found out who the man really was. But the fact is, the rebel Rojok now know that Kip is my son. There was a plot to kidnap him and use him to threaten the Holconcom." He drew in a long breath. "They know that I would sacrifice anything to save my son."

"Was I in danger?" she asked.

His face hardened. "Yes. They would have killed you."

"Where will we go?" she asked miserably.

"To Memcache, but not to my estates, not until I settle the staff issues there. You will go to the fortress, to stay with Ruszel and Komak and Lady Caneese."

"It will be good to see them again," she said. "But Kip will know the truth. He'll know that I've lied to him, all these years."

He smiled. He'd had Kip turn off the white noise device, so he could read her thoughts. "Kip will forgive you." He went to the wall and turned on the vidnet. "Jennings, have you succeeded in reaching Memcache on scramble?"

A smiling face came over the screen. "Indeed I have, sir."

"You really are a magician," Rhemun said with praise.

"Thanks, sir. Here you go." He vanished from the screen, to be replaced by Caneese.

"Your Majesty," Mallory exclaimed. "It's good to see you again!"

"It is very good to see you, Edris. We are all much relieved to know that you are alive and well. I wanted to extend a personal invitation for you and your son to come and stay with us here at the fortress. Madeline and Dtimun are also delighted to find you well. And of course, Komak will be happy to have a playmate like himself."

"It will be a happy reunion for me," Edris said.

"And for me. Farewell."

The screen went dark.

Rhemun laughed. "She was concerned that you might not want to go to the fortress without an invitation. I knew better, but one does not argue with the Empress."

She smiled back. "I would have been concerned," she replied gently. "It was most kind of her."

"Yes." His eyes narrowed. "What of the male on Araman, the one that Kip told me was so persistent in his pursuit of you."

"The one who slapped Kipling?" she asked, and her own eyes flashed. "If I could have gotten my hands on a Gresham," she said with some heat.

He nodded. "I would have gladly killed him for what he did. But it would have involved unfortunate issues with the local authorities." He sighed.

"I think he got the point," she replied, and smiled.

His head lifted. He looked down at her with pure possession, and he morphed, showing her his true face. "It is good to have you back where you belong, Edris," he said softly. "I have missed you."

"I've missed you, too," she said, her eyes adoring him.

He touched her hair, her cheek. "The man bothered me," he murmured. "I hoped that you had not developed...feelings for him."

"After you?" she replied, and she laughed softly. "I could never have looked at another man. Another male," she qualified.

He drew in a long breath. "I should have marked you," he said heavily. "I meant to. But the mark can never be eradicated. One must be certain of the glyph." He smiled slowly. "I could not decide between two marks. Hesitation is usually a mistake." His face tautened. "Even a human male would understand the mark, if he saw it."

"You would never have to worry about that," she said, and the certainty was in her mind, open and vulnerable.

She felt better. He had meant to mark her. So he did feel something for her.

HE READ THAT THOUGHT. He started to tell her what he really felt, to explain further, but the door opened suddenly and Kipling ran into the room, still in his Kahn-Bo garb, excited, with Btnu standing just inside the medical bay.

"I beat both of them with my bo stick!" he explained.

Edris stared at him, stunned. "You're wearing a Kahn-Bo kit," she faltered. "How...?"

"I sent him to a master, on Araman," Rhemun

explained. "I am sorry to have done it without telling you." He turned to Kip. "Whom did you beat?"

Kip didn't know their names. He turned to Btnu.

"He beat Mekashe," he said with quiet pride.

"Mekashe?" Rhemun looked down at Kip with new respect. "He is the Kahn-Bo champion among the entire Holconcom, and the fleet."

Kip's eyes widened. "He is?"

"And you beat him." Rhemun laughed. "I myself can rarely beat him."

"Really?" Kip grinned.

"I don't understand any of this. How did you even contact him?" Edris asked. "It's so dangerous, to use even scrambled comm units…!"

"I spoke to him in his mind, as I am speaking to you, now, in yours," Rhemun said, showing her, at last, his telepathic skills.

She stared at him, aghast. "I didn't know you could do that," she told her son. "I kept saying it was only insight."

"I asked him not to tell you," Rhemun said quietly. "And it is a thing we have little time to discuss, at present. The new offensive is already underway. I asked special permission, which the Dectat provided, because of the threat to both of you. I must deposit you on Memcache and go at once to the front."

"Into battle?" Kip asked, suddenly realizing two things. His friend led the Holconcom, and the ship was going to war. "You won't get killed?" he asked plaintively.

"I will not get killed," he promised drily, and hoped it was a promise he could keep. "I must return to the bridge. I am very proud of you," he told Kip. "Your skills are formidable. I would like to see them for myself. Perhaps once the offensive is past, and we have a lull, I may test them."

Kip grinned. "Whenever you like."

"How will we get to the fortress?" Edris asked, not liking to admit that she was as worried about Rhemun as Kip was.

He saw it in her mind and smiled. "Ruszel will be waiting for you at the spaceport, along with Komak." He looked down at Kip. "He is only a little older than you, and he is also homeschooled. You will have things in common. He is skilled with the bo, himself."

"That will be great!"

"I will see you both again when we dock." Rhemun nodded, and he and Btnu left.

"Keeping secrets from me, huh?" she asked the boy. "And obviously, you know about the white noise sphere."

"Sorry, Mom," he said. "But..."

"Never mind. I'm not mad. Not really."

He hugged her. "That's good."

She hugged him back. She hoped this journey wasn't going to open too many cans of worms.

THERE WAS ONE more hurdle. She discussed it with

Rhemun a few hours before the *Morcai* was due to port at Memcache.

"Which of us is going to tell him who he is?" she asked quietly. "If we wait, he's more likely to find out from someone else."

"I realize that." He looked down at her with soft eyes. He reached out and touched her cheek, and then laid his forehead against hers with a sigh. "We have weathered many storms together, Edris," he said gently. "We will weather this one."

She reached up and locked her arms around him. "It was my fault. I should never have been tricked into leaving Memcache in the first place."

"I never blamed you. I still do not." His arms slid around her and pulled her close. "You are my mate. You will always be. You gave me a son. I have never known such joy, or such happiness, as I have had with you, even when we were apart."

Tears stung her eyes. "We've been apart longer than we were together."

"That will change." He bent his head. "I have… missed you," he whispered.

"And I've missed you!"

She clung to him, fighting down tears, while he bent over her, his cheek on her hair, rocking her in the silence of the room.

The door opened. Kip stood there, startled and curious, to see his mother in the arms of his friend. He didn't know quite what to say.

They noticed him at last. Rhemun lifted his head

with a sigh. "Kip," he said gently. "We must have a talk."

"Now?" Kip asked.

Rhemun nodded. He let Edris go.

"I'll be outside," she said gently. She smiled reassuringly at Kip and touched his shoulder on the way out.

Rhemun lifted the boy and perched him on a table, so that he could see his eyes.

"I know what you're going to say," Kip said. "You like my mother. I guess she likes you, too." He smiled. "It would make me happy, if the two of you were together. It's just that—" he bit his lip "—if you have kids of your own, you won't...well you won't dislike me, because I'm human, will you?" he asked, as if it mattered more than anything that he didn't lose Rhemun's friendship.

Rhemun touched the boy's face gently. "Kip, your mother is my mate," he said gently. "She has been, for many years."

"Your...but, there was my father... How did she...?" he began, confused.

Rhemun drew in a long breath. "This is the difficult part..."

There was a chime. Rhemun touched a spot on the bulkhead. "Yes?"

"The Rojoks are closing," Stern said formally. "Ten standard minutes before they overtake us."

"I will be there shortly," Rhemun promised.

He turned back to Kip. "The Rojoks are the rea-

son you and your mother have to be moved to Memcache."

"They're after Mom?" Kip asked worriedly.

"No. They are after you."

"Me?" Kip was astonished. "But, why?"

Rhemun looked him straight in the eye. "Because
your father commands the Holconcom."

"My...father." He blinked. "You mean, my father's not dead, and he leads the..." Kip broke off.
He stared at the big man with eyes that worshipped
him. "You mean, you...?"

Rhemun nodded.

Kip touched Rhemun's long, curly black hair.
"But...but I don't look like you," he said in almost
a whisper.

Rhemun smiled, touching the boy's hair. "No. You
look like your mother, who is beautiful. Your appearance pleases me very much."

"Part of me is Cehn-Tahr."

"Yes. We think that, perhaps, when you reach
puberty, those traits will advance in you. There is
only one other child of a human mother, and that is
Komak, who was born of Dr. Ruszel and Dtimun.
He, too, has human traits, and his eyes do not yet
change color."

"You are my father." Kip's hand tightened on Rhemun's hair. "My...father!"

He threw his arms around the big man and held
on for dear life, sobbing. Rhemun picked him up
and walked the floor with him, holding him, more

touched than he had been in his long life by the boy's reaction. His eyes closed. He, too, was fighting a display of strong emotion.

The door opened, but neither the boy nor the Cehn-Tahr heard it. Edris looked at her men, at her family, with eyes that also misted with tenderness. She smiled and gently closed the door behind her.

A LONG TIME LATER, Kip came out of the room with Rhemun to find his mother wearing a red uniform.

His mouth fell open.

She shrugged. "I just wanted to see if I could still get into it," she murmured with twinkling eyes.

"You…you are, you were, Holconcom?" Kip faltered.

She nodded. "I took Madeline Ruszel's place as Cularian specialist when she bonded with Dtimun. I served with your father until we bonded and you were on the way."

"Gosh." Kip could hardly take it all in. "You were a combat soldier…"

"Of a sort." She looked up at Rhemun with warm, melting eyes. "Your father and I had some interesting adventures."

"Some of which almost ended in tragedy," Rhemun added quietly. He hid those memories from Kipling, who was too young to see such carnage.

"Can I be a Holconcom, when I grow up?" Kip asked excitedly.

Rhemun chuckled. "Of course. Your Clan status

will give you command of it one day, unless Komak decides to pursue that course. If he does, you will be his executive officer."

"Does he look like me?" Kip asked.

"No," came the soft reply. "But your features may change at adolescence," Rhemun replied.

"The Cehn-Tahr won't like me because I look human..." he began.

"Don't be absurd." Rhemun laughed. "Your mother is a legend among them already. You see, she saved a high-ranking rebel Rojok officer on Ondar. As it happens, he is the foster brother of Chacon."

Edris caught her breath. "I didn't know!"

"They speak of you on Enmehkmehk in respectful whispers." Rhemun chuckled. "You speak their Holy Tongue and you saved an enemy from certain death. That enemy is now your greatest admirer." His face hardened. "Fortunately for him, he is bonded and has a family and will never look at you with covetous eyes. In such case," he added in a husky undertone, "I would be forced to kill him."

Kip shook his head. "My mother, the Holcon-com." He let out a breath. "And I thought you hated the military."

"She meant only to protect you." Rhemun defended her. "She had to keep your true identity secret. If it had become known that I was your father, your life would have been in great danger."

"But why didn't we live with you?" Kip faltered.

"This is why." Rhemun showed him the images

of the years he and Edris were apart, and how, and why, they came to be separate.

"Devroshe, he killed himself?" Kip asked.

Rhemun nodded. His eyes were dark with anger. "I would have gladly done it for him, had I known at the time how he betrayed me."

"But we're together now," Kip said. He went close to his father. "And we won't ever leave you again, will we, Mom?"

She went close, too. "Never while I breathe," she promised.

Rhemun put his arms around them both. "But I must leave you, only for a brief time," he said.

"You promised not to get killed," Kip reminded him firmly.

Rhemun smiled. "Yes. I promised."

"Okay." Kip grinned and hugged him.

CHAPTER FOURTEEN

IT WAS A happy reunion on Memcache for Mallory, when they were met at the spaceport by Madeline Ruszel and Komak.

"Dtimun would have come, too, but there's some financial crisis at the Dectat." Madeline laughed as she hugged Mallory. "You'll see him tonight, anyway, at the fortress. The emperor and Lady Caneese will be there, also."

"The emperor?" Kip exclaimed. "I'm going to meet the emperor?"

"Yes," Rhemun replied, smiling.

"Gosh!" Kip looked at his mother worriedly. "What will we wear, Mom? We don't have that sort of clothes…"

"You will have," Madeline told him. "Come on. I've got a skimmer waiting for us."

Rhemun gave his family a final embrace, reluctantly letting them go.

"You be careful," Edris instructed him.

His eyes laughed at her. He was in his true form, which Kip still found a little intimidating, but he wasn't afraid. He reached up to his father to be lifted and embraced warmly.

"We'll be here when you get back," Kip promised. His eyes were worried. "You have to come back."

Rhemun hugged him again. "I will exercise great caution," he promised, and grinned as he put his son on the ground.

"Can I still talk to you?" Kip asked. "In your mind, I mean?"

"Of course."

"Okay, then."

Rhemun took his leave of Ruszel and Komak formally, and went back to the *Morcai*. He stopped at the entrance to the military berth of the spaceport and sent a last, hungry look toward his family before he went into the building.

Edris herded Kip after the others into the skimmer.

"I read about you, Dr. Ruszel," Kip said, impressed. "There wasn't much on the nexus, but they said you were the first woman ever to serve on a Holconcom ship."

"Yes, I was." She smiled. "And let me tell you, the former commander and I were notorious for our disagreements."

"Were you at Ahkmau?" he asked hesitantly.

She nodded solemnly. "It was a nightmare. We almost lost Dtimun."

"But Dad got you all out of the prison camp,"

Komak said proudly and grinned. "I wish I could have helped!"

"Me, too!" Kip enthused.

"You two weren't even a possibility at that time," Madeline mused. "But I'm sure you would have been formidable. I understand that Kip is excellent with the Kahn-Bo, too," she told her son.

"I can't wait to spar with you," Komak told Kip. "And Dad had them build me this virtual holon, so that I can command armies in battle. You can play with me. It will be great to have someone to talk to," he added. "Not that I don't have people to talk to," he assured his mother. "I mean, somebody like me, my own age."

"I know what you mean," Madeline said complacently. She smiled. "Edris, you've come a long way from that nervous young Lieutenant Commander who had to be dragged aboard the *Morcai*," she teased.

Edris laughed. "And you've come a long way from having your commander blackmail you about your contraband coffee."

The boys wanted to hear all about it, so all the way to the fortress, Madeline told them about the early days of the unit and Edris's first experience of space combat. They listened so attentively that they barely noticed when the skimmer touched down at the fortress.

Kip was stunned at the scope of it. "It's like a castle," he said with awe. "I read about them on the nexus. They were on ancient Earth. Kings and emperors lived there."

"This is where our emperor lives, Kip," Madeline said gently.

"My grandfather," Komak said proudly. "And not only mine…"

"Komak," Madeline cautioned.

"Ooops," he chuckled. "Sorry."

"What?" Kip asked, and tried to probe his new friend's mind. He met a total block.

"Sorry," Komak told him. "I'll have to teach you how to block people, too." He glanced mischeviously at his mother. "There will be things you won't want your relatives to know about."

"You listen here, I may not be a telepath, but your father is, and your grandfather likes me and if I ask them…" Madeline warned.

Komak held up both hands. "Okay, Mom. I'll be good."

She made a face at him, and then laughed affectionately.

KIP WAS STILL exploring the grounds, alone. He turned a corner and came face-to-face with a tall Cehn-Tahr woman in long blue robes with gold trim. She was in her true form, her silver hair down to her waist in back. She was holding a single flower. She smiled.

Kip bowed. He didn't know who she was, but she was very pretty. "If I'm trespassing, I'm very sorry," he said formally.

She cocked her head and studied him intently. "You are Kipling."

He smiled. "Yes, ma'am."

She shook her head. "You are...unique," she said in a soft tone, and her eyes had an odd golden hue, like Kip's father's when he was with Kip or Edris. "A fine young man."

"Thank you," he said hesitantly.

"You do not know me," she said in his mind. There was amusement in her tone. "I am Lady Caneese."

"The Empress." He was spellbound. He bowed again. "Your Highness," he said reverently.

She tipped his face up with a gentle hand. "Lady Caneese," she corrected, and her laugh was like silver bells. "Here, I am only family. Have you met Rognan?"

He frowned. "Rognan? Oh! The Meg-Raven! Kanthor told me about him," he said excitedly.

"He wishes to see you. Come."

She led him toward the fortress, through towering trees with green trunks and spindly leaves, over thick and lush grass dotted here and there with alien flowers like the one she was holding.

"You must not fear for your father," she said, interrupting his thoughts. "I can see the future," she added solemnly. "Your father will live long, like your mother. And," she added with a smile, "you will not be an only child."

"Now I remember," he said, turning to her. "You have the second sight. You're a seer."

She nodded. "I am the only one in my entire Clan with such a gift. It has been both blessing and curse at times." She smiled sadly. "I could not see your mother, or Rhemun would have found you both so much sooner. Any of us could have touched her mind, if she had not used the white noise device so efficiently."

"Dad taught me to turn it off when he and I were talking from a long distance," he said. "If I'd only known…!"

She put an affectionate hand on his shoulder. "The past is an illusion. We cannot touch it. We must live in the time we inhabit."

He smiled at her.

"You are happy with your father."

"So happy," he replied. "He was my friend long before I knew who he really was. I wish… I wish I looked like him," he said sadly.

"You look like your mother. She is truly lovely. You must not wish away your individuality."

He nodded. "I'll try."

"You still have some fear of us," she teased. She morphed back into the more familiar form that Cehn-Tahr used with outworlders. "Is this easier for you?"

"It just takes a little getting used to, but I like the way you look very much," he said, and smiled.

"You do? Well, then…" And she morphed back, laughing.

They walked into a side porch, an open patio, and there was a huge black bird with glowing yellow eyes.

"Rognan!" Kip exclaimed.

The bird turned toward him and made a soft clicking sound. He jumped down from his perch, gingerly because he had a twisted leg, and clomped over to Kip. He towered over the boy. "You are Kipling," he said in Standard. "Many welcomes!"

Kip grinned. "Thank you!"

"I have heard of you from Kanthor. He speaks of you with great praise. He says you will be one day great warrior."

"I hope to be like my father," Kip said with pride. He studied the big bird with utter fascination. "You're so big," he exclaimed.

Rognan chuckled. "My tribe was even bigger. But I have lived here for many, many years. This is now home." He went to Caneese and laid his feathered head against her forehead. "It is warm affection that I give you."

"And that I return," Caneese said, stroking his head. She and the bird had been enemies for almost a generation. But when Ruszel was pregnant with Komak, they made their peace. From enemies they became friends.

"We should join the others," Caneese said gently. "Rognan, you may come if you wish."

"Thank you. Is Kanthor also coming?" he asked Kip.

Kip closed his eyes and searched for Kanthor

in his mind. There was a sudden sharp sound. He opened his eyes, and Kanthor was seated next to Rognan.

"I still can't figure out how you do that," Kip exclaimed.

Kanthor chuckled. "It is secret tech that we share with the Nagaashe."

"Oh, the Nagaashe! I know some live here. Do you think I might get to meet them?" he asked.

"Of a certainty," Caneese answered for the big cat. "But later. Come."

THEY ALL GATHERED in the great room. Above the mantel, above a huge roaring blaze in the fireplace, was a painting of a warrior wielding an energy sword. On the mantel was a moving portrait of a young woman, laughing.

"Lyceria," Caneese told Kip, identifying the woman in the portrait. "My daughter. She is married to the Rojok leader, Chacon."

"A truly great warrior," Kip said with admiration. "They tell stories of him. And the emperor."

Caneese smiled. "No warrior has ever been the equal of Tnurat," she said softly, and her eyes went suddenly to the doorway.

A tall, broad-shouldered man with white hair, wearing a blue uniform with gold trim and many medals, came into the room. He morphed into the true Cehn-Tahr form and approached Kipling.

"Finally," he said gently. "It is an honor to meet you at last, my boy."

"Thank you, sir. Your Highness." Kipling bowed deeply, overwhelmed. This was the emperor of all the Cehn-Tahr and he was actually speaking to him!

"No bowing, no formal addresses." Tnurat chuckled. "Here, we are family."

He moved into the room and drew his fingers down Caneese's cheek before he laid his forehead against hers. He did the same with the other occupants of the room and, finally, Kip.

"It is how we greet each other," he explained to the boy.

"Except, usually, we salute," Dtimun remarked humorously as he joined them. He stopped in front of Kipling. "Sometimes," he added with a grin at his father, because when he led the Holconcom the two were enemies, and his men had standing orders never to salute the emperor. "You look like your father," he said.

Kip's mouth flew open.

"In coloring, not so much," Dtimun conceded. "But you have his mouth and his nose. And," he added on a laugh, "his hair."

"His hair, sir?" Kip asked, and bowed.

Dtimun chuckled. "Your father was forced by his fellows in the *kehmatemer*, the Emperor's Imperial Guard, to wear a helmet. The Rojoks put a price on his head because of his massive head of hair."

"Really?" Kip asked, excited. "And you think I look like my dad?"

Dtimun smiled. "You do."

"Thanks. Nobody else thought so," Kip faltered. "I want my father to be proud of me."

"He should be. You beat Mekashe at the Kahn-Bo, something even I have never been able to do!"

Kip's eyes lit up. The comment made him feel ten feet tall. He didn't stop smiling for a long time.

LATER, WHEN THEY'D eaten and Kip was outside with Lady Caneese looking at the beautiful glowing night bugs, Edris joined them.

"There must be a formal bonding, Edris," Caneese said gently.

"Rhemun mentioned that," Edris replied. "Is it because of his rank?"

"Yes," Caneese said. "This is required."

Edris was uneasy. "I'm not comfortable in crowds," she faltered.

Caneese put a gentle hand on her shoulder. "This will be difficult, of course. But you have become revered by our people. Many want to see you, and Kipling. It will be a happy occasion."

"It won't matter, that I'm human…?"

Caneese actually embraced her. "My son's mate is human, did you notice?" she teased. "I find you, as a species, utterly fascinating."

"Thank you," Edris said softly.

"This will require a trip to the weave master tomorrow," Caneese added. "You must be dressed appropriately. It will be quite formal."

"Now I'm scared." Edris laughed.

"There's nothing to be nervous about," Madeline assured her as she joined them. "I had to do it, too."

"Yes, but you were marrying into the Royal Clan," Edris began.

Caneese cleared her throat. "Your mate commands the Holconcom. It must be done."

Edris sighed. "All right, then. I'll try not to embarrass you all."

"That would not be possible," Caneese assured her. "Everything will be perfect. You will see."

THE GOWN WAS fit for an empress. It was similar to the one Madeline had worn at her own bonding, royal blue with gold trim, and what seemed like a fortune in jewels. They dotted the gown and were echoed in the necklace and earrings and tiara that went with the ensemble. Edris was worried that she was overdressed. But Caneese assured her that it was quite tasteful.

Rhemun returned unexpectedly. Edris and Kipling ran to him, hugging him as if he'd come back from the dead.

He laughed delightedly at the attention and scooped them both up.

"Dtimun says I look like you!" Kip burst out. "He says I have your mouth and your nose."

Rhemun rubbed his cheek against the boy's. "So you do."

"I wish I had gold skin and black hair, though," Kip added.

"I am quite content with the way you look, my son," he replied, ruffling Kip's hair.

"Me, too," Edris said dreamily, pressed to Rhemun's heart.

"Do I get to go to the ceremony?" Kip asked.

"Of course," Rhemun told him. "You will sit with the Imperial family."

"I will? Really? Oh, gosh!"

Rhemun and Edris chuckled. Kipling was so overwhelmed that he was actually quiet for five whole minutes.

THE CEREMONY WAS attended by every race known to the three galaxies. Kipling watched in awe as a pair of bonded Nagaashe took their place outside the aisle. There were Altairians and Rojoks—there was Chacon himself! The famous Rojok field marshal sat beside Kip with his mate, Lyceria, and grinned at him. Kipling stopped looking at the other attendees. He'd read as much about Chacon as he could find. He just stared at him, stunned. Then the emperor walked in, to the sound of music, walking down the aisle attended by his Imperial Guard. He joined the rest of the family on the raised platform. He winked at Kip as he took his seat on the throne next to Lady Caneese. Kip smothered a grin.

Rhemun stood at the altar, regally attired in blue robes with gold trim and a crown about half the size of the one worn by Dtimun. Kipling was surprised at that. His mother was beautiful in her own robes. She wore a tiara. Kip wanted to ask why, but there was utter silence in the huge cathedral.

"You will understand soon," Rhemun said in his mind.

"Okay, Dad," he replied.

There was the faintest chuckle that only he could hear.

Edris joined him at the podium where an Allfaith representative and a high Dectat official stood. They read the service, very solemnly, and first Rhemun and then Edris repeated the words of bonding in the Holy Tongue.

And they were officially bonded. They walked down the aisle together in a solemn procession and into a small antechamber. The guests walked out of the building. Rhemun turned to Edris, drew her tightly into his arms and bent to kiss her with barely contained hunger.

"It's been...so long," she whispered.

"A lifetime."

She kissed him back. There was a slight cough. Flushed, she withdrew from his arms and turned. The emperor, the empress, Princess Lyceria, Chacon, Dtimun, Madeline, Kip and Komak were all standing there, along with Sfilla.

Sfilla, laughing, came forward and embraced

Edris warmly. "I almost didn't make it in time," she told her. "I had to come from a far place. I am so happy to greet you as my daughter, as I have once before, but now more formally."

"And I am happy to greet you as my mother," Edris said, hugging her back.

"Do you not think it time that you told her?" the emperor asked Rhemun with faint amusement.

Rhemun grimaced. He drew in a short breath as he looked down at her. "I have a confession to make."

"You robbed a vendor?" Edris mused.

He shook his head. "No. It is not that sort of confession."

Sfilla raised an eyebrow. "Tell her."

He shrugged. "My father was Alkaasar."

Edris stared at him blankly. Then it registered. Alkaasar had defied an empire to keep his son from being used in genetic experimentation. He was an outlaw to some, a hero to others. But most important of all, he had been Dtimun's older brother. Which meant...

She turned and stared at Rhemun with eyes so wide they seemed like plates.

"What is it?" Kip asked, concerned. He moved to his mother's side. "Mom?"

She swallowed. "Kipling, the emperor is your great-grandfather."

Kip stared at her. "Huh?"

She looked at Tnurat, who was almost rolling with laughter. So were Caneese and the others.

"Do you remember that everyone called Kip *'Da-kaashe'*?" Rhemun asked her. "It means 'son of the royal Clan.'"

"You never said!" Edris gasped.

He touched her cheek gently. "It was not necessary. You loved a soldier first. That was important to me, because in the past, females wanted me for position and wealth."

She shook her head. "I don't know what to say," she faltered. She turned and looked at the others, who were all smiling with affection.

"You say, here I belong," Caneese told her. "Because we are your family."

Edris tried to answer, but she was crying. Rhemun held her close. "And family," he whispered, "is more important than life itself."

"Yes." She hugged him. "Yes!"

Kipling didn't say anything. He was too busy staring at the emperor, whose thoughts were full of amusement and warm affection. It was a lot for a boy to take in, especially one brought up in a situation bordering poverty. His father was the emperor's grandson. His heart swelled with pride. For the first time in his life, he had a real family.

RHEMUN'S ESTATE WAS as beautiful as Edris remembered it. There were familiar faces. The female servants who had been so kind to her were back, smiling to welcome her. There was a new man in Devroshe's place, a kind man with gray hair who welcomed her with a basket of her favorite flowers and knelt at her feet.

Kip went off to explore the grounds with Komak, who was his constant companion now. Edris and Rhemun found privacy in their bedroom.

They were both hungry. It had been years. They barely made it to the bed, and the fever they kindled together was so hot and fierce that Edris almost lost consciousness. Rhemun had forgotten about the dravelzium, so there were some bruises and minor pulled muscles, but Edris laughed as she mended them.

He lay on his back, sated, his laughing eyes on her flushed face. "Well?" he asked.

"I'm looking, I'm looking." She tuned her wrist scanner and held it to her belly. She caught her breath as she watched the colors change. She peered at Rhemun with a secret smile. "Guess."

"A girl." He chuckled.

She just shook her head. "How you could know…?"

"I have been meditating," he teased. He pulled her down into his arms. "And now we must become, again, good friends while we wait for Kip's little sister to be born."

"But we'll have the memories," she reminded him.

He turned and brushed his cheek lovingly against hers. "And what memories!" he whispered huskily.

While she was drinking in his words, he bent his head suddenly and she felt his teeth on her, just below her collarbone. What should have been painful was…exquisite. She moaned softly as he finished and lifted his head.

He studied his work critically, and then smiled. He bent and licked the wounds, sealing them. "Stone," he whispered.

She frowned. "Stone?"

He nodded toward her chest. "The glyph. It is the glyph in Cehn-Tahr for stone."

She cocked her head. "Why?"

"Because it is almost eternal. Like what I feel for you," he whispered.

"Oh." She caught her breath at the look on his face. "Stone." She pulled his mouth down to hers. "Forever."

He smiled against her lips. "Forever."

And for a few minutes, they were lost in their own world of dreams. Until the loud voices of two little boys laughing beneath the window brought them back to the present. They smiled at each other. Because soon there would be three voices, laughing. And one of them would be the second female born into the Royal Clan in its entire history.

* * * * *

Read on for a sneak preview of
DEFENDER,
a stunning story of second-chance love
in Diana Palmer's LONG, TALL TEXANS *series.*

CHAPTER ONE

ISABEL GRAYLING STUCK her head around the study door and peered in. The big desk was empty. The chair hadn't been moved from its position, carefully pushed underneath. Everything on the oak surface was neatly placed; not a pencil wasn't neatly in a cup; not a scrap of paper was out of line. She let out a breath. Her father wasn't home, but the desk kept the fanatical order he insisted on, even when he wasn't here.

She darted out of the office with a relieved sigh and pushed back the long tangle of her reddish-gold hair. Blue, blue eyes were filled with relief. She wrinkled her straight nose, where just a tiny line of freckles ran over its bridge. Her name was Isabel, but only Paul Fiore called her that. To everyone else, she was Sari, just as her sister, Meredith, was always called Merrie.

"Well?" her younger sister, Merrie, asked in a whisper.

Sari turned. The other girl was slender, like herself, but Merrie had hair almost platinum blond, straight and to her waist in back. Her eyes, like Sari's, were

blue, but paler, more the color of a winter sky. Both
girls looked like their late mother, who was pretty
but not beautiful.

"Gone!" Sari said with a wicked grin.

Merrie let out a sigh of relief. "Paul said that
Daddy was going to Germany for a few weeks.
Maybe he'll find some other people to harass once
he's in Europe."

Sari went up to the shorter girl and hugged her.
"It will be all right."

Merrie fought tears. "I only wanted to have my
hair trimmed, not cut. Honestly, Sari, he's so unreasonable…!"

"I know." She didn't dare say more. Paul had told
her things in confidence that she couldn't bear to
share with her baby sister. Their father was far more
dangerous than either of them had known.

To any outsider, the Grayling sisters had everything. Their father was rich beyond any dream. They
lived in a gray stone mansion on acres and acres
of land in Comanche Wells, Texas, where their father kept Thoroughbred horses. Rather, his foreman
kept them. The old man was carefully maneuvered
away from the livestock by the foreman, who'd once
had to save a horse from the man. Darwin Grayling
had beaten animals before. It was rumored that he'd
beaten his wife. She died of a massive concussion,
but Grayling swore that she'd fallen. Not many people in Comanche Wells or nearby Jacobsville, Texas,

wanted to argue with a man who could buy and sell anybody in the state.

That hadn't stopped local physician Jeb "Copper" Coltrain from asking for a coroner's inquest and making accusations that Grayling's description of the accident didn't match the head injuries. But Copper had been called out of town on an emergency by a friend and when he returned, the coroner's inquest was over and accidental death had been put on the death certificate. Case closed.

The Grayling girls didn't know what had truly happened. Sari had been in high school, Merrie in grammar school, when their mother died. They knew only what their father had told them. They were much too afraid of him to ask questions.

Now, Merrie was in her last year of high school and Sari was a senior in college. Sari had majored in history in preparation for a law degree. She went to school in San Antonio, but wasn't allowed to live on campus. Her father had her driven back and forth every day. It was the same with Merrie. Darwin wasn't having either of his daughters around other people. He'd fought and won when Sari tried to move onto the college campus. He was wealthy and his children were targets, he'd said implacably, and they weren't going anywhere without one of his security people.

Which was why Sari and Paul Fiore, head of security for the Grayling Corporation, were such good friends. They'd known each other since Paul moved down from New Jersey to take the job, while Sari was in her last year of high school. Paul drove the girls to school every day.

He'd wondered, but only to Sari, why her father hadn't placed them both in private schools. Sari knew, but she didn't dare say. It was because her father didn't want them out of his sight, where they might say something that he didn't approve of. They knew too much about him, about his business, about the way he treated animals and people.

He was paranoid about his private life. He had women, Sari was certain of it, but never around the house. He had a mistress. She worked for the federal government. Paul had told her, in confidence. He wasn't afraid of Darwin Grayling—Paul wasn't afraid of anyone. But he liked his job and he didn't want to go back to the FBI. He'd worked for the Bureau years ago. Nobody knew why he'd suddenly given up a lucrative government job to become a rent-a-cop for a Texas millionaire in a small town at the back of beyond. Paul never said, either.

Sari touched Merrie's slightly bruised cheek and winced. "I warned you about talking back, honey," she said worriedly. "I'm so sorry!"

"My mouth and my brain don't stay connected," Merrie laughed, but bitterly. Her blue eyes met her sister's. "If we could just tell somebody!"

"We could, and Daddy would make sure they never worked again," Sari said. "That's why I've never told Paul anything..." She bit her lip.

But Merrie knew already. She hugged the taller girl. "I won't tell him. I know how you feel about Paul."

"I wish he felt something for me," Sari said with a long sigh. "He's always been affectionate with me. He takes good care of me. But it's... I don't know how to say it. Impersonal?" She drew away, her expression sad. "He just doesn't get close to people. He dated that out-of-town auditor two years ago, remember? She called here over and over, and he wouldn't talk to her. He said he just wanted someone to go to the movies with, and she was looking at wedding rings." She laughed involuntarily. She shook her head. "He won't get involved."

"Maybe he was involved, and something happened," her sister said softly. "He looks like the sort of person who dives into things headfirst. You know, all or nothing. Maybe he lost somebody he loved, Sari."

"I guess that would explain a lot." She moved away, grimacing. "It's just my luck, to go loopy over a man who thinks a special relationship is something you have with a vehicle."

"It's a very nice vehicle," Merrie began.

"It's a truck, Merrie!" she interrupted, throwing up her hands. "Gosh, you'd think it was a child the way he takes care of it. Special mats, taking it to the car wash once a week. He even waxes it himself." She glowered. "It's a truck!"

"I like trucks," Merrie said. "That cowboy who

worked for us last year had a fancy black one. He wanted to take me to a movie." She shivered. "I thought Daddy was going to kill him."

"So did I." Sari swallowed, hard. She wrapped her arms around her chest. "The cowboy went all the way to Arizona, they said, to make sure Daddy didn't have him followed. He was scared."

"So was I," Merrie confessed. "You know, I'm eighteen years old and I've never gone on a date with a real boy. I've never been kissed, except on the cheek."

"Join the club," her sister laughed softly. "Well, one day we'll break out of here. We'll escape!" she said dramatically. "I'll hire a team of mercenaries to hide us from Daddy!"

"With what money?" Merrie asked sadly. "Neither of us has a dime. Daddy makes sure we can't even get a part-time job to make money. You can't even live at your college campus. I'll bet that gets you talked about."

"It does," Sari confided. "But they figure our father is just eccentric because he's so rich, and they let it go. I don't have any real friends, anyway."

"Just me," Merrie teased.

Sari hugged her. "Just you. You're my best friend, Merrie."

"You're mine, too, even if you are my sister."

Sari drew back. "One day, things will change."

"You've been saying that since we were in grammar school. It hasn't."

"It will."

Merrie touched her cheek and winced. "I told Paul I fell down the steps," she said, when she noticed her sister's worried expression.

"I wonder if he believed you," Sari replied solemnly. "He's not afraid of Daddy."

"He should be. I've heard Daddy has this friend back East," Merrie told her. "He's in with some underworld group. They say he's killed people, that he'll do anything for money." She bit her lower lip. "I don't want Paul hurt any more than you do. The less he knows about what goes on here when he's off duty, the better. He couldn't save us, anyway. He could only be dragged down with us."

"He wouldn't let Daddy hurt us, if he knew," Sari replied.

"So he won't know."

"Someone else might tell him," Sari began.

"Not anybody who works here," Merrie sighed. "Mandy's kept house for over twenty years, since before you were born. She knows stuff, but she's afraid to tell. She has a brother who does illegal things. Daddy told her he could have her brother sent to prison if she ever opened her mouth. She's afraid of him." She looked up. "I'm afraid of him."

Sari winced. "Yes. Me, too."

"I don't ever want to get married, Sari," the younger woman said huskily. "Not ever!"

"One day, you might, if the right man comes along."

Merrie laughed. "He's not likely to come along while Daddy's around, or he'll be leaving in a body bag in the back of a pickup truck."

The dark humor in that statement sent them both into gales of laughter.

PAUL FIORE WAS ITALIAN. He also had a Greek grandmother. It accounted for his olive complexion and thick, jet-black hair and large brown eyes. He was handsome, too, tall and broad-shouldered, muscular without making a point of it. He walked like a panther, light on his feet, and he had a quick mind. He'd been in law enforcement most of his life until he took the job with the Grayling Corporation. He'd wanted to get as far away from federal work—and New Jersey—as he could. Jacobsville, Texas, came close to his ideal place.

He was fond of the girls, Merrie and Sari, and he took charge of the house when Mr. Grayling was out of the country. He could handle any problem that came up. His main responsibility was to keep the girls safe, but he also kept a close watch on the property, especially the very expensive Thoroughbreds Grayling raised for sale.

The housekeeper, Mandy Swilling, was fond of him. She was always baking him the cinnamon cookies he liked so much, and tucking little surprises into his truck when he had to be away on business.

"You've got me ruined," he accused her one morning. "I'll be so spoiled that I'll never be able to get along in the world if I ever get fired from here."

"Mr. Darwin will never fire you," Mandy said confidently. "You keep your mouth shut and you don't ask questions."

His eyes narrowed. "Odd reason to keep a man on, isn't it?"

"Not around here," she said heavily.

He stared at her, his dark eyes twinkling. "You know where all the bodies are buried, huh? That why you still have work?"

She didn't laugh, as he'd expected her to. She just glanced at him and winced. "Don't even joke about things like that, Mr. Paul."

He groaned at her form of addressing him.

"Now, now," she said. "I've always called the boss Mr. Darwin, just like I call the foreman Mr. Edward. It's a way of speaking that Southern folk are raised with. You, being a Yankee…" She stopped and grinned. "Sorry. I meant to say, you, being a northerner, wouldn't know about that."

"I guess so."

"You still sound like a person born up North."

He shrugged and grinned back at her. "We are what we are."

"I suppose so."

He watched her work at making rolls for lunch. She wasn't much to look at. She was about fifty pounds overweight, had short silver hair and dark eyes, and she was slightly stooped over from years of working in gardens with a hoe. But she could cook! The woman was a magician in the kitchen. Paul remembered his tiny little grandmother, making ravioli and antipasto when he was a child, the scent of flour and oil that always seemed to cling to her. Kitchens were comforting to a child who had no real home. His father had worked for a local mob boss, and done all sorts of illegal things, like most of the rest of his family. His mother had died miserable, watching her husband run around with an endless parade of other women, shuddering every time the big boss or law enforcement came to the front door. After his mother died and his father went to jail for the twentieth time, Paul went to live with his little Greek grandmother. He and his cousin Mikey had stayed with her until they were almost grown. Paul watched Mikey go the same route his father had, attached like a tick to the local big crime boss. His father never came around. In fact, he couldn't remember seeing his father more than a dozen times before the man died in a shootout with a rival mob.

It was why he'd gone into law enforcement at seventeen, fresh out of high school. He hated the hold crime had on his family. He hoped he could make a difference, help clean up his old neighborhood and free it from the talons of organized crime. He went from local police right up into the FBI. He'd felt that he was unstoppable, that he could fight crime and win. Pride had blinded him to the reality of life. It had cost him everything.

Still, he missed the Bureau sometimes. But the memories had been lethal. He couldn't face them, not even now, years after the tragedy that had sent him running from New Jersey to Texas on a job tip from a coworker. He'd given up dreams of a home and all the things that went with it. Now, it was just the job, doing the job. He didn't look forward. Ever. One Day at a Time was his credo.

"Why are you hiding in here?" Mandy asked suddenly, breaking into his thoughts.

"It's that obvious, huh?" he asked, the New Jersey accent still prevalent even after the years he'd spent in Texas.

"Yes, it is."

He sipped the black coffee she'd placed in front of him at the table. "Livestock foreman's got a daughter. She came with him today."

"Oh, dear," Mandy replied.

He shrugged. "I took her to lunch at Barbara's Cafe a few weeks ago. Just a casual thing. I met her at the courthouse. She works there. She decided that I was looking for a meaningful relationship. So now she's over here every Saturday like clockwork, hanging out with her dad."

"That will end when Mr. Darwin comes back," she said with feeling. "He doesn't like strangers on the place, even strangers related to people who work here."

He smiled sadly. "Or it will end when I lose my temper and start cursing in Italian."

"You look Italian," she said, studying him.

He chuckled. "You should see my cousin Mikey. He could have auditioned for *The Godfather*. I've got Greek in me, too. My grandmother was from a little town near Athens. She could barely speak English at all. But could she cook! Kind of like you," he added with twinkling eyes. "She'd have liked you, Mandy."

Her hard face softened. "You never speak of your parents."

"I try not to think about them too much. Funny, how we carry our childhoods around on our backs."

She nodded. She was making rolls for lunch and they had to have time to rise. Her hands were floury as she kneaded the soft dough. She nodded toward the rest of the house. "Neither of those poor girls has had a childhood. He keeps them locked up all the time. No parties, no dancing and especially no boys."

He scowled. "I noticed that. I asked the boss once why he didn't let the girls go out occasionally." He took a sip of his coffee.

"What did he tell you?"

"That the last employee who asked him that question is now waiting tables in a little town in the Yukon Territory."

She shook her head. "That's probably true. A cowboy who tried to take Merrie out on a date once got a job in Arizona. They say he's still looking behind him for hired assassins." Her hands stilled in the dough. "Don't you ever mention that outside the house," she advised. "Or to Mr. Darwin. I kind of

like having you around," she added with a smile and
went back to her chore.

"I like this job. No big-city noise, no pressure, no
pressing deadlines on cases."

She glanced up at him, then back down to the
bowl again. "We've never talked about it, but you
were in law enforcement once, weren't you?"

He scowled. "How did you know that?"

"Small towns. Cash Grier let something slip to
a friend, who told Barbara at the café, who told her
cook, who told me."

"Our police chief knew I was in law enforcement? How?" he wondered aloud, feeling insecure.
He didn't want his past widely known here.

She laughed softly. "Nobody knows how he finds
out things. But he worked for the government once."
She glanced at him. "He was a high-level assassin."

His eyes widened. "The police chief?" he exclaimed.

She nodded. "Then he was a Texas Ranger—that
ended when he slugged the temporary captain and
got fired. Afterward he worked for the DA in San
Antonio and then he came here."

He whistled. "Slugged the captain." He chuckled.
"He's still a pretty tough customer, despite the gorgeous wife and two little kids."

"That's what everyone says. We're pretty protective of him. Our late mayor—who was heavily
into drug smuggling on the side—tried to fire Chief
Grier, and the whole city police force and fire depart-

ment, and all our city employees, said they'd quit on the spot if he did."

"Obviously he wasn't fired."

She smiled. "Not hardly. It turns out that the state attorney general, Simon Hart, is Cash Grier's cousin. He showed up, along with some reporters, at the hearing they had to discuss the firing of the chief's patrol officers. They arrested a drunk politician and he told the mayor to fire them. The chief said over his dead body."

"I've been here for years, and I heard gossip about it, but that's the first time I've heard the whole story."

"An amazing man, our chief."

"Oh, yes." He finished his coffee. "Nobody makes coffee like you do, Mandy. Never weak and pitiful, always strong and robust!"

"Yes, and the coffee usually comes out that way, too!" she said with a wicked grin.

He laughed as he got up from the table, and went back to work.

THAT NIGHT HE was researching a story about an attempted Texas Thoroughbred kidnapping on the internet when Sari walked in the open door. He was perched on the bed in just his pajama bottoms with the laptop beside him. Sari had on a long blue cotton nightgown with a thick, ruffled matching housecoat buttoned way up to the throat. She jumped onto the bed with him, her long hair in a braid, her eyes twinkling as she crossed her legs under the voluminous garment.

"Do that when your dad comes home, and we'll both be sitting on the front lawn with the door locked," he teased.

"You know I never do it when he's home. What are you looking up?"

"Remember that story last week about the so-called traveling horse groomer who turned up at the White Stables in Lexington, Kentucky, and walked off with a Thoroughbred in the middle of the night?"

"Yes, I do."

"Well, just in case he headed south when he jumped bail, I'm checking out similar attempts. I found one in Texas that happened two weeks ago. So I'm reading about his possible MO."

She frowned. "MO?"

"Modus operandi," he said. "It's Latin. It means…"

"Please," she said. "I know Latin. It means method of operation."

"Close enough," he said with a gentle smile. His eyes went back to the computer screen. "Generally speaking, once a criminal finds a method that works, he uses it over and over until he's caught. I want to make sure that he doesn't sashay in here while your dad's gone and make off with Grayling's Pride."

"Sashay?" she teased.

He wrinkled his nose. "You're a bad influence on me," he mused, his eyes still on the computer screen. "That's one of your favorite words."

"It's just a useful one. *Snit* is my favorite one."

He raised an eyebrow at her.

"And lately you're in a snit more than you're not," she pointed out.

He managed a smile. "Bad memories. Anniversaries hit hard."

She bit her tongue. She'd never discussed really personal things with him. She'd tried once and he'd closed up immediately. So she smiled impersonally. "So they say," she said instead of posing the question she was dying to.

He admired her tact. He didn't say so, of course. She couldn't know the memories that tormented him, that had him up walking the floor late at night. She couldn't know the guilt that ate at him night and day because he was in the wrong place at the wrong time when it really mattered.

"Are you okay?" she asked suddenly.

His dark eyebrows went up. "What?"

She shrugged. "You looked wounded just then."

She was more perceptive than he'd realized. He scrolled down the story he was reading online. "Wounded. Odd choice of words there, Isabel."

"You're the only person who ever called me that."

"What? Isabel?" He looked up, studying her softly rounded face, her lovely complexion, her blue, blue eyes. "You look like an Isabel."

"Is that a compliment or something else?"

"Definitely a compliment." He looked back at the computer screen. "I used to love to read about your namesake. She was queen of Spain in the fifteenth century. She and her husband led a crusade to push foreigners out of their country. They succeeded in 1492."

Her lips parted. "Isabella la Catolica."

His chiseled lips pursed. "My God. You know your history."

She laughed softly. "I'm a history major," she reminded him. "Also a Spanish scholar. I'm doing a semester of Spanish immersion. English isn't spoken in the classroom, ever. And we read some of the classic novels in Spanish."

He chuckled softly. "My favorite was Pio Baroja. He was Basque, something of a legend in the early twentieth century."

"Mine was *Sangre y Arena*."

"Blasco Ibáñez," he shot back. "*Blood and Sand*. Bullfighting?" he added in a surprised tone.

She laughed. "Yes, well, I didn't realize what the book would be about until I got into it, and then I couldn't put it down."

"They made a movie about it back in the forties, I think it was," he told her. "It starred Tyrone Power and Rita Hayworth. Painful, bittersweet story. He ran around on his saintly wife with a woman who was little more than a prostitute."

"I suppose saintly women weren't much in demand in some circles in those days. And especially not today," she added with a wistful little sigh. "Men want experienced women."

"Not all of them," he said, looking away from her.

"Really?"

He forced himself to keep his eyes on the computer screen. "Think about it. A man would have to be crazy to risk STDs or HIV for an hour's pleasure with a woman who knew her way around bedrooms."

She fought a blush and lost.

He saw it and laughed. "Honey, you aren't worldly at all, are you?"

"I'm alternately backward or unliberated, to hear my classmates tell it. But mostly they tolerate my odd point of view. I think one of them actually feels sorry for me."

"Twenty years down the road, they may wish they'd had your sterling morals," he replied. He looked up, into her eyes, and for a few endless seconds, he didn't look away. She felt her body glowing, burning with sensations she'd never felt before. But just when she thought she'd go crazy if she didn't do something, footsteps sounded in the hall.

"So there you are," Mandy exclaimed. "I've looked everywhere." She stared at them.

Paul made a face. "Do I look like a suicidal man looking for the unemployment line to you?" he asked sourly.

Both women laughed.

"All the same, don't do that when your dad's home," she told Sari firmly.

"I never would, you know that," Sari said gently. "Why were you looking for me?"

"That girl at college who can't ever find her history notes wants to talk to you about tomorrow's test."

"Nancy," she groaned. "Honestly, I don't know how she passed anything until I came along! She actually called up one of our professors at night and asked if he could give her the high points of his lecture. He hung up on her."

"I'm not surprised," Paul said. "Better go answer the questions, tidbit," he added to Sari.

"I guess so," she said. She got off the bed, reluctantly. The way he'd looked at her had made her feel shaky inside. She wanted him to do it again. But he was already buried in his computer screen.

"There was an attempted horse heist just two days ago up near San Antonio," he was muttering. "I think I'll call the DA up there and see if he's made any arrests."

"Good night, Paul," Sari said as she left the room.

"Night, sprout. Sleep well."

"You, too."

MANDY LED HER into the kitchen and pointed to the phone.

"Hello, Nancy?" Sari said.

"Oh, thank goodness," the other girl rushed. "I'm in such a mess! I can't find my notes, and I'll fail the test…!"

"No worries. Let me get mine and I'll read them to you."

"You could fax them…"

"You'd never read my handwriting," Sari laughed. "Besides, it will help me remember what I need for tomorrow's test."

"In that case, thanks," Nancy said.

"You're welcome. Give me your number and I'll call you back. I'll have to hunt up my own notes."

Nancy gave it to her and hung up.

Sari came back down with the notes she'd retrieved from her bulky book bag. She phoned Nancy from the kitchen, where Mandy was cleaning up, and read the notes to her. It didn't take long.

"I'll see you in class," Nancy said. "And thanks! You've saved my life!" She hung up.

"She says I saved her life," Sari said, chuckling.

Mandy gave her a glance. "If you want to save two lives, you'll stay out of Mr. Paul's bedroom."

"Mandy, it's perfectly innocent. The door's always open when I'm in there."

"You don't understand. It's how it looks, that easy familiarity between you two. It will carry over to other times, in daylight. If your father sees it, even *thinks* that there might be something going on…"

"I don't do it when he's here."

"I know that. It's just…" She grimaced. "I don't know where he put all the cameras."

Sari's heart jumped. "What cameras?"

"He had it done while you girls were at school. He had three security cameras installed. He sent me out of the house on an errand while they were put in place. I don't know where they are."

"Surely he wouldn't have them put in our bedrooms," Sari began worriedly.

"There's no telling," Mandy said. "I only know that he didn't put one in here. I'd have noticed if anything was moved or displaced. Nothing was."

Sari chewed on a fingernail. "Gosh, now I'll worry if I talk in my sleep!"

"The cameras are why you should stay out of Mr. Paul's bedroom. Besides that," she added under her breath, "you're tempting fate."

"I am? How?" Sari asked blankly.

"Honey, Mr. Paul takes a woman out for a sandwich or a quick dinner. He never goes home with them."

Sari flushed with sudden pleasure.

"My point is," the older woman went on, "that he's a man starved of...well...satisfaction," she faltered. "You might say something or do something to tempt him, is what I'm trying to say."

Sari sighed and rested her face on her palms, propped on her elbows. "That would be a fine thing," she mused. "He's never even touched me except to help me out of a car," she added on a wistful sigh.

"If he ever did touch you, your father would be sure to hear about it. And I don't like to think of the consequences. He's a violent man, Sari," she added gently.

"I know that." Her face showed her misery. She was too innocent to hide her responses.

"So, don't tempt fate," Mandy said softly. She hugged the younger woman tight. "I know how you feel about him. But if you start something, he'll be out on his ear. And what your father would do to you…" She drew back with a grimace. "I love Mr. Paul," she added. "He's the kindest man I know. You don't want to get him fired."

"Of course I don't," Sari replied. "I promise I'll behave."

"You always have," Mandy said with a tender smile. "It all ends, you know," she said suddenly.

"Ends?"

"Misery. Unrequited love. Even life. It all ends. We live in pieces of emotion. Pieces of life. It doesn't all get put together until we're old and ready for the long sleep."

"Okay, when you get philosophical, I know it's past my bedtime," Sari teased.

Mandy hugged her one last time. "You're a sweet child. Go to bed. Sleep well."

"You, too." She went to the doorway and paused. She turned. "Thanks."

"What for?"

"Caring about me and Merrie," Sari said gently. "Nobody else has, since Mama died."

"It's because I care that I sometimes say things you don't want to hear, my darling."

Sari smiled. "I know." She turned and left the room.

MANDY, OLDER AND WISER, saw what Sari and Paul really felt for each other, and she worried at the possible consequences if that tsunami of emotion ever turned loose in them.

She went back to her chores, closing the kitchen up for the night.

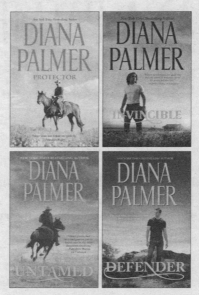

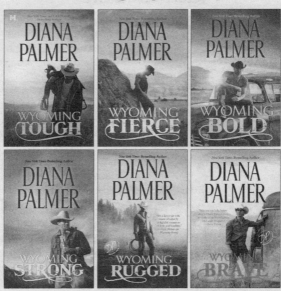

Get 2 Free Books,
<u>Plus</u> 2 Free Gifts –
just for trying the Reader Service!

STRS17